Infinite Search

Life of a Lighter

Maja Molan

Cover Art by Marina Benkovič
Book Design by Jaka Tomc
Edit by Alice Shepherd Erlač
Photo by Petra Molan
Web page by Leja Potočnik

www.infinitesearchbook.com

Language: English
Publication city/country: Ljubljana, Slovenia

Published by Zavod Ustvar'

To the lighter crew:

May they never steal your last lighter.

Table of Contents:

ACKNOWLEDGMENTS & INTRODUCTION

Fuerteventura, June 2019

"What if a lighter could record all the interactions it witnesses? Can you imagine all the stories it would tell? I wish it had a camera so we could playback the footage and reminisce about all its meetings and conversations." A friend said this as she picked up a lighter from the table in our Fuerteventura holiday apartment.

Just minutes before, we had confronted her for always stealing our lighters and constantly leaving us unable to light candles, the stove, or cigarettes. The rest of the night was filled with vivid conversation and laughs about what a lighter would record if it had a tiny camera inserted in it, and that idea got stuck in my head.

In the night I woke up, opened the notebook I'd brought with me for a totally different purpose, and started writing this book. By the time I left Fuerteventura, I had finished the first three chapters and the rest of the book came pouring out over the subsequent two and half months.

I came to that island broken. And with this book, I started to heal.

Maja Molan

GRATITUDE

Thank you to my family and closest friends who have supported and tolerated me over the almost two years I've ramped on about this book (you know who you are), to the people who have been there for me in the newness of the publishing process, especially Alice Burden, to Urša Kodela and Nevenka Kamenik for astrological advice, to Leja Potočnik for reading, marketing advice and web page development, and her sister Verena for the hook idea, to Tadea Vahčič, Zanna Dear, Anja Molan, Nadja Rijavec, and Corina Graff for reading and commenting on the story, to my amazing editor and friend Alice Shepherd Erlač, to the outstanding artist Marina Benkovič who created the dream cover with little to no explanation about the ideas floating around my head, to Petra Molan for beautiful photos, and finally for the book formatting, thank you Jaka Tomc.

FB Page: Infinite search (BOOK)

Instagram: @infinitesearchbook

Web page: www.infinitesearchbook.com

Prologue

People want everything instantly... instant solutions to patch holes but not heal.

I was made in China. I know, dear reader, you expected something more spectacular, and so I must disappoint you at the very start. I was one in a line of one thousand moulded lighters.

My first human interaction was with Lin-Ji, a joyful little girl with small, fast fingers, who clipped my guard and spark wheel together. She was a factory worker, earning two dollars a day, and had just turned eight. Eight is a lucky number in China but not for Lin-Ji. She was incinerated in an explosion after I was shipped out and her too small body was laid to rest.

After setting my hood, I was sent to the final pre-shipping room in the factory. A grumpy old lady, whose name I never learnt since she didn't speak to anyone nor did anyone address her directly, automatically taped a small white label on me. This mechanic movement had been her work for the past 40 years. She put me in a five-by-ten box with other lighters made that day. We were transferred to Europe in a gigantic cargo ship. The process was fast, impersonal, and cold.

And so we arrive at the start of my journey.

I learnt, as I passed from person to person, that everything exists in a time, space, and society full of promises: rapid success, solutions, love, and money.

People are connected virtually but physically disconnected. I have witnessed the annoyance they feel if asked to wait for anything, and I have accompanied their frustration when forced to be without their comforts.

Nature teaches everyone that each plant has its cycle, that nothing sprouts from the ground and reaches maturity in a day, that there are no fast solutions which repeatedly wreak rewards. But many people want everything instantly: instant pasta, instant coffee, instant friends, and instant solutions to their problems, instant solutions to patch holes but not heal. They are forgetful and thoughtless. They want to dispose of things, animals, and others after use. But let's be frank. There is no instant coffee that tastes as good as that which is freshly ground, and there are no instant solutions.

The people I travelled with taught me a lot. Through them I learnt that people want to reap, but not sow the good seeds. Through them I also learnt that it is never too late to grow.

A cyclic observation of time teaches that everything exists within loops of elapsing time. The cycle begins when a physical process takes its first metaphorical step and closes when the steps stop. These processes repeat time and again: a constant starting and finishing of time. But I hope my story will teach you something other than cycles. I hope it will show that there is in fact no beginning and end, that every end is not a close but the beginning of something else. Cycles are an illusion that people create to comfort their past decisions.

One: NICK

People use each other, purely, selfishly, with no thought, instantaneously, like animals.

I was shipped to London and distributed to Oxford Street. It was an exciting start, full of people and traffic. I saw a diverse, mixed society while waiting on that stand: tourists searching for souvenirs and people talking, screaming, laughing, stealing.

Nick bought me in a hurry. He didn't even look to pick me.

There was a hard pain settling in his stomach, but he was dressed nicely for his new job and that concealed his inner turmoil.

He was the type of boy that mothers loved more than their daughters. He behaved and did everything correctly, as expected. He finished his law degree amongst the top five students at his university; he quickly found a prestigious job in a law office; he was incredibly bright and knowledgeable. But he lacked the determination and charm that equate to overall success.

If one used a colour to describe Nick, it would be a kind of beige absent of any special spark. He was overtaken many times by less able yet more savvy and charming peers.

He was stiff and careful and forever accidently aiding those who grabbed life by the balls. You liked him instantly and forgot him as soon as he walked away. He was a faceless man.

Tonight was the engagement party of Nick's friend and long-time crush, Linda.

She'd been shopping days before to prepare for the event and everything was ready. But as the time of her wedding drew nearer, Linda saw Nick slipping from her grasp. During the party, when she knew Nick would be on his way, she smashed a shop-sealed bottle of vodka in an attempt to draw him closer. She called her loyally infatuated friend asking for, "Another bottle and a lighter for someone that's come without. Thank you so much, Nick. You're amazing." She hung up, smiling at his eagerness to jump to the rescue and save her night.

He never told her how he felt, never tried really. Friend-zoned from the beginning.

"You are amazing, Nick. I wish I had a boyfriend like you." Was something he'd hear at least once a week. In Linda's weeks of heartache, it would be multiple times a day.

Over the past two years, the phrase was adapted to, "I wish Mike would be more like you." But she didn't mean that. She loved the crazy temperament and adventurous spirit of Mike. They fought with passion and made-up in bed with even greater fire.

Linda liked Nick and was well aware of his feelings for her. But she didn't fancy Nick. She didn't love Nick. All the same, she didn't want to lose his calming, safe presence, so she kept him close for whenever she needed to feel good or desired.

His thoughts travelled to the moment he saw her ginger hair in the lecture hall for the first time. He sat next to her pale skin and big green eyes and felt pulled to her.

When she looked into his eyes, his heart stopped and it faltered every time from then on. He never noticed other girls; they were bad imitations next to Linda.

Walking down the street to the bus stop, he remembered the time in Greece when she stumbled drunk into his room.

School was finished. This was their celebration. This was everyone's celebration.

She was crying and screaming hysterically about a guy she'd met that night, "Why doesn't he like me?" She stripped off her clothes. "What is wrong with me?" She did it right in front of him. "Am I ugly?" Showing him her blooming body. "Am I not appealing? Look at me!"

He stared at her naked form, trembling with the most rigid erection of his life. She started kissing him, but he grabbed a sheet from the bed next to them and covered her. Nick held her with the sheets between them. They fell asleep hugged together, him listening to her drunk snores while trying to breathe through intense groin pain.

In the morning, Linda woke and looked at Nick in horror. She sat on the bed, pulled up her knees, and hugged her bent legs. She lowered her chin, turned her big green eyes on him, and said, "Did we...?"

Nick shook his head, confirming nothing happened, and Linda opened her mouth to release a hysteric laugh of relief. She hugged him and said, "You are the best. I wish I had a boyfriend like you."

Nick got on the bus from Oxford Street and remembered that that same evening in Greece Linda found a new love interest, a Spanish guy tattooed from head to toe. He fucked her on the beach and took her favourite bra as a souvenir. It's possible that the bra is still hanging in a local bar, dusted and forgotten.

That same night, Nick stumbled across a Dutch girl swaying, like him, from too much drink.

Without words, they led each other to the beach and undressed. As Nick screwed her mechanically, he thought about Linda's small breasts and pert nipples. He pulled out before climaxing and came all over the unnamed girl, then left her lying on the beach smiling and half-asleep.

Returning to the bar, Nick drank twelve ouzos in a minute, quickly stumbled out, cried to the stars, and turned to puke under a tree.

People use each other, Nick thought to himself, *purely, selfishly, with no thought, instantaneously, like animals.*

Off the bus and walking slowly to Linda and Mike's apartment, Nick clutched the bag containing vodka and me. Memories flashed through his mind: all-night study parties, picnics at the campus park, bike rides to the city centre, graduation, the moment Linda called him screaming and crying simultaneously, "I just got engaged. He proposed! Isn't it bliss?!"

The hard pain in Nick's stomach got worse. If someone looked in his eyes, the struggle and growing devastation would be quite visible, but he was practiced at hiding himself behind a smile.

Mike opened the door.

"Hey, chap." Turning his head to the room, he shouted, "Linda, your bell boy's here." He gave Nick a smiling slap on the shoulder which was so hard that Nick stepped back. "Just kidding. Come in. We missed you."

The room was crowded. People were mingling, drinking, celebrating, and in the middle of it all was Linda.

"Nick!" Linda screamed, jumping around his neck and squeezing hard. "Look. Look! Goldsmith's finally fixed my engagement ring. Isn't it amazing?"

He nodded and smiled, stomach clenching.

Linda took the bottle of vodka from his hand and pointed to a tall, elegant looking foreign girl.

"That's Mike's friend Marie, from France. She's the one annoying us for a lighter. Could you go give it to her?" And with that, she left Nick alone in the middle of the room.

A newly arrived couple was welcomed to the party by Linda, Mike, and her diamond accessory. Nick watched her clutch chipmunk-like onto Mike's arm.

Marie glared at Nick from under her long eyelashes and lifted an eyebrow as if to tell him nonverbally, "How dare you come to me?"

"Hi, you need a lighter?" He asked, waving me under her nose.

"Oh, Mon ami," she replied in a soft, theatrical voice. "Come with me!" She didn't wait for consent but pulled Nick to the balcony. "Oh, Mon Dieu! I lost my lighter in the morning. I can't believe everyone here vapes or doesn't smoke at all! What is this, healthier? We will die of health!" She lit a cigarette with me and talked while continually waving the hand that held the cigarette underneath Nick's nose. In her other hand she cradled me like her most significant treasure. "A room with fifty people and not a single lighter. Not even one. You smoke?"

"No."

She carried on, "Oh, so healthy with no smoking but then all the drugs. I know you English people."

He stoically stared at Marie as she continued without any prompt. This was a familiar situation for Nick, where he was a voiceless ear. He didn't want to confess that he'd never tried any drugs, other than alcohol. Besides, Marie left little space for contributions.

Back in the experimental days, Nick had been the master of faking puffs while his friends explored. Nobody ever noticed he wasn't actually joining in. Nick's fear of drugs was bigger than his interest because at five-years old he'd seen his older brother overdose. That was enough of an experience for him.

Marie carried on. "You English, so stiff. French people are so relaxed. You need to be more relaxed, like French, sipping red wine, eating well." She never stopped. She spoke to fill the space.

She talked to Nick because she needed an audience, but there was no attempt to form a connection in the conversation, or rather the monologue. She described in detail her trip to the United States, how she spent the summer in the United Kingdom, and how, now, she had to return home to take her place in the family company. Marie informed Nick that she doesn't want to marry too young, yet not too old, that she doesn't want children but she knows that it's expected of her.

Eventually, Nick stopped pretending to listen but Marie persisted. They stood side by side all night, Nick leaning on the balustrade and watching Linda flash her ring around the room. He imagined how it would feel to stand next to Linda, as her fiancée. His thoughts wandered, showing every mute moment where his heart had wished to speak, and he reimagined how the conversations should have gone.

"Why can't I meet someone like you?" Linda would ask.

"You met me," Nick would reply. "Be with me. Love me. Hold me. Laugh with me."

In reality he was perpetually quiet and chance after chance passed by. *What could I have lost, a friend? Instead, I denied myself, failed myself, put myself last.* For a brief moment, he felt disposable. *If you behave like you are disposable, people throw you away when they are done with you.*

Linda felt Nick's eyes on her and released a quiet, private giggle.

A memory from two years previous came to Nick. It was the trip where Linda met Mike; the memory stung like a wasp to the heart.

A group of five friends, including Nick and Linda, travelled to Scotland to visit old friends from school. It was New Years.

They slept in a beautiful cabin on an island in the North Hebrides, and during this time Linda and Nick became closer.

Linda was tired of the jerks she kept meeting and slowly opened up to Nick, who was afraid to be too quick, too sudden, especially since their summer in Greece.

One evening, the duo lay by the fire and found themselves gazing into each others' eyes. The distance from home invited bravery. The warmth and crackle of the fire encouraged them, but Nick did not pull Linda close, did not kiss her. She was waiting and wanting, and still, he didn't - couldn't.

People find it hard to cross lines. I was not willing to gamble, not even a bit. Nick comforted himself as history repeated in his mind.

The next day, Mike joined the group. He was a friend's cousin, and his car had broken down meaning his plans to go to the other side of the island had fallen apart. That evening, Nick put the final nail in his own coffin when Mike asked, "Hey, lad. What's up with you and Linda? Are you a couple?"

"No." Nick replied. "No. Just friends." He couldn't stop the words coming out.

The next day, Mike invited Linda for a walk. They came back holding hands and their relationship continued in London.

Linda, in all her engagement glitter, came to Nick's side and shook him gently. Marie was on the phone.

"Hey, here you are. I missed you." Her words pulled Nick back to the moment. "You didn't need to keep Marie company all night." Linda said in a jealous tone. It meant she wanted more attention, more from Nick on her evening.

"Well, she dragged me out. She talked. I didn't mind listening to her ramble."

Linda caressed his arm with the tips of her fingers.

"Oh, Nick. You don't need to be polite to her and talk all night just because she's alone here. You're always so kind." Then she hugged him close and whispered in his ear. "Isn't it ironic? Everything could have gone differently that day, the day Mike and I met." He looked at her in pained confusion. "If you'd made a move in Scotland, who knows, maybe *we* would be together today." She giggled, pulling him against her.

A darkness covered Nick's eyes. Regret's bomb of self-hate, sadness, weakness, and resentment exploded and travelled through him as naturally as a wave coming to the shore.

It sent small pieces of himself hurling towards his head and triggered a migraine.

It travelled to his stomach and stirred everything up, setting his intestines aflame. His body felt the pain of her words.

"I do hope you find someone as good as you," said Linda, hugging him before running back to Mike and leaving Nick statuesque.

Marie swooped by. "My cab's on the way. You are such a good listener." She didn't use his name. "You must visit me in Paris. Could you give me your card? My phone died. "

Nick opened his wallet without thinking and gave her a business card that was so new one could smell the fresh ink. Marie gave him a brief hug and kissed the air by each of his cheeks, grabbed her designer handbag, and ran out to a cab for the airport. En route, she put the card down to stow me in her bag and in doing so forgot the card and Nick all together.

Stepping into the fresh air at Paris Airport, Marie lit a cigarette and tapped her leg nervously. Her flight had landed early and her driver was late, which left her at a loose end. She placed me on a bench next to her bag and moments later her driver appeared. Grabbing her handbag and luggage, Marie went off and left me right there at Arrivals.

* * *

I lay on that bench for forty-eight hours. The airport buzz was intense with people running for their check-in, others trying to waste time between transfers, workers taking cigarette breaks, and drivers coming and going. One airport worker picked me up on his break between throwing suitcases on and off planes. Later, a cleaning lady borrowed me for a much needed cigarette in the VIP lounge. I was forgotten there for a while and then brought back to the same bench where a young girl picked me up.

Two: JACQUELINE and STORM

People can master many things, and one of the most profound masteries is self-torture.

Jacqueline was at the airport following a vacation to Monte Carlo with her sister and father. Her father liked taking them to extravagant places now to assuage his guilt for the marriage he had slowly torn apart.

He met his new love interest at work. She was his personal secretary, young, well-dressed, and pampered beyond natural flaws. The Barbie-like assistant appealed to him because she was the absolute opposite of Jacqueline's mother who was free spirited, arty, and refused to be reshaped by his success.

Ironically, the free spirit that Jacqueline's father opposed so much at this moment in time had consumed him, mind and body, when their eyes first locked on the dance floor in Normandy almost sixteen years ago. She had run to him, pulled him under the disco ball, and encouraged his hands to her hips. He was shy at the time and instantly smitten with her boldness. She introduced him to the art world, loved painting, and was intent on pursuing her passions.

The universe, however, had other plans, and soon after they started dating she got pregnant. Jacqueline arrived not long after a fast, fashionable wedding.

The young parents laughed and explained that she was born prematurely and, of course, conceived within wedlock. Three years later, Chloe entered their lives and their mother's dreams were pushed further aside.

For the next fifteen years, their mother's primary focus was raising her daughters and taking care of her husband. She took a job as an art teacher at a primary school. The desire to exhibit her own artwork was slowly subdued. Her canvases were tucked away in a corner and crowded by things that the family gathered over the years: objects that made them feel momentarily alive, successful, worthy before they were stacked up and made meaningless. Meanwhile, their father worked hard to move up from their three-room apartment to a small condo, and then on to a big house. With each move, they changed friends, schools, and activities.

Somehow, the mother was unaltered by this success and resisted the expectations of their new business world. She did not follow the well-established rules of hosting. She still wore inappropriate, artsy clothes and enjoyed laughing. The father became a successful CEO first and a husband second. He changed. She stayed the same.

For two years, his thoughts and time were occupied with Nicole, the secretary.

The ex-artist, wife and mother suspected foul play and felt trapped in her marriage but would not be the one to propose divorce. They were both from old, Christian, French families and she didn't wish to disgrace either side. In those same two years, their daughters were distracted by adolescent obligations. So, husband and children mostly absent, the solitary mother dusted off her canvases and started to paint again.

She reached out to now-distant arty peers who welcomed her back with open arms and her passion was rekindled.

When Jacqueline's father proposed divorce, her mother felt a physical weight lifted from her back.

She got an apartment in Montmartre as part of the settlement, one she had been secretly eyeing for some months, and an excessive monthly allowance for her daughters. This allowed her to keep all the perks of a wealthy family life while enabling her to play the artist once more.

* * *

Back at Paris Airport, Jacqueline, our fifteen-year-old student from a recently divorced home, pushed me into her pocket. She was in the last development phases of physical maturity and a stunning girl, but she belittled herself every day, thinking her ears were too big and her nose too long.

Since the divorce, Jacqueline tried to skip each meal her mother was absent from and she had become quite thin. Her mother failed to notice that her perfectly behaved, piano playing, model student, president of the class daughter was fading away.

Chloe, on the other hand, got her parents attention for everything. She was wild from the minute she entered this world and counterbalanced Jacqueline's seemingly calm nature. Chloe acted out, even more so since the divorce, and demanded all their parents' concern and attention. She suited the diverse, bohemian Montmartre crowd more than Jacqueline. Since moving here, she skipped school more frequently, started wearing heavy make-up stolen from fancy shops while her mother wasn't looking, dated, and had even begun experimenting with drugs. Chloe did everything teenage and good that was against Jacqueline's nature. Jacqueline, Vierge Marie.

As Jacqueline rotated me in the pocket of her jeans, I heard her whisper the name, "Storm."

She looked to her father, who was on the phone, trying to keep his voice low and inch away from the girls in order to speak in private. Chloe wasn't supposed to know about Nicole yet, but Jacqueline was well aware.

She could hear Nicole screaming on the other end of the line, all jealousy and control. Jacqueline's father whispered and explained why he hadn't told Chloe yet.

He was muttering something like, "The timing's still not right. Chloe needs smaller steps."

Jacqueline noted with interest that men, even successful ones like her father, can physically fight battles whilst simultaneously being afraid to look into someone's eyes and embrace their emotions.

Chloe smiled from under her cap as her father squirmed.

Some meters away, Jacqueline tried to relax her growing anxiety as she rotated me in hand and dreamily repeated, "Storm. Storm. Storm."

* * *

The Roche family moved from Fuerteventura to Montmartre, Paris, some time after Jacqueline and her reduced family.

The Roche parents were free spirited hippies with dreadlocks and piercings. They preferred to talk about the water and sun movements than what was happening in society. The father was a musician and mother an IT consultant. She had gone to Fuerte to surf her last free summer away after graduating from college and before 'real life' began. She was French and focused, and he was a young, blonde, surf teacher, musician, fisherman, artist type. He looked like Thor and groups of girls followed him everywhere he went. She ignored him which made her unwittingly attractive. After weeks of partying, long conversations at beach bonfires, smoking hash under the stars, and serenading, her walls slowly cracked and then fell down all together during one mighty island storm. Their love was primal, pure, passionate, and unending.

Deciding to stay on the island, the future mother of the Roche family began to work online and slowly got better at winning paid IT jobs, while the future father opened a surf store. Their family quickly grew until they had five boys: Storm, Rider, Sunny, Reef, and Cliff. Over time, they grew in success and could provide more than just love for their family.

The Roche mother unintentionally programmed a successful app which led them, temporarily, to Paris. A deal was struck within the family that this move would only be for a year so that everything needed to redefine the company from a start-up was fixed, and then they would return to Fuerteventura. The father and boys resentfully relocated to the mainland and this was where Jacqueline and Storm met.

They first crossed paths in the school hallway and even from a distance Jacqueline became breathless. She was naturally introverted, but in Storm's presence she became mute. Jacqueline's peers had always mocked the way she presented herself as a young lady but this never bothered her before. Now she was interested in Storm, who looked ultimately free with skin darkened and hair lightened by the sun, her reputation made her uneasy. He carried himself differently to anyone else she knew. He looked like a lion, captured and caged, and her heart longed for him.

Storm had spent the first five years of his life living in a camp trailer on the beach of Fuerte without running water or electricity. For the next ten years, the family lived in a beach shack. The younger boys can't remember the trailer, but for Storm it was the best place to grow up, a trailer on the beach with the ocean and sun all around. The elements were his best friends and thorough teachers. He was someone that could survive with a Swiss Army knife, his connection to nature, and his practical mind. He missed the island, missed the wind, missed the colours of the soil, and the smell of salt. He missed surfing and skating and enjoying his endless, free surroundings.

Jacqueline became infatuated by him, while Storm failed to notice her existence.

But as luck would have it, Jacqueline's mother and Storm's father met on the streets of Paris. Jacqueline's mother listened to his melancholic guitar playing as he sat under a tree, and his tortured voice and pathos connected with her.

After some casual conversation, Storm's father invited Jacqueline's mother to meet the family. Soon, they started to share evenings together and accidently created a new tribe. The two artists joined forces to cooperate on an exhibition that they entitled, *Broken.* This meant Jacqueline's mother spent more and more time there, so Jacqueline and Chloe had to tag along.

Chloe made friends with Rider, the second-eldest, sharing a passion for skating. And Jacqueline waited and watched for the perfect moment to start a conversation with Storm. But he often moved around the space like an army of clouds gathering and his unstable, unpredictable movements stopped her.

Eventually, they bumped into each other on the hallway of the large Roche apartment. Storm casually leaned towards her and asked, "Do you smoke?"

Jacqueline, shocked by the direct contact and unsure about what he actually meant, gathered her breath and managed to reply, "Yes."

Smiling, Storm instructed, "Okay. Next time you're here, bring a lighter. I'll bring the stuff. We've got to divide and conquer." And, as quickly as he'd appeared, he was gone.

Since returning from the two long weeks away with her father, time had stopped for Jacqueline. She had become restless and burned inside from his attempts to buy out his guilt. She had been unable to shake these angry feelings, but this brief moment with Storm pulled her, heart racing, back to the present.

Jacqueline's mother burst into her bedroom, phone in hand and one finger over the speaker. "Is it a problem if we have a sleepover at the Roche's place?" She asked in a rush. "I know they're not your type of people, too free for your taste, but we really want to finish plans for the opening. If you prefer to stay home, I can call someone?"

Jacqueline felt a flood of excitement and panic cover her. She composed herself, took a breath, and calmly replied, "I can go with you. It's okay."

As soon as her mother left, Jacqueline began to flit about the room, gathering clothes and taking me from a pink box where I'd been safely hidden atop a velvet cloth. She put me in her bag and repeatedly checked I was there before leaving the apartment.

Chloe would spend the night with their father. He'd decided it was time to tell her about Nicole. Jacqueline had been kind enough to hear him out in Monte Carlo over breakfast. She'd never forget how he tortured his breakfast, stabbing at a sausage on his plate whilst choking over the phrase step-mum. Now it was Chloe's turn, but she wouldn't be so easy on him.

Jacqueline had given her father the space to talk because she always wanted to please people, even in her early days.

Walking towards the Roche's, she remembered that as a child she had been given a dress for her birthday and subsequently performed for her family in it like a well-trained dog. Every time a relative requested, "Hey princess, twirl for me. Aren't you just the cutest?!" She would do it. She would twirl and spin, especially for her granny, and ignore the sickness building in her stomach. She would please them all. Thinking about it now made her boil inside, but she didn't understand why. Anger and fear bubbled inside her and made her want to scream. But before she could make a sound, a tension took hold of her neck. Jacqueline tried to breathe, break it down, and relax.

At the Roche apartment, the oldest brothers, Storm and Rider, were out. Jacqueline distracted herself playing with the twins, Sunny and Reef. The youngest, Cliff, slept on his mother's lap.

"She is my rock, my amazing young lady." Said Jacqueline's mum, watching from a distance. "She was so stable throughout the divorce, unlike Chloe. Chloe's wilder." The adults looked at Jacqueline and smiled.

She nodded to her mum but wanted to shout, wishing to break everything in the room, rip the pictures apart, smash the frames, and tear the pillows to feathery pieces. *Stable,* she thought and became crazed inside. Imagining raging through the room made her calmer, mentally releasing tension, but too soon a feeling of shame arrived. She was ashamed of even fantasising about acting out like that. *I would never follow such impulses.* Jacqueline took a long, intentional breath.

People can master many things, and one of the most profound masteries is self-torture: something Jacqueline was good at. On bad days, she would return to events years passed and dissect them with surgical precision. Then she would spin in mental cycles over the memory: for a moment, an hour, a day, quietly, so no one noticed, until blame and regret filled her.

We choose not to forgive those that disappoint us. She thought as she sat between an unknowing Sunny and Reef. *We doggedly hold on to love that has left. We continuously punish ourselves for something long gone. Curious. That moment has passed, that person has left, and they've forgotten. It's impossible to turn back time. So what exactly is the point of these thoughts?* Jacqueline's mind carried on twirling as the twins played in front of her.

My father does not live with us anymore. I am thinking about him. He is thinking about Nicole, not mum, not me. The old him is no more. He has changed. He has moved on and forgotten. And me? Have I grown, learned, risen, fallen?

Destructive voices filled her head, but one quiet nurturing one broke through and confirmed, *Breaking down doesn't help.* The voice was very small, but Jacqueline knew it to be true. She didn't have the tools to allow the voice to heal her yet, but it brought a brief reprise.

At that moment, Storm returned like a powerful wind. Jacqueline felt his presence before the door opened and it brought her back to the here and now.

Bursting in, Storm leant a skateboard against the wall and started, "Bloody city folk with no manners." On seeing the native Parisian guests, he stopped what would have been an impressive rant and moved on to the next feeling. "I'm hungry."

Rider arrived soon after with a ripped knee and dejected expression. He put a bandage on the cut, grabbed a box of cookies, and disappeared to his room. Storm sat on the kitchen counter, devoured a plate of left-over moussaka, cleaned the dishes, and then just sat unmoving.

After some minutes of calm, Storm's mother asked him to show Jacqueline to the study, her room for the night, and announced, "I'll finish dinner, so we can all eat together."

Storm looked at Jacqueline and nodded that she should follow him. Quickly standing up and grabbing her bag, Jacqueline left the twins to their play and her thoughts on the ground with them.

Storm showed her to a small study room equipped with a computer, bookshelf, and bunk bed. It doubled up as a store room and housed all the unusual items the family couldn't seem to leave in Fuerte but that had no place here in Paris, remnants from the life they couldn't wait to return to.

Before the moment was lost, Jacqueline opened her bag and presented me to Storm as though I were pure gold.

"As promised," She attempted a casual smile, "I have a lighter. We can smoke!" Jacqueline wanted to be cool but had no idea if she'd pulled it off.

Storm leaned on the desk and half smiled, half smirked. "Cool. I managed to pinch some stuff from dad."

Her heart pounded fast as she asked, "Where can we go?" But what she really wanted to know was is this safe? Is it good stuff? She'd heard people talk about *good stuff* but never even tried to smoke a cigarette. Fear and excitement crashed together inside her like waves on a cliff. She tried to hide her boiling emotions but the blood exploding in her head gave her away.

Burning redness filled Jacqueline's so she looked away. She wasn't sure what embarrassed her exactly. Was it smoking? Was it the feeling of Storm's closeness and confidence?

Sensing her discomfort and excitement, Storm appeased, "Don't worry. Everything's good. You're safe with me. We'll go smoke at the cemetery and I'll take care of you. Okay?"

Storm's mother's voice came booming across the apartment. "Dinner!" They smiled quickly to each other before leaving the study and joining the rest of the family.

For Jacqueline days passed at the dinner table as her body buzzed in anticipation. She couldn't taste food. Her palette was totally overcome by the emotions speeding through her. She tried to hide herself and avoided looking at Storm, but butterflies flew around her stomach and utterly new sensations took over. She ate mechanically, smiled when spoken to, and politely replied to questions when needed.

It was a short, efficient meal for everyone else. The artists rushed to continue plotting and talked about plans as they ate. The younger children had a bedtime routine to adhere to which got them and their mother eating and moving on quickly.

As they all went about their business, Storm and Jacqueline said their goodbyes and headed for the door.

"Come back before midnight," yelled Storm's mother.

Jacqueline's mother didn't want to press for an earlier curfew, even though midnight felt too late for her daughter's safety. Her renewed free spirit wouldn't allow that kind of stuffiness and control to come through.

Jacqueline and Storm walked towards the cemetery in silence, with Jacqueline rotating me in her pocket every step of the way. Storm led her to an empty crypt. Disrespecting the dead horrified her but she didn't share her opinion.

Instead, she let the silence of the walk and the cemetery and the crypt and Storm fill her body with a new kind of hum for life. It gave her great calm in spite of her fears of the vengeful, offended dead.

Storm gathered his blonde hair in a bun at the top of his head and hugged Jacqueline, sheltering her from the chilled air. "Don't worry, sweet Jacqueline. Just enjoy."

If he only knew how hard *just enjoying* was for her. For some it's simple, let go of everything and just enjoy, but not for Jacqueline.

Storm produced a pre-rolled joint and smiled. Jacqueline clutched me hard, making me hot like I'd been burning for an hour. She pulled me out, wiped her sweat from my casing, and gave me to Storm. Taking me in hand, Storm lit the joint. Their excitement was visible. My flame filled the darkness and encased them in an experience utterly new to Jacqueline. Storm inhaled, paused, and slowly exhaled. Aromatic smoke rolled out of his mouth and he pulled Jacqueline closer again, passing her the joint.

"You haven't smoked before. Don't try to deny it." He smiled. "It's okay. Inhale into your lungs, slowly. Then exhale, slowly."

Jacqueline took the lit joint in her fumbling hand, terrified, and tried to push her emotions aside. *Enjoy,* she reminded herself. *Just try to enjoy.* She inhaled and fell to instant choking and coughing. Her throat grew tight and she couldn't stop coughing on. Storm gently tapped her back, giggling.

"It's okay. It's always like that the first time. Next time, slowly inhale," he extended the word slowly to emphasise his point, "and then exhale." He took her by the shoulders opening up her ribs and then leaned her against him while taking two quick puffs and returning the joint to her hand.

This time she successfully inhaled, paused, and exhaled. A strange sensation spread across her head as if her brain were being pinched by a million little needless, not painful ones - little ones, tiny ones.

Her previously uncontrollable thoughts stopped and left only one drifting around like a living, floating, twitching thing: *My father told me some people are leaders and others are followers. But he was wrong. We're all the leaders of our own lives. Everything we do is a decision leading us to our future. Even when we decide to do nothing, to keep our opinion in, it's still a decision. And it's our own. I can't blame anyone for their decisions. If I wake up and let myself be happy, or wake up and let myself be miserable, it's my choice. I organise and lead my life.* The tiny, little needles carried on tickling her brain. *My father fed me the idea that only some of us are important, that only they can lead. I'm not a leader, but I am important. Being successful and rich won't give me the life I want.*

"I am chasing goals that aren't my own." She said into the empty space surrounding them. "I'm living the expectations of my father, but not my own. I'm desperate to prove my worth, capability, and drive to society and to him.

And I'm desperate not to offend anyone. I'm desperate." She spoke to herself, quietly but with absolute clarity.

Storm was in his own world of thoughts and unaware Jacqueline was experiencing a eureka moment. He didn't hear her revelation and broke her thoughts by saying, "I hate this city."

Jacqueline snapped into a state of confused shock. *How could anyone find Paris anything but the most gorgeous city in the world?*

"Why?!" She asked accusingly. "Paris is amazing. It's the best capital in the world. Its culture is unbelievable and the whole city is rich with history and a beautiful mix of cultures and ethnicities."

As she spoke, the world slowed down. Her body became mellow, and for the first time in her young life, she was still. Storm's opinion didn't matter. Her anger floated away, and she allowed herself to relax on his shoulder and embrace his warmth.

Storm stroked her hair, playing with her curls, and shared stories of his paradise, Fuerte. He seemed to be speaking from far, far away and for a very, very long time before his voice grew closer.

"Here, in Paris, you can't smell the air." He said. "It's dirty and there are so many poor people living on the street. I miss the sensation of sand between my toes. I miss the smell of salt. I miss the wind in my hair and the sun kissing the top of my head and my skin."

Jacqueline realised that the beauty of her Paris escaped Storm because he could only focus on the ugly things. Storm took me from his pocket, closed one eye, and looked through me to the sky.

"In Fuerte, the sky is blue and clouds are white. They dance together with the wind. And it's always warm." She could picture him there. "I was free. There are no curfews because it's safe..." Storm's voice cracked.

Jacqueline felt every stroke of Storm's hand on her head as a gentle electric current. She felt alive and paralysed simultaneously.

His voice deepened her relaxed state and she felt she could listen for hours.

The beaches, the white houses with flat roofs, the Moroccan markets, the excitement of riding a wave, the taste of fresh fish caught and prepared on the beach that day, all his scenes were vivid in her mind. Carefree tourists enjoying and relaxing. Locals with a mañana mentality that she couldn't dream of. She wished Storm would take her there. She wished to live together in a trailer on the beach and imagined this shared life so intensely that when Storm gently shook her, saying, "We've got to put some food in you," she felt shocked and tricked.

He guided her on wobbly legs to a bakery and bought her a croissant. Crossing the street, they sat on a bench across from the Moulin Rouge and ate quietly.

"This is the best pastry I've ever eaten." She said passionately, "The chocolate is so good, and it melts in my mouth. OMG! This is so good. Have I tasted food before now?

In my fifteen years, I don't think I ever enjoyed food until this croissant." She stressed the word this to show the importance of this experience and this croissant. "Is this normal? Is everyone else stressed at my age? Why can't I enjoy life? It's so good not thinking about everything at once." Storm let her ramble. "This is really the best. Mmmm... So good. Love it. I have to do this more often: to just stop, enjoy, let go of all the unnecessary thoughts."

As Jacqueline verbally ambled on, Storm watched crowds of people trying to take perfect selfies in front of the Moulin Rouge. He flicked my spark wheel, sending amber flecks into the air. "Idiots. They take photos and don't even look at the building. Then they run to the next building or statue and take more blind selfies.

36

That's how they go through life, collecting points and running around like Super Mario in a video game, unable to stop, feel, enjoy. I hate that." Storm exhaled with frustration. "We have to go. We're already late. Are you ok?"

Sugar rushed through Jacqueline's veins so she could say optimistically and honestly, "Yes! Let's go."

When they arrived back at the Roche apartment, Storm directed Jacqueline straight to his room. Fortunately, his room was near the front door so they could sneak in undetected. Storm left her for a moment to go to the living room where his parents, Jacqueline's mother, and the exhibition curator were working away. They were totally immersed in the creative flow.

"We're home. We're going to watch a movie in my room." Storm announced, grabbing juice, chips, and cheese, and leaving quickly.

The adults approved their return without looking up to see that Storm and Jacqueline were in fact half an hour late. After hearing Storm shut his bedroom door, they enhanced their exhibition creativity with red wine and the same plant Storm and Jacqueline had used for mental distraction.

Storm heard his father declare enthusiastically, "This will be the most spectacular opening of an exhibition since Picasso lived and worked in Paris!" And turned to see a sleepy Jacqueline sprawled out on his bed. He instructed her to drink juice. She sat up obediently, like the good student she was, and drank. As the liquid spread across her tongue, Jacqueline became aware of how dry her mouth was. She took a longer gulp and felt the moisture returning. It brought great satisfaction.

Storm put a movie on as Jacqueline drifted off to sleep beside him. Sailing in her own world, she watched her thoughts flash without logical connection or direction.

* * *

Jacqueline woke early in the morning to find herself fully dressed in Storm's bed. Her body ached suggesting she'd slept in the same position all night. She was horrified. Storm, the gentleman, was breathing heavily on the floor in a sleeping bag.

She stood up as quietly and quickly as she could and ran to the study where she was supposed to be sleeping.

Lying on the bunk bed, Jacqueline tried to reimagine the walk home but her memory was blurry. *Storm's bed was so cosy,* she thought as a wave of guilt swallowed her. She couldn't tell if the guilt came from her actions or because she enjoyed it all so much.

She tried, again, to remember the way home and what she'd been thinking. It had been powerful. Just hours ago she had the answers to everything, but now, nothing was clear. Jacqueline took a breath but was unwillingly overcome by confused feelings about Storm. She'd never met anyone like him, never felt like this for anyone before him. A warmth embraced her in her bunk. *Does he like me?* She questioned, taking another deep breath. *It'd be great if he did...* Before her young mind could flitter any further, the darkness of night sunk in and she slept again.

* * *

Jacqueline's mother shook her awake. "Hey, baby. Time for breakfast. Then we have to go home. There's still so much to do!" She squeaked.

Jacqueline looked at her mother closely and realised she was too focused on her exhibition to see her daughter: she didn't see Jacqueline was dressed in the same clothes as the night before, puffy eyed and dreary. *Why would today be any different? She never sees me. She's busy with Chloe, her divorce, and her exhibition. Full stop.* Jacqueline felt relieved that her rebellion would go unpunished but also resented this neglect.

She didn't want trouble, but she felt truly invisible to her mother and didn't want that either.

At breakfast, Jacqueline played with her food, staring at her plate. She didn't look at Storm once in case he or anybody else would read her mind.

When the torturous feast was done, Jacqueline's mother asked her to wait for her by the front door.

Here Jacqueline nervously wished to run away. Storm came over and squeezed me into the palm of her hand, whispering, "For next time, after the exhibition." He smiled, leaving Jacqueline to wait with a pounding heart.

She spent the rest of the day unsuccessfully scanning the internet for a social media account for Storm and filled the subsequent three days over-analysing every second of the interactions she could remember clearly. She wished Storm had kissed her. All her friends had been kissed by now: in a school toilet cubicle, on the bus, behind a curtain, some had even gone all the way. But Jacqueline was still waiting for her first and yearned that this be with Storm.

Although, I'm glad he didn't kiss me in the cemetery. She daydreamed. *That wouldn't be a romantic story to tell. So does he like me or am I just someone he's hanging out with because he doesn't have friends here?*

Or, even worse, was he forced by his parents? Her thoughts twirled. Later, she would learn that nobody could force Storm to do anything he didn't want to and that he always prefers solitude over bad company. But for now, she questioned motives and criticised herself.

* * *

After three painful days of searching and questioning, Jacqueline lay in the bath with only candle light brightening the room.

She looked at the candle's flame through me and mumbled, "Why didn't he take my number? We could be texting at this moment. Why did he give this lighter back? Was it mockery or an excuse to meet again?"

Jacqueline created a wild movie in her head, an Oscar-worthy scenario for best dramatic scene, where she was left rejected and unwanted.

She tortured herself, neglected her well-established schedule, stayed in the solitude of her wild imagination, and no one noticed.

* * *

On the day of the exhibition, Jacqueline changed her outfit several times and couldn't recognise herself in any of them. She had always been efficient and focused, but now, she didn't know how to present herself. With every change of clothes, she grew more and more frustrated. *What's happened to my brain? Have I lost my identity or is this love?* Eventually, she decided to go dressed totally in black as if attending one of her many piano recitals. She made a bun at the top of her head to present herself as a serious musician and was satisfied. If nothing else, the musician was a role that she knew to be truly her.

Jacqueline's mother dragged her and Chloe along early to oversee the final setting up and embrace the room one more time before spectators arrived. Storm, Rider, and their father arrived soon after, but their mother had stayed home because the younger ones' babysitter had cancelled. Chloe ran to Rider as soon she spotted him and they headed straight for the street.

Jacqueline, the true opposite of her sister in every way, waited at a casual distance. She observed Storm, who wore light blue trousers and a colourful patterned t-shirt. His appearance and hers stood in direct contrast. He was a gust of fresh air, lightening everything and causing Jacqueline's heart to beat at her ribs. She turned me over in her hand, realising she'd lost the cool she wanted to maintain and cursed herself.

Storm politely greeted her mother and the gallery staff before making his way around the space.

A painting entitled, *Broken,* hung before Jacqueline. It was entirely black with a single golden crack running through its core. She stared at the image to distract herself but soon found she was in fact looking at her own portrait.

She had been covering herself in serious black and now, with Storm, something had broken. An oppressed light was starting to break out of her.

Storm spoke close to her. "Surely it's not that bad, Jacqueline. Why are you dressed for a funeral?" She faltered. Storm placed his hand above her gaze and released her tightly wound bun of hair. Overwhelmed and unresponsive, Storm could touch Jacqueline freely and he did so with no regard for their parents on the other side of the room. He moved a strand of hair from her face.

Storm called across the room, "We're going for a walk." Notifying rather than asking. To Storm the freedom to roam was a birthright.

"Yes. Yes." Jacqueline's mother replied. "Just be back in time for the opening." Her dream was finally coming true so she didn't care where they were going.

The gallery space was close to the Sacré-Coeur, the Sacred Heart of Paris, inviting Jacqueline and Storm to walk towards the church. A group of loud Italian tourists approached from the other direction and Storm found himself taking Jacqueline's hand and pulling her in front of himself, away from them.

Jacqueline flushed with inexplicable anger. "I have lived in Paris my whole life, Storm. What was that, playing the hero?" *I can take care of myself. I don't need a prince.*

"What?" He asked. The crowd passed without incident.

Her anger dissipated and was replaced by something close to comfort. This feeling was special and new: being cared for, wanted, next to each other. It was a feeling many yearn for. Jacqueline had yearned for it.

"Nothing." She replied and was grateful that he didn't ask again.

They settled on a bench in a quiet street. Jacqueline pulled me from her bag and handed me over.

A small laugh escaped Storm's lips as he put me on the bench between them. Raising a hand towards her cheek, Storm's fingers travelled through Jacqueline's hair and he moved closer. They held each other's gaze, clearly feeling the same excitement, and Storm leaned forward, kissing Jacqueline on the lips. They opened their eyes to find each other smiling. There was no need to say a word.

Storm produced a joint and brought it to his lips, tilted his head, hair falling in front of his face, and attempted to light me. A strong wind killed my flame which made him laugh again. This time he laughed so hard tears came to his eyes. "One would think that couldn't happen to me since I learnt to light fires under the winds of Fuerte!" Smiling, he kissed Jacqueline again, quickly, sweetly. And on the second try, he was successful.

They smoked and watched the stars, talking sparingly and enjoying each other's warmth.

When they returned to the gallery, Jacqueline felt like she'd landed on another planet. It was minutes before the opening and she was crossing galaxies and planes of reality. She stood quietly next to Storm throughout the evening, her body alive and buzzing.

After that night, they became a couple. It was a natural partnership where words were rarely needed.

Storm teased her out of her shell like a little crab, and she made staying in Paris bearable, even enjoyable at times.

But the summer arrived fast, meaning the Roche family's year on the mainland was coming to an end.

The young couple met in their crypt one more time before Storm returned to Fuerteventura. Jacqueline cried, even though she knew this was coming. They were both mournful but ready. They shared a final joint, after which Jacqueline gave me as a memento to her soon to be ex-lover, Storm.

Jacqueline would periodically search for Storm online in the following years, even when they were grown and very different from these teenage days. It was nostalgia searching for comfort. But she would never find a profile for him. The closest she came was an account entitled, *StormforRider*, which she discovered some years after their separation.

And with that, we come to the finale of my romantic period. But as this story draws to a close, the next is on the horizon.

* * *

And, bloody hell, was Storm right; Fuerteventura is windy.

Soon after arriving, Storm was surrounded by awaiting friends. I travelled in many circles with him on evening sessions after the sea, next to bonfires. He told stories about Paris and Jacqueline, about the city and how she made it better. They stayed in touch for a while. But, with time, their texts got shorter, calls more and more infrequent, until eventually contact ceased. But it was nothing tragic. It was just time. New excitement came into both of their lives and they grew apart naturally.

Storm became occupied with tourists and promoting his friends' booths where you could buy knickknacks and beach-made art. He'd befriend small groups, normally English girls, and take them to the markets. He'd use all his charm to animate milky-white-soon-to-be-lobster-red ladies into investing in his friends' artwork, pointing out hand-crafted pictures made from Fuerte stones and sculpted into seaside motifs. It was a win-win-win.

The tourists bought nice stuff, his friends made a profit, and in return, Storm got something for free from their stall, a cut of the sale, or an exchange of favours another time.

"This is the perfect reminder of our magical island and me." He'd say with an irresistible smile. "It will bring summer energy and harmony to your home." He'd flutter his eyelashes over blue eyes, decorated by sun-whitened curls.

That part, where he stared adoringly, was even more successful than his cheesy lines. And he'd play with me in his hand as he went about his daily life, socialising and hustling.

One day, as a tourist invested in Storm's spiel, he put me down on a stand and hugged the new beach-art owner. Her already sunburnt skin grew redder, and they walked away without a second glance at the stand. I assume, at some point, Storm realised that he'd lost me. But he was one who understood the natural flow of things coming and going, the tide rising and falling, night replacing day, lighters coming into one person's life and going away with another, the easy separation of people and places, like Jacqueline and Paris.

And so I found myself floating around the Fuerte market scene for a while, another incredible shift and turn of the universe.

Life on the market was vivid, colourful, loud, and exciting. My time there started with burning sage on the stand of a young artist that created stories out of stones intended to dissolve negative energy. But because the market place is a sharing community, I travelled between the hands of many.

After burning sage, I lit cigarettes for an old hippy who made tin-candlesticks. He had long grey dreadlocks and a body full of washed-out tattoos from the seventies. Over thirty years, he'd developed a unique technique for making his candle sticks from the only material he had access to: empty cans of beans. He lived on a diet of beans and day-old bread, more or less leftovers and hand-outs from friends working around the area.

His wife, a heavy lady, sold knitted bags that were so old fashioned they had become fashionable again, especially with the retro- loving millennials.

The candle maker poured gas in me, greeted a young lady selling motivational quotes written on wooden boards, and offered me to light her camp stove. The lady's children grew up crawling between stands on the market.

She passed me on to a group of Moroccan women creating traditional flower decorations from orange peel. Then, I was handed to a young couple crafting accessories from old T-shirts. Each day brought love and connection between these people.

Eventually, a female tourist asked the upcycling craftsman to borrow a lighter as she rummaged in a gigantic bag for her own misplaced one. As her search became desperate, she bent forward for a more thorough investigation, which sent her sunglasses cascading from her head. Without any sign of distress, she caught them in a free hand and searched on. It looked like this was a reoccurring predicament for her. From the depths of her bag, she pulled out another pair of sunglasses, a napkin, a makeup bag, but failed to produce what she was after.

"Here you go." The young craftsman said, handing me over.

She lit a slim cigarette and clutched me in her fist. "I'll take five of your necklaces, please." She said after exhaling a cloud of much longed for smoke.

The craftsman politely asked, "What colours would you like?"

"Could you just pick five different ones for me. We're on an official ladies holiday at a yoga house just over there." She pointed in a random direction that didn't suggest any house in particular.

The craftsman nodded and picked five necklaces, each subtly different from the other.

She gave him money, snatched the prepared bag, and almost ran off, shouting, "Thanks," as she hurried away. Tucked away in her clenched fist, I travelled on from the market to the next adventure.

Three: KARA, TINA, ANA, EVA, MARINA

It's easier to meddle in other people's business than to go within and look at my own demons.

"I'm back and I've got gifts." Kara announced to the house of friends. She pulled the five necklaces from her bag and laid them on the table for people to choose their favourite.

Kara was a hectic lady who seemed to be constantly searching for something in her pockets, her purse, or her bag.

"And I got a complimentary lighter." She giggled. "Let's hope we don't lose this one any time soon." She hunched over and started digging through the bag that hung off her shoulder. "I just have to find it," she became hurried and flustered, "in this bloody bag." But I was waiting in her sweating palm. Placing the bag on the coffee table, Kara started to pull items from it like a magician pulling silk scarves from a hat: a bottle of water, lip gloss, glasses, a long sleeved shirt, a pack of cigarettes, chewing gum, hairpins, tampons. "I can't believe I've lost the lighter already! No way ..." And then she noticed her hand and me tucked away there. "Oh, there you are." Kara smiled as she opened her palm. "We must not lose this one, ladies!"

It was 11a.m. The first coffee pot of the day simmered on the hob.

Tina led the breakfast preparations. She was a personal assistant at a digital agency, married to a banker (who spent more time in Brussels than home), a mother of three boys, and a classic new-age-eco-bio-fasting-wannabe-vegan-who-loves-eggs-and-seafood-too-much-to-commit-fully. Tina excused her dietary shortcomings with the logic that she ate so few animal products it practically didn't count, and when she did, they were always sourced from local, free-range farms or seasonal fisherman, which was highly responsible. She would often say, "I'm basically supporting those living in poverty when I eat meat, so it's not in any way a contribution to the harmful meat industry."

Tina broadcast from the kitchen, "Ladies, we have coconut, almond, and vanilla soya milk. The almond is sugar-free."

"Do we have any normal milk?" Asked Ana from another room.

"This is normal milk." Tina retorted, "You're not a calf."

Tina annoyed Ana hugely. In Ana's mind, Tina tried too hard to appear morally responsible and present herself as pure and virginal. Everything Tina said, the tone in which she said it, and the way she animated herself as she said it annoyed Ana. Each time they met, Ana's tolerance for her decreased.

Thinks she's a bloody moral compass. Ana thought. *The high school 'it girl', master of social organisation and not just of this group of friends but of everything.* But Ana had seen Tina in quite a compromising situation a few weeks before this holiday and now knew Tina was merely a flawed performer.

Tina worked tirelessly every day to act as the perfect wife, mother, friend, assistant, humanitarian, superwoman, and every day she punished herself for failing to fully embody these titles. She needed everyone around her, everyone who could see her, even from a distance, to believe that she could master any challenge and do it looking perfect.

What's more, Tina was unhappy. But she could never admit this truth, not even to her high school friends.

She'd have to be honest with herself before confiding in anyone else, and that wasn't going to happen any time soon.

Tina had extended her list of punishable flaws recently by overstepping a flirtation with a close friend of her husband. She'd actually continued overstepping for some months. *Not very superwomanly,* she scolded herself. *Two weeks of fasting will make it better.* And so Tina purged her bad actions by denying her body the possibility of holding on to anything. She cut ties with her lover, telling herself, *It was just a misstep. Nobody got hurt.* But she felt something hot and molten inside that wouldn't go away.

Needless to say, Ana and Tina were totally different from each other. Tina was control. Ana was impulse. During Ana's school years she was considered the outrageous member of the group because she skipped between the beds of multiple guys on what she called, "A good weekend." Now she'd calmed down and settled with a nice, composed man that offered her structure and stability. He showed her how to be internally level, something she had no idea she yearned for. In the past, she'd fullfil herself with sex and sport, and her friends quietly judged her for it thinking she was giving herself away for validation. When she found her kindred spirit, she realised that she'd been bedding ugly frogs as a distraction rather than what she originally thought was plain fun. No one said the search for Prince Charming came easy.

Marina gave Ana a small carton of milk that she'd smuggled in without Tina detecting. "Here." She whispered. "I knew this would happen."

Ana hugged her. "You are the real humanitarian and, above all, my best friend."

The group's friendship persevered for twenty years because of Kara.

She was the glue that kept contact with each friend individually on a monthly basis over the phone and with the friends collaboratively bi-monthly over group email.

The five friends were much changed from their school days, but that didn't dampen Kara's determination to keep them close. She was the mediator during personality clashes, the compassionate ear for anyone's struggles or errors. She readily dropped her own life when her friends needed her. And she never complained, even when she was struggling with her own life.

It wasn't that Kara withheld her personal struggles but none of her friends seemed to notice them. Hidden in plain sight. She filled her single life with cats, organising social events, ladies' nights and excursions. The biggest event of her year was coordinating their annual vacation.

This year, Fuerteventura was the destination. Kara heard an acquaintance talking about the magical island, how the energy of the place changed her, and had to find out more. She was told about a yoga house and a Slovenian yoga teacher with black hair and dark skin. "An amazon woman with the power of a lion and the wit of old medicine folk. She can read your astrology chart and open up all your internal energy in her sessions. Urša's her name, pronounced *Ur-sha*. She makes magic happen on Fuerte."

And so these five friends, whose paths couldn't diverge even if they wanted to, sat down to breakfast on Fuerte and awaited their meeting with Urša.

Eva yelled. "Can we eat?" She always waited to be catered for and assumed the role of clean-up crew rather than ever cooking or baking. Her kitchen at home was practically new, only being used to boil eggs, tea, or coffee. She would occasionally open the microwave to heat up a ready meal but that was the extent of her culinary skills.

And when on occasion the stove was lit for something more complex than heating water, her friends would mock her and declare that a national holiday be created in celebration of the miraculous event.

Tina brought the last plates through and finished curating the table. It was fit for an exhibition.

"So we have fruit, hummus, avocado, and a tomato, capris and olive salad." Tina smiled a glistening smile. "For Ana, Kara, and Eva, there's goat's cheese. Then there's a vegan cheese for those who respect their bodies and don't want to contaminate them with milk products which support the starvation of young animals. Bon appetit!"

Kara squished Ana and Eva's hands to placate them. The group feasted on delicious local food, and Tina's comments were forgotten.

After breakfast, the friends walked to the beach. Tina wore a dirty pink, designer bikini and carried a matching towel and bag. Eva wore all black. Ana donned her sporty shorts despite being the skinniest and fittest of the group as an ex-competitive runner. Marina was in a mismatched bikini, of which both top and bottom were old and slightly see-through, and carried a bag that she got as a complimentary gift with sun cream. Kara dragged her gigantic handbag and covered herself in a baggy linen shirt which she rarely came off. She claimed to fear getting sunburnt, but in reality, she felt like a whale next to her friends. They were fit and slim and so she covered herself with a sports hat and towel and hid in the shade. Ironically, she'd always end up burnt despite the shade and have to return home with stark red stripes highlighting small patches of her body.

Settled on the beach, Kara began to search through her bag. I lay between a pile of unnecessary things that for some reason Kara's felt bound to. The endless insignificant things in her bag reflected the many, equally unnecessary, thoughts trapped in her head.

She had a bag full of stuff she didn't want or need and a head full of disappointment and self-loathing.

Kara would historically dip in and out of extreme diets to take control of these thoughts. Just before Fuerte, she'd overheard colleagues talking about her appearance and relapsed into a new radical diet. *Attempt one hundred,* she'd thought to herself.

And while this was exhausting, she was unable to break her habits and ignore the negative things said about her.

Instead, she'd just shove the comments in her bag and carry them around. She'd make changes: meditation, yoga, affirmations, chanting, but nothing worked. She followed different gurus and read a plethora of books but was never able to let go.

People are like dogs. Kara thought, imagining herself covered in fur and waddling around. *They behave according to their training. If a dog's trained to stay in the garden, it'll bark and run to the fence but it won't jump over. It won't step out, even if the door is left open.*

Needless to say, Kara's diet ended before they landed on Fuerteventura.

After some minutes, she discovered me with an, "Aha!" And threw me on her towel to presume the second round of searching for cigarettes. She placed a slim cigarette between her fingers and took a long inhale. "Anyone want one?"

Tina rotated from her back to her stomach, commenting, "We haven't even had a drink yet, so there goes my usual excuse for a cig."

Eva waved, signalling participation. Kara threw me and the pack of cigarettes in her direction. "It is a vacation after all; we're allowed to enjoy ourselves. Don't be so uptight, Tina." In reality, Eva often smoked in secret, puffing away under the stars.

She managed stress by smoking or eating and knew it was better to smoke because it was easy to replace clothes when they smelt of smoke but tough to lose weight. Her dear friend Kara was a constant reminder of that. So smoking and drinking were her coping mechanisms and guilty pleasures.

Eva placed the cigarette between her lips and shielded me with a cupped hand from the wind. She held me while leaning over bent legs and taking in big breaths of nicotine.

She watched windsurfers sail in the distance. She'd wanted to try but never collected the courage to. Eva reminded herself that she couldn't afford broken nails let alone bones. But, truly, she never challenged herself with anything.

If she didn't know she'd be the best, she wouldn't take the risk of failing. Being a loser was not Eva's thing. That's why she never stayed in a relationship very long. One burn was more than enough. Now she preferred romances light and quick and called her exploits sweet treats. Every fling was the same: barely legal, picked up from fitness sessions, and naïve. She'd let them, "Help me relax." And when they got attached, she'd end it.

"We should get some hash or weed!" Shouted Marina from the middle of the group silence. "We've all got our struggles. What about a quick fix for today, to mellow us?"

"Yes, great idea." Ana replied.

"My poison is still alcohol. You know I can't handle joints. But you go for it." Eva said rolling her eyes and playfully pushing Ana.

"Oh, come on!" Said Ana. "Just one or two puffs for old times sake, Eva. Drift off for a while." Eva didn't look convinced. "Or everything's so blooming wonderful in your life that you want to stay totally sober here?" Ana had lost her job a few months before the holiday and had to move to the in-law's house. She was living with her prince of stability and his controlling, possessive mother.

Ana could only come to Fuerte because Kara insisted on paying for her. She felt life was far from rosy and it embarrassed her to come along as the freeloading friend.

"No." Replied Eva, "It's the regular combination of flowers and shit, but it's up to me how I choose to deal with that shit." She turned away to avoid Ana's reaction. This was the first time she'd stood up to her and it worried her for some reason.

Eva became aware of a pain in her side and searched for a distraction.

Her regulars were boys, alcohol, cigarettes, ice cream in extreme moments, and despite what she just told Ana, occasionally drugs. She rotated her coping strategies to avoid becoming reliant on any. "Ooo, look at that bo-oooo-dy!" She theatrically whispered so everyone would hear.

"Oh, dear." Tina commented. "That's a child, Eva. Don't be such a cougar."

"Hey! I'm a MILF. Except I'm nobody's mother." Eva retorted in fits of laughter. "And now, I'm going to fix you some gear." She adjusted her bikini to reveal her newly enhanced breasts and walked towards the young target. He was knelt on the ground tightening the ropes of his windsurf as Eva's shadow engulfed him. He looked up straight into Eva's balloons, and she tactically welcomed him by bending down to say hello.

The remaining women watched open-mouthed. Some time passed where no one commented. As Kara lit her third cigarette with me I realised the person Eva was speaking to was Storm. He looked happy and healthy on his favourite place on earth, the seashore. The friends gasped to see Eva following her young man to a house near the beach. Tina visibly twitched. Kara flicked my spark wheel nervously. Marina and Ana quietly sniggered to each other.

Eva and Storm resurfaced after some minutes. She strode back to the towels smiling to grab her wallet.

54

Storm took her money openly and gave her a paper bag. Then he disappeared without seeing me tucked in Kara's hand.

"I have it. It's Fuerteventura hash, special edition! Or so my young sexy friend pledges." That was how Eva operated: identify the need; find the solution. When she knew she could win, it was game on. Of course, except when it came to challenges of the heart. They were something she never touched.

"Amazing!" Said Marina, giving her friend a big hug. "Today, after yoga and dinner, we're having gin tonics and joints. Let's get the party started."

Lunch, at the nearest beach bar, was late and small: one green salad each with gin and tonics on the side. Afterwards, Kara was still hungry but too ashamed to admit it because Tina and Eva kept moaning that their portions were too big and impossible to finish. They left half their food on the plate and Kara wanted so much to finish it but didn't. Luckily, Ana wanted ice cream so Kara got her fill there.

As they waited, Kara felt compelled to unload some of her thoughts. She wanted to say, "I think I'm a stress eater, Ana. And I get really pissed off when people say things like, 'It's too much. My body is telling me to stop. You have to listen to your body.' I'm like, 'Really?! My body tells me it wants pizza, pasta with truffles, ice cream, bread with cheeses and spread, and to drink gallons of red wine at every meal. Should I listen to that?' I eat to fill something inside me, to smother it."

But she didn't know how to make herself speak those words so instead she said, "I think I have a problem with food, Ana."

Ana smiled and hugged her without prejudice, welcoming Kara's honesty. She loved her and could understand issues surrounding food. At one point, Ana was obsessed with eating *clean* and doing endless fitness sessions. She would train for up to five hours a day and sometimes even that didn't feel like enough. She was well aware of the way addictions work.

* * *

At their evening yoga class, the five friends tried to follow Urša, their teacher. Kara was surprised by how flexible she was, finding herself more bendy than most of her friends. Marina had been practicing Kundalini yoga at home and thought she would be good in this session, but she was shocked by the rapid pose changes of Asana and kept falling behind.

Ana sweated like crazy but was determined to finish one hundred percent of the class. Tina and Eva lost interest and photographed each other in sexy Asana poses. The Amazonian yoga teacher was not impressed with this behaviour.

"If you need a break," she instructed, "Lay down on the mat and relax in child's pose. The time that we practice yoga is a time for focusing on our inner selves."

Tina and Eva giggled, putting their phones away, and lay on their mats trying not to laugh out loud.

After shavasana meditation, the group packed away and thanked Urša. At home, they prepared a colourful dinner of salads, cauliflower mash with almonds, tomatoes, and olives, a vegan one-pot, and grilled shrimps. They invited Urša to join them to make amends for the less than serious session. The food was enjoyed by all and the company easy. After eating and once Eva had cleaned the dishes, they moved to the terrace and rolled the first joint.

Marina commented, "Sometimes, I feel like we're children pretending to be grownups." Which made them all smile.

Urša lit the joint and inhaled deeply before passing it on. Eva took a puff despite her protest on the beach. "Call it peer pressure." She joked.

The pressure doesn't disappear once you're an adult, thought Ana as she watched Eva from across their circle.

Talk soon moved to astrology. Kara itched for Urša to read her chart but didn't want to ask directly. After some time discussing the suns and moons, Urša said, "I can read your charts, you know?" Kara's eyes sparkled. "All you have to do is insert your data on my phone and then I can begin." Urša offered her mobile open on an astrology page to the group.

"My chart first." Kara said, grabbing the phone. The circle breathed and relaxed and no one but Kara had the compulsion to jump for their chart reading.

Urša started to explain the influence of different planets in the birth chart as she read through what Kara's. "So, Kara, you have the Sun and Chiron in your sixth house. It's important to know that the sixth house represents health, lifestyle, and acceptance of yourself and your daily cycles. People with the Sun here should focus on trying to begin each day cheerfully. Since the Sun is here, it is what you would need in life: to shine. But Chiron is a very different story and your biggest pain. Do you know the story of Chiron?"

Urša lit a new joint. Eva, the non smoker, sat next to her and stared longingly. Urša held me in her left hand and the joint and her phone in the right. She looked around the circle of women who waited to hear about Chiron.

They realised with a sudden jolt that Urša had asked a question and simultaneously replied, "No."

"Who's Chiron?" asked Kara.

"Okay, Chiron was one of the Greek half-gods: half horse, half man. He is recognised as a compassionate, nurturing, and youthful spirit, someone loved by all. I'll give you the short version of his story. Chiron dropped an arrow on his foot that had been dipped in Lernaean Hydra venom and this poisoned him. He was a masterful healer, so he gathered every herb he knew could help his ailment and began treatment. But his knowledge was no match for the venom and he failed.

Left in constant suffering and unable to ease the struggle, his half-brother, Zeus, killed him to release him from the pain." The circle was entranced in Urša's story.

"The point is, Chiron couldn't die naturally because he was half god, so his pain would have been eternal. Where we have Chiron in our chart, Kara, there is pain.

If one is able to overcome that pain, it will be their biggest success. Guilt, pain, powerlessness, and manipulation are all Chiron."

The joint in Urša's hand had gone out. She relit it as Eva watched in irritation. She wanted it so badly and found it hard to wait. It would seem this *was* one way she chose to deal with her shit.

Tina didn't believe in astrology, so she drank her gin and tonic and hoped for something intelligent to come up in the conversation.

Urša finally passed the joint to Eva, who dragged on it like it was air.

"So there are three stages of Chiron." Urša continued. "In the first, Chiron is screaming. He is the injured one. In the second, he is accepting his pain and sharing it with others. He is the one who hurts others. In the third, he transcends to become the healer." Urša looked around the group, evaluating if she was being clear. She paid close attention to Kara. "So in your case, Kara, Chiron must affect your health, workout, or diet." She seemed to quickly assess Kara's body and then added, "Or both health and diet."

Kara swallowed. A hot pain rose inside that she likened to being repeatedly stabbed.

"Well, I know I'm healthy." An awkward silence hung over the group. "So, I guess, it's diet."

Urša was unapologetic in her approach. Gently and without prejudice, she asked, "Are you happy with your body, Kara? Are you happy with the way you look?"

Eva's mouth fell open. *Are we talking about this?*

Kara hugged herself. She'd always claimed to be content with her looks. This lie was reinforced by her friends who neglected to address the fact she was gaining kilos year after year. They cheered her as she swung from one diet hit promising, 'unbelievable results in a couple of weeks,' to the next.

Ana prepared exercise routines. But Kara never lasted more than six months. It always started with a special occasion, then a weekly cheat treat, until she'd throw the whole thing out the window and dispose of another diet book or self-help manual. She'd put the weight back on and then some, and no one would say a word.

You could cut the silence around the circle with a knife. Ana and Marina looked at each other, then stared at the floor. Tina got up and practically ran to the toilet.

Kara swallowed one more time. "Well, I'm big-boned. And I like to eat. You can see the results." She tried to laugh but it sounded awkward, almost hysterical.

Urša calmly replied, "I love eating too, and I eat a lot. But I am aware that everything I put into my body is fuel and I don't take more than I need. Food creates chemical reactions that influence how I feel. The fuel you need depends on your blood type and metabolism. This defines how much and what is good for you."

Kara pinched her thighs. *How is this happening?* She didn't want to cry in front of a stranger or her friends but she was finding it hard to hold the tears back.

Tina was still absent. The others looked away, shrinking to become invisible.

"Are you happy, Kara?" Urša wanted to reach out and grab her. "Or do you feel hollow? Do you feel a void?"

Kara stared at the question.

Tina hid behind a wall, waiting for the air to clear. She'd witnessed at least twenty of Kara's diets since school. It pained her that she couldn't help and annoyed her that Kara's food issues had been embraced by their group. She overlooked the fact that she had never said anything constructive to her friend.

"You know, negative food relationships are widely supported by our society.

I think we're not even aware of how many different kinds there are, but they're all supported by the media and social media: overeating and obesity, malnutrition from junk food, eating obsessively 'clean' and 'healthy', low-carb high-fibre diets, eating based on blood type. There's loads of them.

When you give too much importance to one thing, it can consume you. And it happens easily with food." The silence lingered now and covered them like a cloak. Urša took a few short puffs and sent the joint on.

Exhaling, she continued, "For example, I am vegan eighty percent of the time. But when I come here, I eat goats cheese and fish. The food that gives you energy is good food. Again, it depends on your body. If I ate a lot of cheese and processed food, I would be big and tired."

"Me too!" Eva proudly contributed to the conversation.

Urša couldn't help feeling she wasn't taking this seriously and was irritated by Eva. "It is all about balance. You should only eat when you are hungry and give your body good food as fuel."

Kara bit her lip, trying hard to fight back the tears. Marina sat in lotus position and looked intensely at her friend, thinking, *Maybe this will be the fundamental moment that breaks her.*

"I am quite happy the way I am. I accept myself." Kara stoically declared.

Time stopped.

"It's not possible. You see, the problem with Chiron is that even if you weighed fifty kilos you wouldn't be happy. I think you need an extreme change. You need to accept the pain that is inside you. It's the only way to get to the third stage and become the healer. The good news is that you are completely able to do this, and when you do, you'll shine like the sun.

You will be fully expressed. But that will only happen if you complete this path honestly."

Silence.

"First, you must decide if you've had enough pain and if you're ready to feel it in its entirety, to overcome it, and to step from hell into paradise."

"Okay." Kara replied with certainty.

Her thoughts travelled back to a diet with the great Elan, where she lost masses of weight but never found any feeling of success. She always felt fat. Her thoughts travelled further to when she got slim after school and for the first time men noticed her. Soon after, her heart was broken and she was landed with a novel, unwanted pain. So she returned to her first love, food. Food was the only thing that brought fulfilment.

But Kara was active and she did love fresh, healthy food. She also loved to eat her way through heartbreak, stressful work days, home troubles, and friends' misfortunes.

She found salvation in binge eating mountains of spaghetti with an avalanche of parmesan on top. She'd follow that with a bar of chocolate, then microwaved popcorn, and finally, a tub of ice cream. There were variations to her repertoire but it always looked like a list too long for one human meal.

With every bite she felt her stomach becoming full, and she only stopped when at the point of suffocation.

Kara realised, now, that she was surrounded by her closest friends and still unwilling to confess honestly to her habits. *At least I can admit to myself now, in silence.* She thought. *Could that be a step in the right direction?*

Marina stood up, taking control of the silence engulfing her friends. "Can I be next?"

With that, Tina felt safe to re-join the circle. She excused herself saying, "I forgot that too much alcohol with a joint isn't a good idea. You guys should have reminded me."

The group remained uncomfortable.

Marina inserted her data into Urša's mobile and passed it back.

"Oh, you have Mars in your ninth house and it's in Libra. Interesting. You must be a humanitarian. You can make a big difference to your immediate world by helping others."

The friends looked to each other in amazement.

"I am!" Marina declared. "I run my own local charity. This is crazy. I don't even believe in horoscopes."

Urša looked critically, "This is astrology; horoscopes are in the newspaper." Marina blush. "It would appear you always put yourself last. You should make an effort to look after yourself and learn how to balance your humanitarian work and your life. If not, you'll suffer burn out or illness. "

The group nodded in stoned unison and almost simultaneously agreed, "That's true."

Marina smiled and gathered papers, tobacco and weed. "In the name of balance, I'll treat myself to a new joint." She rolled while Ana put her information in the phone.

"So your main challenge, as I see it Ana, is your family. This could be your primary family or your chosen one. You also have Chiron, but he's in your fourth house. It would seem you had some pain or lack of acceptance in your primary family. This will continue to cause you pain until you embrace, realise, and overcome it." Urša held eye contact with Ana, who looked shocked.

"Well, my dad left us." She confessed. "I still don't have any contact with him. He tried to reach out some years ago, but I just can't see him. I'm still too angry. He disappointed me."

She looked down at the floor. "And we've just moved to my husband's mother's house. And now -- oh man, this is so stupid. But, now, I have a feeling my husband left me for his mother. He is there for me, but that nasty old witch comes first when we're there."

Urša looked at Ana's chart again. "I'm sorry, Ana, but before you can go further in your current relationships, you have to forgive your father. You need a father in your life. And it's better that he left you.

I believe the alternative would have been abusive for your mother or you. He did his best. Sometimes it's hard to know what is best for you."

Ana was speechless.

Tina rolled her eyes sceptically. She didn't want to hear about everyone's problems and the fact that Urša nailed it with Kara, Marina, and Ana made her nervous.

Ana felt a heavy weight fall from her chest and as it crashed to the ground she began to cry. Kara embraced her tiny body. Tina noticed the muscles moving in Kara's arms like she was protecting Ana from the whole world. Kara seemed to embrace Ana's pain and cry with her.

It was absurd, but Tina understood for the first time that she wasn't alone in her secret pain. Each of her friends was fighting a battle and carrying pain.

Eva fought internally over what she wanted and what she feared. She wasn't sure she could take the cold-blooded truth from Urša, aware that she created a bubble around herself that no one was allowed to penetrate. Eventually, she took the phone from Urša's hand and entered her data. Want won over fear. She returned the phone without a word and waited.

"Rose coloured glasses," Urša stated to everyone's confusion. "You idealise everything. You have Neptune in your first house.

That means that you don't see things as they really are. You make them better or worse, so your view is never true. You don't even see yourself realistically."

Eva contradicted, "No. I have a very analytical mind. I assess the risks and opportunities of every situation I face. What do you mean?"

Urša laughed. "Yes, I can see this is true since you have Mars in the tenth house. You shine there. But that is the house of career and public appearance." Urša took the joint from Kara and leaned back. She closed her eyes, inhaled, opened them, and re-lit. Lying back, she inhaled one more time and stayed like that with her eyes shut, leaning her head against the wall.

"I'm saying you don't see yourself. That or you oversell or undersell your talents. It depends on your beliefs. But you don't know who you are."

The others started to giggle like crazy.

"She thinks she's a good driver." Marina said. "But she's so unfocused, always talking on the phone, and driving over half the lane."

"She undersells her pastries." Added Ana. "She thinks they're not as beautiful as Tina's, but they're so tasty. I think that's why she doesn't try to be more creative."

Eva rolled her eyes.

Tina carried on the social commentary, "And you're so afraid to be hurt again that you don't see the good possibilities around you. I know there's a nice man out there for you, not just these young, stupid boys."

For the first time, the circle of friends cradled their secret pains rather than ignoring them. *We all have our wars,* thought Tina.

Urša looked seriously at Eva. "Start loving yourself, now." She turned to the circle.

"All of you. You're amazing people full of light and love, but you can't share that love if you don't love yourself. You can't love yourself if you feel anger, disappointment, or hate towards yourselves or others." Urša tried to assess if they were listening or understanding. "There is no better time to start loving yourself than now, even if you feel you have too much weight on your shoulders with debt or relationships. It may sound silly, but if you start loving yourself, you can feel good and be happy, in spite of the weight of life."

It was Tina's turn, but she wasn't ready to hear anything true about herself. Her feelings were a Pandora's box that would remain locked tonight. "I am so tired." She stood, play-yawning. "I'm going to clock out for today."

Marina protested, "Oh, come on. It's your turn, Tina. It's just fun."

"Tomorrow. We don't have to do everything in one night. Like the fisherman told us: relax, mañana." She rushed inside before anyone could protest further. Tina showered, changed, and brushed her teeth in less than ten minutes. Then she jumped into bed and curled up into the foetal position.

How can I keep pretending? How can I look in Robert's eyes after spending so much time with his best friend? How did I get into this mess?

Tina had spent the past few months in secret with Tom but had recently cut all contact. Now she was heartbroken. Something clicked when she was with him. She still didn't really know when or how it started, but Robert was away and becoming physically and emotionally absent. They'd stopped talking to each other.

If they didn't have children, she would've walked away or at least that's what she told herself. Infuriatingly, Tom had been around since the beginning of Tina and Robert. *How didn't I see him then? Robert was more handsome and athletic, but I always liked Tom too.* He was the type that everyone liked but was often overshadowed by egos.

Tom had loved Tina in silence for years but never told her. One day, she called him to look after her younger boys while she took the eldest to a sleepover. Robert was away and when she came back to Tom's for the boys, they opened a bottle of wine and sat talking on the balcony.

After a couple glasses, Tina was giggling hysterically. "You are like my second husband. I should have picked you, Tom. In the end, even with all Robert's money, I just want to share a nice evening drinking and talking." Tina looked up at the stars in silence.

Supported by strong wine, Tom collected his courage and while also looking at the stars confessed, "I've loved you from the moment I met you, Tina."

A universal story, thought Tina as she cradled her sadness. *People always realise what they've missed when it's too late.*

Outside, Eva laughed asking, "What was that? Kara, what's up with Tina?"

Kara was preoccupied. *Why do I put myself last time and again? How has nobody ever asked if I need help, if I'm hurt or sad or worried?*

She pulled herself away from her thoughts for long enough to reply, "How should I know?"

"Oh, you know everything." Marina meant this as a compliment, but Kara heard it mockingly. "We all tell you everything. That's how it is, always was. You are our Kara, the superglue."

They say the wind uncovers everything. And the Fuerteventura wind was certainly doing that.

I took the easy road, thought Kara. *It's easier to meddle in other people's business than to go within and look at my own demons.* Kara's emotions piled up and she felt close to exploding. She took me from Urša's hand, grabbed a joint that sat unclaimed in an ashtray, and started drawing in extended breaths like meditation.

Eva, Ana, Marina, and Urša watched. Kara's gaze travelled up through the glass ceiling of the terrace unable to see the stars through her own reflection. She bit her tongue to prevent herself screaming or crying.

"Just so you know, this is powerful local hash." Urša warned. She'd seen this reaction after reading charts in the past, where something clicks. Something had clicked for Kara, or rather, burst. *But, now,* Urša questioned internally, *will Kara be able to overcome her pain. The hardest part is admitting something's wrong. We let the stories and dramas of others consume and blinker us. We get distracted by false perfection on social media. We get lost in the game. But it is one big illusion, Kara. The Earth will not stop for us. The sun will not stop shining. The world just is. It doesn't care if we are heart broken, lost a job, or have a bad marriage. It doesn't care if we have a lousy self-image. Life just is. But you should care about yourself.*

The friends fell to confused silence again. They weren't used to Kara being unpleasant or rude. So each one slowly retired taking a plate or glass with them. They left Kara entirely alone on the terrace with a cup and a bottle of water. Kara pushed the sofa out from under the glass ceiling so she could see the sky. She lay down, let herself rest in the darkness, and observed the stars.

From a short distance away, Urša opened her window and played Lotus Sutra. Kara relaxed in a cloud of music, hash, and stars. She reeled through the decisions that had led her here. She breathed into her epiphany and declared to the sky, "If I'm going to change my life, I have to stop making the same old fear-based decisions. I have to start creating a new life centred around me."

* * *

The next morning, Tina carefully applied her make up. No matter the occasion (dinner, the gym, a doctor's appointment, a windy beach) she had to look effortlessly immaculate with cheeks lightly blushed and eyelashes painted with just a touch of mascara. This was the desired effect, but in reality, she used two different foundations and three shades of correctors to cover any irregularity on her face.

She opened a jewellery box and took out a new pair of earrings. They were inlaid with small diamonds, and Tina looked at them proudly: a trophy, a fix to distract her thoughts from Tom and Robert. She thought about Urša's words. *Are you filling a void?*

Tina put the earrings on and observed herself in the mirror. She could pass for ten years younger than she was, but she criticised her appearance. Grabbing her breasts and pushing them higher, she frowned, then let them fall to their natural position. She touched her stomach. It wasn't just flat but concave. *And all I do is run twice a week and rigidly control my food consumption.* She allowed herself one fast-food treat a month: a big pizza or a burger with chips. This would be eaten quickly, in the car, away from public view, and always alone.

Tina's fingers gently drifted over her body. She was thinking about Tom: his calm, how she could be without make-up in front of him, how he ruffled her hair out of perfection. He joked, "Messy hair. I don't care." She whispered it into the privacy of her room and ran both hands through her hair, disrupting it.

But I can't do it. Instantaneously, she corrected herself so that every hair was in place. *Inhale. Exhale.* She placed a slightly crooked smile on her face, took another controlled breath, and joined her friends.

Breathing, Urša had explained in their yoga session the day before, connects your whole body. "People smoke so they can remember how to breathe. How to inhale and exhale." She said as they moved between poses.

"When people stop breathing well, they are in trouble." Change pose. "Half of their problems could be solved with deep breathing." Change. "Breaths that provide cells, the blood, and organs with enough oxygen to work to their full capacity."

Change. "But people are strange." She'd commented as Tina and Eva snapped selfies. "They prefer prescribed drugs, illegal drugs, smoking, drinking, sex, anything that quickly cheats the body in to thinking it's breathing well," Change, "Happy," Change, "healthy, okay." Change. "It's impolite to be in a bad mood or place in life." Change. "It means you failed. You stopped breathing."

Tina tried to remember this, telling herself, "Breathe."

Kara overslept on the terrace and missed morning yoga. She woke with the sun on her face, then moved to the porch where Marina was busily laying the table for breakfast. Ana and Eva brought fresh fruit, yogurt, porridge, eggs, toast, cheese, and ham. Tina had everything prepared and decorated on plates. It was perfect. Finally, Tina joined with a coffee pot and freshly squeezed juice on a tray.

Kara noticed Tina was too poised and sensed she was battling herself this morning. But rather than sympathise, as would have been her default response, Kara flashed in hatred. She hated Tina's perfect make-up and designer appearance. She hated her exhibition food. She hated her.

Eva poured Kara and herself a coffee, adding soya milk to her own. She sat next to Kara, took a cigarette, and lit her first of the day. Eva played with me, picking me up and putting me down, turning me in her fingers, flicking my spark wheel. She indirectly stared at Kara, deciding whether to acknowledge her pain or not. Finally, Eva put me on the table and decided to carry on pretending.

"Crazy, huh." Eva gently nudged Kara in the ribs. "Yesterday was crazy. Right? I don't believe this mumbo jumbo astrology shit."

Kara sipped her coffee without response.

It's hard when things are off balance. Thought Eva.

She didn't want to cause any more upset and gently tried to tease Kara back to happiness. *I just want her to feel comfortable, content, even if it's an illusion. I'll play along.*

"Exceptional preparation. Compliments to the breakfast team!" Eva applauded and raised her mug.

They ate in silence, each swimming in thoughts. Kara used breakfast to show herself she could make better decisions about food, but in the end, she ate everything that was offered twice over. She stuffed herself with small portions of this and that and then did the same again until her stomach was comforting and full.

Marina counted her blessings as she watched Kara. *I have a fantastic family, beautiful friends, and I get to do what I love most in life - help people.*

Ana stabbed at a tomato, visualising her mother-in-law's face and thinking, *Just die. Just die, bitch.*

Eva filled her plate and mentally calculated the calories before eating. She pushed Tina's words to the back of her mind, thinking, *No. No. NO. I am not afraid of a relationship. I just don't want it. Big difference! Why would I need someone? To steady their social expectations? No.*

Tina dissected an orange, a well tested system where she would labour over playing with what was on her plate to the point where she no longer wanted it. Tina had taught herself to become numb to her thoughts during the day with games like this. She made herself so focused on the orange that there was no space to think about anything else.

If one could light the stress in that room, it would cause a mighty explosion.

Kara, despite eating the most, finished first. She moved to the pool side and lay down in a shadow looking glum.

Others cleared the table, while Tina remained seated with her coconut milk coffee.

Urša dropped by to see what morning had brought the group and headed straight to Kara. "May I join?"

Kara nodded, granting Urša license to play meditation music on her mobile. She wept silently. Wiping her tears Kara asked, "What did you mean when you said I can conquer Chiron?"

Urša stared at the clouds satisfied that Kara had listened. "I will try to explain with an example. One month before I moved here, I played the Euro Jackpot. Before I even checked my numbers, I began to worry about the amount of money I could potentially win and how I'd invest it. I worried about spending it wisely when all I'd done was buy the ticket. I realised that I was limiting myself in my own mind. I couldn't just buy the ticket and enjoy the thought of a vacation or a big villa next to the sea. And then I had an Aha! moment. I realised that I did this in many areas of life, and in every one where I worried, I was failing.

I would hope to begin something and then my dreams would run away from me and I would stop myself before I started because I was scared. I allowed the expectation to become too great." She looked at Kara again. "I was blocking myself from being free."

"You need something radical, Kara." Urša continued, "I don't know. Go to an ashram for half a year and start fasting. Change diet. Find one that is good for you long-term. Study eating by your blood type and see how it feels. Or start intermittent fasting. Or go to a sweat lodge. Try ayahuasca. Try something supported and guided. Everyone has to find their own recipe."

Urša paused. A breeze ran over the pool's surface and Kara watched the ripples spread, grow, and then settle.

"You need your brain to reset and switch. You need something that will make you believe you deserve the body you want, that you can handle it, and that there is a sexy, happy person inside you. Don't get me wrong. You are perfect now.

But if you really want to heal, you have to do more. You have to focus totally on yourself. Normally, new routines take at least twenty-one days to settle in. That's why guidance helps. You need that time so that the new routine becomes part of you, so that it feels your own. When you feel like it's part of you, you won't relapse. And know that relapsing is okay at the beginning. It's okay as long as you learn from it."

"What's aya-something? Sounds exotic." Kara said interested.

"It is a challenging but rewarding path. The experience is different for everyone. Let's say, each person gets exactly what is needed for their journey."

"How does it work?"

"You drink this medicine twice in one night and then you have visions. You see things, patterns, connections with others, solutions for how to guide yourself.

In the process, you relive your traumas, fears, and demons. There can also be puking and diarrhoea; it's your body cleansing toxins. By the end you travel to a beautiful, magical place and find new dimensions to life. You need to fast beforehand. It's best if you can fast for a month but it varies. It's kind of semi-illegal. "

Urša lit a cigarette and leaned towards Kara. "You really have to be ready to meet your demons. It's hard, but if you don't have any medical problems, this is something that can shake you hard. But," She inhaled and made a pause for dramatic effect, "You have to know this is a beginning. You must continue to set goals and make good decisions every day. It's not a quick fix. Life won't change if you don't follow the answers Aya gives you on your trip. The experience is a kind of wake-up call."

Urša smiled. "It's never too late to discover you're still alive. And it is a medicine. The medicines found in native cultures, where people are still connected to nature, are where people get what they really need for personal growth and progress.

No two people can have the same experience, each one is special." Urša lay down.

Kara, comforted, processed Urša's suggestions.

Tina quietly joined them, removed her dress, and spread out on a sun lounger. She took a deep breath and collected her courage.

She started and then stopped herself, swallowed, took a breath and then calmly, as if uninterested, said, "Urša, can you read my chart now?"

Kara glanced at Tina in surprise. The two had been best friends for years, and Kara always knew what was going on with Tina. But recently, the friends had been absent and Kara was in the dark.

"Sure, give me your phone."

Tina entered her data and passed the phone back to Urša.

"Oh." Said Urša, lighting a new cigarette. "You have Libra in your sign and moon. You can't live with chaos. You love beautiful things, to be dressed well, and to enjoy the expensive pleasures of life." Urša scrolled through the chart. There was nothing shocking so far. "Oh, and you have Pluto *and* Chiron in your fourth house. Do you have problems with your primary family?" She stared right past Tina's mask. "That means the one you were born in and the one you have now."

Tina objected, "No. I have an amazing husband and three beautiful boys, so no."

But Kara added, "Her parents divorced when she was very young. They fought hard, so she didn't see her father after. He died soon after the split. Tina was never able to make peace with him. And, if she's honest with herself, she's still angry with her mother for not letting her see her dad."

Urša scrolled the phone. "That's your biggest pain. Pluto is an unconscious energy. You can feel it but not observe it. You can't really influence him. With Pluto, you can only cooperate.

He is hidden deep so you must always go deeper. And we already know what Chiron means. It is hard for you to express your pain."

Tina maintained stoicism. "What were the three stages of Chiron again? I missed that. I wasn't focused."

Urša repeated, "Chiron has three phases or archetypes: the Wounded Healer, the Shaman, and the Alchemist. They represent where your soul is on its journey.

In the first phase, you suffer and explore primal pain: the Wounded Healer. In the second, you attempt to heal and embrace the pain: the Shaman. When you explore the first and second, you can then turn your pain into a gift, and that is when you become the Alchemist. If you are interested, you should search for it online. It is super easy, same for the planets."

Urša changed the topic. "How's your partner?"

"I'm married. I have three boys." Repeated Tina.

"I heard you the first time." Urša put the phone down. "But since you have Pluto here, it's not just your parents causing you pain. You have to forgive both of them for how they behaved. They did the best they could. But there is more to this." She scrolled the phone again.

"Do you still love your husband? Do you make time for each other?"

No and no, flashed in both Kara and Tina's heads.

"We have three boys," she said. "There's not enough time for us. My husband is away a lot on business trips, sometimes for up to two weeks. When he's home, we have more or less a full house because we're always hosting his partners. We have a very fulfilling life. We are a stable family." *And I am in love with his best friend, with whom I find more than enough time. He's always with us. All I need is a sleepover with him and we become a delightful family.*

But her thoughts wouldn't betray her. She smiled, appearing tranquil and holy.

This was the first secret she'd kept from Kara. It was too big. If nobody knew, it wasn't there and everything could carry on in blissful ignorance. Tina was afraid, now, that if she started talking the box would burst wide open and she wouldn't be able to hide her secret anymore.

Urša raised an eyebrow. "My question was if you still have a relationship with your husband? Or are you living as friends, roommates? When I look at your chart, I see divorce lingering if you don't fix things soon. In fact, now."

Tina stared at Urša trying to sell a lie, but she wasn't able to speak. After what felt like a long time, she said, "Yes. We have a good relationship."

Come on. What's wrong with you? You are the picture of happiness and have been for some time. Everyone believes it but you can't lie to a stranger? You'll never see this woman again. Come on!

Kara knew something was off in Tina's marriage. Tina had been unavailable for months, keeping herself busy as her and Robert continually fell out. Kara could see a pattern but not the cause. What's more, she didn't want to push Tina to tell her.

After a long and painful silence, Tina tried again. "Yes, we're happy." Urša stared into Tina's cold blue eyes, knowing there was a different story. But it wasn't her place to ask any more. Afterall, she was merely the reader.

Kara saw again that they all shared great pains, albeit from different causes. She also realised there was nothing to be done to help Tina. Similarly, nothing external could placate her at this time. *Each of us stands alone when facing our challenges.* Kara lectured internally. *Tina needs to learn to put down her mask and face herself.*

"If you need additional information, I'll be around. I have a yoga session on the beach in half an hour so I've got to go. Have fun, ladies. See you in the evening." She left Kara and Tina looking at each other in the silence of acceptance and regret.

Marina joined them. "What's the plan for today? We can go to the south end of the beach if you guys want. I've just got to pick up the car at the rental place in the next hour."

* * *

Marina drove. Kara sat in front. The other three squished in the back.

"Next time, I'll book a car too." Eva said, annoyed with the sweat dripping down her body. She hated sweating, even after a workout or sex. She wanted a shower.

Kara searched for me, again, in her bag. I was jammed between a small make-up bag and her mobile. She managed to miss me on every scan and started pulling everything out. When her bag was empty enough, she found the pack of cigarettes and me.

"Let's stop in this town and get a coffee." Kara proposed.

"Oh, for the flying kite." Replied Tina. "Why are you smoking so much lately, Kara? You really want to kill yourself or what?" Tina's voice grated Kara.

Eva jumped in. "Hey, chill everyone! We're on vacation." She held her hands out like a police officer. "I agree. We should get a coffee and enjoy a cigarette or, even better, a gin and tonic. It's not good for your health to drink too much coffee. You know?" She laughed hysterically, enjoying her joke.

Kara turned on Tina in anger. "Well, Ms Perfect, I am so sorry that I don't reach your high standards. It would be a very dull world if everyone was as controlled as you, with your perfect house, perfect husband, perfect boys, perfect dog, and your perfect shit." She held Tina's gaze.

Ana covered her mouth with both hands to stop herself laughing out loud but she couldn't hold it in. Kara's explosion was a blessing to her. It was exactly what she'd wanted to say to Tina since arriving on Fuerteventura. This was the highlight of Ana's vacation, and she was loving it, laughing from the bottom of her stomach.

But Kara hadn't finished yet. It was like watching a fractured dam spill over. No one could prevent the coming damage. The water pressed and slowly forced each crack apart. The cracks became holes that got bigger, and bigger, until ... BOOM.

"What's wrong with you and your life that you feel you have to pity us? You talk about your happy marriage -- tell us what's really happening. Or don't. You can hide things if you want, but in the end, you won't be able to hide it from yourself.

What the fuck is happening with you, Ms Self-Control, Ms Everything-Has-To-Be-Perfect?

What are you so busy with that you don't even have time for coffee any more? And what? Now I'm ruining your vision of a perfect vacation?"

Tina sat shocked and unable to speak.

Ana wasn't laughing anymore. It wasn't funny anymore.

Eva, who was sitting behind Kara, wanted to calm her down so reached forward and stroked her arms. Marina pulled over and pointed to a coffee shop not far from them.

"Everybody out." She shouted. "Sit somewhere outside. Get space." Marina ordered coffee for herself and shots for everyone else. A young waiter helped her bring them to the table along with a selection of pastries cut into small sharing pieces.

She looked round at the pity party. Kara smoked with her back to the table. She stared at the clouds too scared to make eye contact with anyone. Ana looked at the floor, feeling guilty for laughing.

Tina silently cried, trying not to disrupt her make-up. Eva hugged and reassured her. "There, there. Everything's alright."

"Ok, girls, time for shots." Marina broke in. "No excuses." Marina always saved a crisis with coffee, alcohol, and sugar.

"I'm cheating on Robert with his friend Tom." Tina screamed into the air. "We've been having an affair for months." She slammed her shot down and continued crying in a less ladylike manner, deafeningly hyperventilating between sobs.

"Shit." Said Marina. "We need the whole bottle." She came back quickly with a bottle of local spirits and started pouring more shots.

Ana looked at the weeping Tina. "I knew about it." She said. "I saw you two." Ana gasped.

"And, in the spirit of honesty, I hate my mother in law with a burning passion. I have never hated anyone so intensely in all my life. She's ruining my marriage. I had no idea he was such a mummy's boy. It's repulsive. I hate it. I want her to die a painful death. It's horrible, but it's true!"

Kara prepped herself and went for it, "I hate myself. I hate the way I look." She took a breath. "I have to change something. I can't carry on like this."

Eva screamed, desperate to speak before she could chicken out. "I have a crush on a co-worker." She was doing it. "He's newly divorced, but I'm terrified. I don't want to be hurt. It's crazy. I push him away every time he says something sweet and distract myself with guys that give me a quick rush. I use them and throw them away as soon as I'm done and I don't let this co-worker get close."

The four friends had tears running down their cheeks but they were also smiling. Finally, they'd let go of their individual frustrations.

Marina encouraged them. "Bless the drink! We can drown our problems for a bit." She refilled glasses and took her turn to share. "I'm stressed too." There was no crying or shouting. She was very controlled. "Our Kate is pregnant, bless her, which means I have to find a new assistant. I am so used to her way of doing things; I don't know how I'm going to cope without her."

The four red-eyed confessors looked at Marina and burst into laughter.

"She's from another planet," giggled Ana. "Marina, you just accept life as it is. No labelling it good or bad. It's just happening. You're always kind and content. Thank god one of us is."

The pressure was off. The eruption had run its course, and the friends started to really talk for the first time in years, without masks, without pretending.

They spoke long into the night, emptied local alcohol supplies of liquor and gin and tonics. They never settled the costs with each other for that day, but they did start along a path that made them stronger and brought them closer.

* * *

The next day was their last on the island. The ladies left in a hurry and with massive headaches. Marina, as the designated driver, was the only one unscathed. In the rush, they forgot me in the living room but I was soon scooped up by Urša. She tucked me away in the pocket of her giant bag.

It was a Sunday morning and Urša went walking through Corralejo. The street was a clash of Saturday's night life and Sunday's early risers. The final drunken party goers crawled back home, while others rushed to their jobs. Hookers and pimps analysed the night's success as morning joggers passed on their routes. Cleaners slowly disposed of the evidence of parties, gathering cigarette butts, forgotten cups, and glasses that were scattered around the city centre.

Waiters opened coffee shops and tried to wash away the stink of booze with cooked breakfasts.

I fell out of her bag somewhere along the way. Urša disappeared into the distance.

* * *

Many people passed without noticing me. Eventually, an old fisherman spotted me and picked me up. He lit me, declaring I was, "A happy surprise and a good start to the morning. I am truly blessed. You're just what I needed."

He'd returned from a fishing trip and would now take me along on his hectic morning routine. The old fisherman spent the best part of the day bringing boxes and boxes of fish and shellfish to restaurants along the bay. He stopped in a bar where many fishermen gathered after their day's toil and enjoyed a beer.

It seemed an obligatory after-work meeting where they compared how each other ranked in terms of fishing success. They'd take time drinking and then return to their wives who were ready and waiting with a freshly made lunch.

A young couple sat down at the same bar and the fisherman observed them. They eyed each other playfully and so lovingly that it could melt a heart of stone. They giggled like teenagers and appeared to be in a private seclusion from the rest of the world.

One of the pair left for the bathroom, and the other headed towards the old fisherman. "Ola. Pardon. We're newlyweds and I'm organising a romantic dinner for us on the beach. I really need a lighter to set the romantic scene, but I can't just buy it or my partner will suspect my plan. I see you've got a lighter there. Can I buy it from you? What do you say?"

The old fisherman looked at him without expression, then started to laugh wholeheartedly revealing many missing teeth. "Newlyweds?" His laugh went on.

"Sure. Take it. May it bring light to your marriage. Half of a good marriage is happiness you know?!"

The newly married man went back to his table and stowed me in his pocket. He wasn't alone for long.

"And?" Asked his partner.

"Got it. Three to me, still two for you. I'm winning!"

His gloating was met by a gentle punch in the stomach. "Cheeky little devil."

They loved practical jokes and pranks, any type of challenge where they had to act and use their brains. Waving to the fisherman, they took off holding hands. And so we move on once more.

Four: JACOPO AND ROCCO

We have placed ourselves in separate boxes where we can't communicate. Our values, our dreams have slipped apart from one another.

Jacopo came from a religious Italian family that never imagined he would be anything but a conventional heterosexual man. As a result, he lived his early years in a lie. His high school girlfriend, Vanessa, was a smart, beautiful, young woman that he admired. In their parents' eyes, Jacopo and Vanessa had been coupled since they were babies cradled side by side at family picnics.

Jacopo found the courage to step out of the closet after finishing school. It wasn't easy.

At school, Jacopo competed for the football team and Vanessa played mandolin in the orchestra. He did love her and enjoyed her company, but the more their relationship developed the more he became aware that something was missing. He didn't mind kissing Vanessa, hugging her, but she was never in his mind when an unwelcome teenage erection popped up. He didn't feel aroused by her but rather loved her like a sister.

One day after football training, Jacopo and his team mates were fooling about on the pitch.

A friend tackled Jacopo to the floor and as they rolled on top of each other and laughed, Jacopo noticed the friend's warm breath against his neck and strong muscles holding him.

Before he knew it, Jacopo got his first full-on erection and pushed his friend away in panic. He was overcome by a sudden mix of emotions that instructed him to hide.

"You idiot. You kicked me." Jacopo shouted, trying to compensate for what was really hurting him.

He lay in the foetal position for a while and wished the blood out of his groin and back to his head. Gasping for air, Jacopo tried to fight back tears and think about Vanessa's breasts. She'd presented herself to him, all blossoming and beautiful, the night before, but it didn't affect him. She guided his hand to her breast, and he felt nothing. It was like handling a warm ball of fat. She, on the other hand, got excited. Her nipples became hard and her face animated with wicked thoughts.

In his last year of school, Jacopo noticed that the smell of some of his male friends aroused him, that he enjoyed watching muscles moving across their torsos as they changed for football, and that he loved the way pubic hair spreads across a man's stomach.

Vanessa wanted to be more intimate in the middle of their last year.

"Come on." She'd plead. "We'll stay together forever anyway. You'll be my one and only, Jacopo. What does it matter if we have sex now or in a year, after marriage?" She looked at him with big, imploring eyes, completely unaware that her feminine charm had no impact.

In the face of these conversations, panic built in Jacopo's chest. He knew Vanessa was one of the fairest and most unique people he would ever meet, but it wasn't enough. The thought of entering her made him want to vomit, like someone squeezing his stomach intent on forcing his organs from his mouth.

"No." He'd soothe her. "Be patient. You know what Father Giovanni said in his last sermon. 'The one who is patient can meet paradise on Earth.'

You said it yourself; we have our whole lives together. I respect you and don't want to rush." This time, their shared faith helped persuade her and she understood clearly that he wanted to be married before anything happened below the waist.

But, then, the graduation party came along and alcohol lowered inhibitions. Vanessa, intoxicated for the first time, begged him to set a date for their wedding. She wanted to be married and have sex so badly that it consumed her thoughts even when unable to think clearly.

Jacopo couldn't do it anymore. "Vanessa, I'm sorry. I love you," she smiled drunkenly without realising what was coming, "but I've realised I love you as a friend. I can't marry you." He could see the words slowly processing, but she didn't understand yet. "I'm breaking off the engagement, Vanessa." The words hit her hard bringing new horrors as she embraced them.

Vanessa locked herself in the bathroom for the rest of the night and was surrounded by her closest friends. Jacopo more or less ruined their class's graduation party. It felt like everyone was sucked into his very private and very personal drama and there was nothing he could do about it. The girls comforted Vanessa while the boys, like Jacopo, absented from their first sexual experiences. They would hold onto that grudge for the rest of the summer.

Both families couldn't understand how the lovers had ceased to be. Their parents would cry down the phone to each other, "They were meant to be together. What changed?"

Jacopo moved to Rome for university without confiding in anyone about his big secret. He just left, disappointed Vanessa and their families, and dropped all expectations of the life they had planned for him.

University meant a new life for Jacopo. Nobody cared who he was attracted to. There was a shared agreement among students that it didn't matter how you looked or who you fucked. Everything was accepted.

Still, Jacopo needed some time to come out of his shell and embrace this new freedom. To start off with, he was an observer of the liberated dynamics of university. He noted that everybody was experimenting; you just had to decide and be what you wanted to be. You could try it for a while and move on to something new when you wished.

The first time Jacopo braved a gay bar was in his second year of study. He'd wanted to go since day one in Rome, but something held him back. When he finally made it through the door, Jacopo thought he'd landed in a fairy tale. The colours were bold. The faces were even bolder, happy, and flirtatious. Some people were in costume and everyone seemed to openly embrace themselves.

Sitting in a corner at the end of the bar, Jacopo ordered a beer and tried to acclimatise. He felt comfortable hidden from the main crowd, and from here, he could watch the groups around him, breathe in the scent of the place. A breeze of longed-for freedom overtook him. Jacopo watched beautiful bodies dance and touch each other without constraint. The people surrounding him were the most handsome and happy he had ever seen. He sipped his beer and smiled and took pleasure in being where he belonged.

And then he noticed one dancer in particular, Rocco. Jacopo tried to mentally etch this man into his brain. He didn't know his name or anything about him at this point, but Jacopo was mesmerised. *He's a vision. His dark skin sparkles with dancing sweat. That black curly hair is angelic; I love the way it jumps with his movements.* Jacopo was smitten from afar. *And his smile, a mouth full of teeth that shine like precious diamonds.*

Rocco wore an open white shirt and white jeans which emphasised his dark skin. He was the epitome of an old Roman statue, curved to perfection.

Jacopo returned to that bar every weekend for five weeks. He would sit in the same corner and wait until Rocco arrived.

When he did, Jacopo would find himself unable to approach and say hello. Instead, he'd observe and ignore the troops of ripped young men marching around him, some smiling flirtatiously in his direction and others approaching him directly as a conquest.

Rocco and Jacopo finally met at the bar on the fifth weekend. Rocco could feel Jacopo's green eyes staring at him. He glanced over to the young man thinking, *This youngster still smells of his mother's milk. But he's quite beautiful, blossoming from boy to man.*

"Rocco." He said, presenting a welcoming hand.

"Jacopo."

They shook and started talking, then drinking, then flirting. Jacopo was nervous. *Is this how to flirt with a man?* And Rocco felt like a king seeing Jacopo's soul beg for healing and love. Jacopo the wobbly, new-born chick wishing desperately to play with the roosters.

Rocco and Jacopo talked the whole night and never found themselves in an awkward pause. And it was the same from that night on. Rocco, aged forty, became the first romantic love of Jacopo, aged twenty-two.

* * *

A little over four years later, Jacopo finished university with a minor extension. The long-term lovers discussed their relationship at length and eventually decided to immortalise their passion with a civil partnership. They celebrated with a wild marriage party surrounded by friends, and Jacopo finally felt whole and complete.

Rocco was also in love but went into the partnership with the belief that it was time to settle down more than anything else. Telling himself, *I'm older and we've had a fun four years, so why not?*

When he proposed on their favourite square, under the shadow of trees from an adjacent park, Jacopo replied with an ecstatic, "Yes."

Fuerteventura was their honeymoon destination and where I came to know their story.

* * *

"OK. Next task!" Jacopo announced joyfully.

"No more tasks today." Rocco interrupted. "It's time to relax on the beach."

They walked towards the sea. Rocco settled on a towel and began to oil his skin. Youthful Jacopo ran straight to the water and revelled in the cool lapping against his hot body.

As Jacopo made his way back, all sea soaked and sun kissed, Rocco watched with admiration. He adored Jacopo's well-sculpted, football-player body. Rocco was even jealous of his young spouse at times, especially when others noticed his beauty. Man, woman, straight, gay, it didn't matter. In Rocco's mind, they all looked at Jacopo with lust.

Lying on the sand next to Rocco, Jacopo stared at slow floating clouds. He closed his eyes to rest, but the words he'd read in a text on Rocco's phone by mistake were burning hotter than the sun.

> Still miss your touch. Let's meet.
> I'll be in Rome next month.
> Love. Ted

When challenged, Rocco explained that Ted was an ex from a short exchange programme in New York. After the relationship ended, they met once for coffee but otherwise didn't keep contact. "Now, eighteen years later, I have pleasant memories of that period, but nothing more." Rocco comforted.

That would've been enough of an explanation if Jacopo hadn't found letters to disprove this story.

Uncovering them was a genuine mistake; Jacopo wasn't searching for trouble. But just before their honeymoon they fell in his lap, and now, they were slowly driving him crazy.

* * *

Both Rocco and Jacopo loved to dress up and be silly, so Jacopo planned to take superhero outfits on honeymoon as a surprise. Rocco had lots of them and he stored them at his mother's house. So Jacopo and his mother-in-law conspired in the surprise, and off Jacopo went to search through her basement.

Rocco's mother and Jacopo liked each other instantly, but since Jacopo had come out as gay to his family she'd been even more attentive. Jacopo's family wouldn't speak with him after he refused their offer of divine intervention.

"This is unacceptable, Jacopo." They cried down the phone. "We'll speak with Father Giovanni and find a way to heal you of this disease." As they protested, Rocco's mother offered support and acceptance.

In the basements, Rocco's mother pointed Jacopo in the right direction, saying, "That closet there, dear. Good luck on your quest." She smiled. "Take your time. And when you're finished, lock the door and bring the key over to the neighbour's. I promised to fix her hair, and I get told off if I am late. She's very old-fashioned. So I've got to run." Jacopo hugged her and kissed the top of her head. She left the room with no idea what Jacopo would find.

He opened the closet doors and quickly located the right box. Rocco labelled everything with descriptions, so it was an easy task. Jacopo felt like a happy child as he tucked the costumes away into his backpack. He smiled, imagining the look on Rocco's face when seeing the outfits in Fuerteventura. A wave of excitement flooded over him and he laughed out loud in the basement. Jacopo had been counting down the hours until their honeymoon, anticipating a new intimacy in their relationship, and he was ready for the good times to begin.

Shoving other disrupted boxes back into Rocco's closet caused a small shoebox to fall from above. The box flung open and a torrent of letters flowed out. Jacopo looked around the room to check he was alone and no one had seen his clumsy handling of Rocco's possessions. As he gathered the letters to put them away, he noticed they were all from the same person. It was a name Jacopo recognised. It was Ted.

"Shit." Jacopo whispered into the room. He knelt down and inspected under the closet, ensuring every single one had been picked up. In his hand he held a postcard. He stared at it knowing that the postcard and the whole box were private. But he read on all the same.

MOMENTS WITH YOU ARE DIAMONDS
I WILL CHERISH FOREVER.

YOU WILL ALWAYS BE MY VALENTINE

XOXO

TED

Jacopo heard himself gasp as his brain went into overdrive. There was no date. The card must have been on a gift given in person. *This is Ted.* Jacopo reeled. *Rocco told me it was a fling, nothing special.* He looked at the letters. There were many.

Why does my husband still have these letters? He should have burnt them, thrown them away. Jacopo grabbed his head to stop the exploding pain that ripped through him.

"What is this? Why are these still here?" Jacopo sat and looked for dates on the letters. *Okay, these are old: eighteen years old. That makes sense.* He continued to sit and stare at what was in his hands, waiting to make a decision. They reminded him of a time Vanessa left him in a room with her open diary as a test. He had not, for even a split second, wanted to read her thoughts. But he wanted to read these.

Jacopo took the letters and piled them by date. *Twelve letters,* he noted.

90

He put them back in the box and closed it, then reopened it. *Just one.* He knew it wasn't right but didn't care, operating on a desire to know and nothing else. *What's the harm? They're almost two decades old. It's in the past. It's like reading a historical documentary about young Rocco. It'll help me understand him better.*

NYC, October 6th, 1999

Dear Rocco,

I can't believe you're really back in Europe. You are so far from me now. I cried myself to sleep last night, and when I woke up this morning, all I wanted was to see you. But that's impossible.

You are always in my head, on my mind. Before I go to sleep and when I wake up, all I can think about is you.

How are you? How was your return? Did you travel well? I hope so.

I am here, moody and depressed because you're gone from my life. I don't know what to write or say. I feel the pain of your absence all over my body.

I love you.

Ted

Jacopo panicked. *It was tough for Ted to accept Rocco was gone.* He didn't contemplate it this time and opened the next letter.

Dear Rocco,

They say time heals all wounds. But my pain grows more significant with each week that passes. I feel so bad that I am becoming crazy. I want so much to see your face and your beautiful brown eyes one more time. Now I can only remember them. I never got to say the things I wanted to because my pride wouldn't allow me. Now, I'm trying to cherish the memory of our time together and to remember the details: every laugh, what we spoke about, how you looked.

Thank you for your last beautiful letter. As you see, I can't express myself as well as you. I've put the photo you sent me on my wall so I can watch you before I go to bed and see you when I wake up.

I love you,

Ted

This does not read like a fling or a one-night stand. Jacopo's breathing became heavy. *This was Ted's real, deep, first love. Rocco was loved by Ted and maybe loved him in return. And he called this a fling.* Jacopo opened the next letter.

NYC, November 11th, 1999

Dear Rocco,

I can't get you out of my head. I put on our music and it makes me remember every moment we spent together. I wish I could hold you, kiss your lips, play with your hair, touch your beautiful skin. I wish I could hear your loud laughter.

I wish I'd expressed myself openly to you from the beginning, from the moment we met. I played so hard to get, and now, you have possessed me. I am completely obsessed.

Remember the park, climbing on trees, and picnics under the old oak? Our tree.

I love you,

Ted

Somewhere in Jacopo's brain he wanted to stop, but he couldn't. He opened and read the letters until he'd read them all. He sat alone in the basement and cried. Jacopo felt Ted's pain close to him and it was unbearable.

A noise came from upstairs, so Jacopo took a quick picture of the back of one envelope to capture Ted's address. He packed the twelve letters into their box and returned them to the closet of Rocco's history. Grabbing his backpack, Jacopo ran upstairs to find Rocco's mother home again.

"Thank you." He said as he quickly hugged her and moved to leave.

"I can't believe you're still here, Jacopo. Did you find your outfits?" Rocco's mother asked.

"Yes, I was searching for a mask." He lied, "Somehow it fell under the closet, so I didn't find it for a while. Thanks again." He felt blood colouring his cheeks as he lied to the woman that had given him unending support.

"Will you stay for dinner?"

"I have to go and get ready for work I'm afraid." Jacopo excused himself. "I've got to help a co-worker. They just called me." He was out the door with tears in his eyes. "Love you. Ciao." Emotional drills bored into his head as he said goodbye.

His ears burnt. He had no idea he could feel such devastation, anger, and jealousy.

He knew that Rocco had previous partners, that he'd fucked half the gay community in Rome, *But why lie to me? Why call it a fling when it was serious? And now they're back in contact. What does that mean?*

Jacopo became obsessed with trying to find Ted on social media but had no luck. *What kind of person doesn't have social media, not one?* He would curse and start to judge the Ted that was hidden from him. Eventually, Jacopo found him on LinkedIn and learned the face of Rocco's ex-love. From here, Jacopo uncovered a few pages connected to Ted's company and his name under seminars where he had presented. He looked well-groomed, handsome even.

I wonder what they did when they were together? Jacopo compared his fictitious creation of Ted and Rocco's relationship with his own relationship. It turned his stomach.

NYC, December 10th, 1999

Dear Rocco,

Time is slowly passing without you, and I am still raging around my apartment. I am not fun company. I made a box, like a child, and filled it with our pictures. We're so handsome together. I also put our concert tickets and a leaf you accidentally brought back from one of our park picnics in there. These small mementoes allow me to relive some of the happiest times of my life.

I still can't believe I've fallen so hard for you, and so quickly. I wish I could pick you up in my arms now, take you to the coast, and hold you while we watch the sunrise.

The Christmas season is coming. Our holiday time together was such fun. It was the time of my life, in fact. Every moment was special.

The lights are on in the mall, and the city's glowing, but I can't find holiday cheer in me. I search for you everywhere I go. I smelt your perfume at the store, but it's not the same. Your natural scent is missing. I enviously watched young lovers shopping together, laughing together. I can't believe that this time last year we were skating side by side.

I can't believe time has passed so quickly and that we made no plan. Why is it so difficult to have you, for us to be together?

I want us to hold each other one more time.

I love you

Ted

* * *

"Where are you?" Rocco asked, agitated and jealous as they lay on the beach.

"Thinking of someone else." Jacopo wasn't lying. He had another man on his mind but for entirely different reasons than Rocco suspected. Jacopo turned on his side to face Rocco and supported his head on his hand. "And he's gorgeous." He mocked, grabbing Rocco by the waist and kissing him. Jacopo gazed into Rocco's eyes and to cover his feelings teased him more.

Can I ask about Ted again? He questioned as the sun and sand warmed him. *I can't stop repeating this story of Ted. But now is not the right time.*

Rocco and Jacopo sizzled in toxicity.

They needed each other to feel complete, but they were torturing themselves with jealousy and crazy scenarios of ex-lovers. One thing united them; they loved each other and didn't want to be alone. But they were being divided but everything unsaid.

Rocco saw a playful, fearful glint in Jacopo's eye and wondered, *Is this good love, mature love? Do we love each other more than anyone else? Why do I feel this need to claim him as my own? He's not my property. Mature love exists in people who spend time together and create memories without unhealthy attachment. Is that us?*

Each swallowed their doubt and covered it with a laugh. Jacopo kissed Rocco one more time before taking a blueberry cigarillo from his bag. He searched around himself, cigarillo hanging from his mouth, and asked for the lighter. Rocco lit me as Jacopo bent his knees and hugged them. They sat silently together and watched the sun set into the sea. As the light dimmed, Jacopo remembered another letter.

NYC, December 31st, 1999

Dear Rocco,

Sorry for the messy handwriting. I'm drunk. I wish you were here now so we could lie on the bed and look at each other. I want to look into your eyes.

I drove to your apartment. Then I realised you're not there. That place belongs to some other foreign student now.

I wait for the year 2000 alone. I don't want to party; there's a feeling deep inside me that my life is over. I don't find any joy... I will never find someone like you again... I know it sounds pathetic, but it's true.

I love you forever.

Ted

P.S.

Happy New Year! HAPPY 2000. May it bring us together again... xoxo (January 1st, 2000).

"Where are you, now?" Rocco nervously asked. The letter smeared with red wine disappeared from Jacopo's mind.

"Do you prefer sunrise or sunset?" Jacopo asked, fixed on the sunset before them and avoiding looking at Rocco. He smoked and rolled me over in his hand.

"What kind of question is that?" Rocco asked, confused. With each of Jacopo's seemingly random questions Rocco's restlessness grew.

Jacopo repeated calmly, "Do you prefer sunrise or sunset? Easy. Which is more intriguing to you, waiting for the sun to rise or watching her set?" For Jacopo, there was only one answer.

"I like the sunrise. The hope of a new day brings me joy. But when you're enjoying the company of someone special, either is perfect." Rocco was pleased with himself.

Wrong. Jacopo clenched his fists so hard he could crack me open.

Sensing the tension and willing a change in mood, Rocco suggested, "Let's go. We have a reservation. Maybe we'll see the sunrise as well as sunset tonight." He hugged a silent Jacopo.

At the hotel, they freshened up for dinner. Both tried to look fabulous in celebration of their union. But the celebration couldn't stop Jacopo's haunting memories.

NYC, February 1st, 2000

Dear Rocco,

You are always on my mind. We have to think of ways to be together again. I was checking the tickets to Rome, but they're incredibly expensive. I don't know how I will ever afford to get to you.

All I want to do is hold you and look in your eyes. I'm going crazy away from you. We spent the best part of a year together, side by side, and now we are four months apart. Even after four months, every cell of my body misses you.

We were in a bubble with eyes solely for each other, as you so nicely put in your last letter.

I had stopped writing because I thought it would help me forget you. I even asked my roommate not to tell me when I have messages from you on the phone. But now I feel broken. Your second letter broke my heart.

You have to know that this separation is incredibly hard for me. You cloud my mind, make me a crazy person who's unable to think about anything else... but you... just you... all the time... every second. It's like your memory is constantly searching for me, hunting me.

I love you forever.

Ted

* * *

The restaurant had a perfect view of Lobos. Rocco lit a candle to enhance the romance and, while doing so, got distracted by a handsome man in the company of a young, enthused woman.

Jacopo noticed and the words were out before he could stop them. "Do you find him attractive?" He reprimanded himself.

98

Of course you find him attractive. I couldn't be the only one on your mind. Why do you look at others if I'm here? Why was Ted so special? Why did you create a bubble with him and not me?

Jacopo took a long sip of wine, accidentally emptying his glass.

"Who? What?" Rocco replied, genuinely confused. "What's up with you today? We should be the happiest couple here. For sure, we are the most handsome." Rocco tried to touch Jacopo's hand but his young partner pulled away and poured himself another glass of wine.

"Hey, we should make a toast." Rocco countered to lighten the mood.

"I saw it." Jacopo interrupted. "How you looked at that tall guy eating with the blonde. Do you find him attractive? You're here with me, and still, you look at other guys. Aren't I enough?"

Rocco laughed theatrically which made it hard to tell if this humoured him or if he was deflecting the attack. "What's wrong with you today? Why all these weird questions? You are the most beautiful man on this island, if not in the whole world. At the very least, you're the most beautiful in Europe." He smiled and tried to take Jacopo's hand again.

"You really think that?" Jacopo spat his words. "For real? So there's no one more handsome in the U.S., for example?" Jacopo could see he was destroying their honeymoon, but he couldn't forget the letters and every time Rocco refused to mention them his jealousy intensified.

NYC, March 5th, 2000

Dear Rocco,

I have been busy. Hell, I'm always busy, but that doesn't mean I'm not missing you still, even after six months.

You are gone and it kills me every day. I'm dreaming of you again. I lie awake sometimes thinking about why I didn't kiss you for longer, hold you for longer, make love with you for longer. I think of calling, but it's too expensive and the time difference never fits. What can we do?

Every day I see you vividly in my room, where you sat, lay, and danced. You are the most beautiful person I ever met, inside and out. I met the most amazing man in the world and lost him.

Do you remember how everyone noticed us at parties? We were always the most beautiful couple in the room. We are blessed with looks, wits, and brains. And, dear Rocco, you wrote that I am the most handsome man you know, but I think you are the most beautiful creature I ever encountered and ever will.

Come back to me, please.

I love you to the moon and back again.

Ted

Jacopo had always been told he was beautiful, classically handsome. But this knowledge didn't calm him. It didn't make him feel better knowing that him and Rocco were beautiful together. He was afraid that he wasn't enough and would never be enough. In this moment, Jacopo called himself ugly and fixated on the beauty of the man on the other table with the blonde and on Ted. The part of his soul that loved Rocco fell silent and jealousy rampaged. It stopped him seeing Rocco's attempts to be kind and reassuring. It was blind to the light in Rocco's eyes. Jacopo rolled his glass in circles and asked, "Who did you love the most?"

Rocco almost choked on his wine, "What are you talking about?"

"Was it Ted or is it me?" Jacopo held me up and observed Rocco as though looking through a lens. *Why can't I put my ego aside and speak clearly, ask honestly?*

NYC, April 19th, 2000

My love, Rocco,

They say time heals. Why is it still not healing me? I feel such pain.

I hear your voice in my dreams. You are the perfect man for me. I think all the other men are dull and unattractive in your shadow.

I went out recently and it bored me. I prefer us, our little world, away from everyone — just you and me in the eternity of our emotions.

Send me more pictures, preferably topless.

I will wait for you forever.

I love you,

Ted

"Where are these questions coming from, Jacopo?" Rocco demanded.

Jacopo couldn't be honest. He made Rocco wait as he searched for an explanation, but he couldn't find one. He needed to conceal his invasion of Rocco's privacy, so after some time, he shrugged.

"Why all these questions, Jacopo?" Rocco wasn't going to let it go any longer. "I already told you, Ted was a fling in the US.

It lasted two months, we had almost no contact beyond those two months."

NYC, May 23rd, 2000

Rocco, my love,

I'm still waiting for your letter. I'm getting crazier with waiting. I think it would be good if you opened an email account. You probably have libraries near you if you don't have the internet at home. Please, consider doing this for me.

I've developed the film from my camera, and I'm sending you a picture of us together. Do you remember this trip?

You are so handsome. Aren't we such a lovely couple? We complete each other like a puzzle finally solved.

How can the pain still burn so much? If this is love, why does it hurt so much?

I love your soul and body and presence.

Always yours

Ted

Every time Rocco lied, Jacopo felt like someone was pulling his skin off with claws. Everything hurt. Every part of his body burned from disappointment.

This was not the evening they had planned.

"But will you meet him if he comes to Rome?" Jacopo asked directly.

"I don't know. Probably not." Rocco turned away and confessed, "Although, it would be nice to see Ted again after all these years."

Jacopo felt sick. His mind went blank. He stood up in the middle of their dinner and walked away. Tears marked his cheeks on the way to the hotel, and before he knew it, he was running to stop them, to get the sick feeling out of his body. He raced passed the hotel and ran and ran and ran until he collapsed near the beach with nothing but the waves as his witness.

Rocco paid the bill and followed after him, but Jacopo was too fast in his escape. Rocco tried to call but couldn't get through. He typed a message, "Jacopo, don't be childish. Come back. Let's talk." But Jacopo's phone was on silent and his eyes were lost in the dark sky. Rocco lay down in their honeymoon sweet and wept from abandonment.

Sitting alone, Jacopo thought about Rocco's words at dinner, "Almost no contact since then." *How can he tell such lies?*

NYC, June 30th, 2000

Rocco,

Congratulations! I was so excited to finally get an email from you. Welcome to this century.

I'm getting better. I still miss you like crazy. I don't know if the news that you still think of me helps. Although, I see so much is happening to you that it is certainly a comfort to know I'm still in your heart. It's almost a momentary cure to my madness.

How is it possible that two people are made for each other and not together? Why don't you come back? I'd love to go to Rome, but what can I do in Italy? I don't know the language and the opportunities in the States are better for both of us.

Anyway, every week is a little better. It turns out, time and a lack of closeness do eventually heal broken hearts.

Love,

Ted

They stayed in contact, intimate contact. Jacopo took deep breaths. *What if they started to fool around again?* But as quickly as he exhaled, he found his thoughts kicking off. *But when? When he was in the U.S. on that three week training course? He said he had a super busy schedule. And even with the time difference he wrote every day, quite extensively. He couldn't have. Could he?*

Jacopo lay down on the cool evening ground and felt the rhythm of the sea through the earth. Too tired to challenge his ideas about Rocco any further, he let the waves lap in his mind and allowed himself to drift off to sleep.

* * *

In the morning, Jacopo woke to the open air, stiff and tired. He headed directly to the hotel breakfast room, where Rocco was already dressed and seated. Rocco didn't look up even when Jacopo cleared his throat to announce his arrival. Pissed was the only word that could describe Rocco's mood. He couldn't believe the man he'd married had actually run away for a whole night on their honeymoon.

"Are you still behaving like a child?" Rocco questioned without raising his eyes from where he pretended to scan the news on his phone. "Have I married a child, Jacopo?"

Jacopo felt guilty. He would be furious if Rocco ran away from him, especially in his current state of paranoia, and he didn't want to argue so said, "No. I'm sorry I left you like that."

After breakfast, Jacopo showered and washed the panic from his skin. As the water cleansed him, Ted's voice snuck in.

NYC, August 25th, 2000

Rocco,

I hope you're well. I am extremely busy with my new work and studying. I know that I took a long time to write back, but I've been so very busy with everything that I didn't get the chance before now.

If I'm honest with you, which I have always tried to be, I needed time to heal. I needed to not be in contact with you, to have a crazy summer and let go. I'd mourned the loss of you for eight months. My sister implored me to stop punishing myself. She invited me to join her on some charity work in Brazil and didn't allow me to open any mail without her being at my side.

I have so much on my plate. Be good.

All the best,

Ted

A ferry took Jacopo and Rocco from Fuerteventura to Morocco for a three-day, pre-booked trip. As soon as they boarded, a fight ensued. Rocco lit a cigarillo with me and dropped me under a bench. They screamed at each other as Jacopo seethed, invasive words filling his head.

Rocco, my dearest,

A year has passed.

I will always be glad I met you. In some ways, you defined me. It was fun. It was wonderful. I still visit our places from time to time and fondly remember being there together.

I hope your plans are becoming reality.

With love, your friend,

Ted

Jacopo disengaged from their argument, preoccupied. Rocco, frustrated, left him sitting on a bench alone.

Jacopo took a moment, inhaled and thought, *We have placed ourselves in separate boxes where we can't communicate. Our values, our dreams, have slipped apart from one another.*

The thought made him want to cry. *How did this happen so quickly?* With an inhale, his mind switched and expanded and he saw that there was a diverging path before them and a choice to be made. *We need to decide whether we walk it together or alone. Can we continue? Can we find appreciation, peace, and love for each other again?*

Jacopo stood up abruptly and left to figure out his next steps. And I was left alone once more.

Five: EMA, JAN and MAKS

They all teach us 'the right way' to do things. But maybe they're not right at all.

An infant named Maks picked me up on the ferry and shoved me into his mouth. That was a first. After some sucking and exploring with his tongue, Maks tried to swallow me but, thankfully, his mother Ema intervened.

"Maks, that's yucky! You shouldn't put things you find lying around in your mouth." Said Ema, pulling me away from Maks' grip and throwing me thoughtlessly in her bag. It was a new-mum reflex that ensured nothing meaningful got left behind.

Ema picked up her son and began reflecting on the trip they were returning from. She'd visited Morocco before as a student, and everything about her time there had been fantastic. It was a trip she could never forget. But this time, the holiday dragged out before her like feet pulled through deep wet mud. Morocco hadn't changed, but for Ema travelling with an infant was not fun. She'd imagined the family supporting each other and smiling in the face of adventure, but it wasn't like that at all. She couldn't relax, despite willing herself to, and was unable to enjoy it. She realised that, tragically, she wasn't the hip, free-flowing traveller she wanted to be.

Ema spotted her husband, Jan, and called out to him. "Got him! He'd snuck under a bench somehow. I swear, he'll give me a heart attack one of these days. I hope we manage to keep our sanity until he comes of age."

She wanted to speak in good humour but sounded genuinely concerned about pending madness.

Jan took Maks in his arms and hugged him tight. He noticed the pitch in Ema's voice, and his heart sank. *When will we break these cycles?*

Jan and Ema had been communicating badly for some time and it was really starting to show. *This is ridiculous.* He cursed to himself. *It's the same scene replaying: choice, change, sacrifice, disappointment, desperation, misery, new choice, repeat. The cycle of my whole life. What did I do to deserve this?*

Jan dreamt of simplicity. He wanted to love his wife, protect his son and teach him what it felt like to be truly loved, and that was it.

"What if," He started, "We are all so thoroughly trained by our parents, society, and religion that we're unable to diverge from the path they've set us on?" The words fell from his mouth heavily.

Ema looked horrified, which prompted Jan to soothe her and caress her back. It was a habit he'd developed in their years trying to get pregnant.

"What do you mean?" Ema exhaled a desperate breath.

"You know." He cautiously tried to explain. "They all teach us 'the right way' to do things. But maybe they're not right at all." Jan read his wife's confused expression. *Does she get it?* He continued. "From a young age, my mother taught me one way to hang the laundry. She said it was the only and right way to do it. She obsessed about the 'right way'. Her methods were ingrained in me, so I never tried to hang laundry any other way. I accepted her truth as absolute."

Ema broke eye contact. "I needed time living away from her ways to change my own. A friend showed me the trick with the hanger a few years after I'd moved out, and it made so much more sense than my mother's way. Now I hang all my clothes on the hanger.

108

After they're dry, I fold the pieces for the drawer and the rest stays hanging. I barely have to do any ironing. It's the perfect way for me."

Jan paused his monologue and ran after Maks who was quickly wriggling away. It gave Jan a moment's break from the conversation but not from his point. He grabbed the sprawling child and thought, *Fuck. This again. Why did I start this conversation, the meaning of bloody life, again?! Good one, Jan.* He smiled from a distance at the nervous looking Ema. *She's going to over-analyse every stupid irrelevant thing I just said. Why couldn't I talk about music or sport or the bloody weather? How can we shift our energy and break this cycle?*

Jan watched Ema for a moment as Maks reached out to sea from the safety of his father's arms. *She's become just like my mother: never satisfied, always worried.*

Jan, with Maks in tow, took his seat next to Ema suggested, "Let's go inside otherwise Maks is going to make a jump for the water." He hoped a change of location would change the topic.

Inside, Jan picked a quiet spot away from bright ferry lights and other passengers and laid his jacket on a seat for Ema. She settled into the warmth and continued what Jan started. "Each year, it feels more and more important to me to watch what's going on in the world around us, to observe human behaviour and reflect on how we live our own lives."

Jan knew where this conversation was going, and he didn't want to listen.

"Whenever I travel," Ema continued, "I'm fascinated by the way people from different cultures do things. It sounds simple, but because I look around myself I'm constantly adapting my life processes." She raised her eyebrows to ensure he was listening. Jan nodded in false attentiveness. "It's all part of growing as a person, but for me it's about becoming more true to my real nature. I'm trying to make big changes every time I adjust the way I function."

Jan thought but would never say, *I've seen so many adjustments that I can't remember who you truly were when we started anymore.*

"Each time I change a process," Ema explained, "I crush an outdated belief of how something should be done or an idea of what's perfect. I say goodbye to 'the right way'." She didn't say anymore but let Jan soak in her wisdom and feel her judgment that he was not able to crush outdated beliefs in the same way she could.

He turned away and rolled his eyes. *It's true: she's alway trying new things. She is constantly trying to become a greater, more reflective soul, but in doing so, she pushes me out of her favour, out of her practices, and forces me from her affection. I can't listen to another one of her sermons. They aren't her true nature at all.*

He'd tried every way he knew to support her 'true nature' over the years, then to support her through their failed pregnancies, and post natal depression. But he was starting to realise he couldn't stop her feeling disappointed by life. Jan was at breaking point. *How much longer can she search for happiness. When will she ever feel happy?*

As a boy, Jan's mum had preached to him as well. It made his mood swing from free and happy to heavy and low. Sitting next to Ema, with the water ebbing below them, Jan imagined his mother, remembered the efforts he went to to calm her down, to reassure her he was there for her, that he'd always be there.

Jan's voice escaped revealing his annoyance. "I'm quite aware of how you change processes all the time, Ema, because we share a life and so change together. It's slowly driving me crazy." Ema turned shooting waves of pain in his direction. He'd gone too far. "Maybe our system should be that we don't have one anymore." He continued trying to be supportive. "We have travelled down a long and winding path, and it will continue ahead of us. But it should be an amazing and liberating journey.

People are unconscious of the path for a lot of their life, but eventually, we have to start making choices about which turns to take. The question now is, when will you start walking the path consciously and stick to it?" He let the word 'you' sink in.

"For the past ten years, I've been consciously coordinating and adjusting my life for your wishes." He continued. "I set goals and really challenged deeply rooted beliefs for you. I followed you. But the last seven years have been a nightmare, for you especially. I know this. But I've changed lots of aspects of my life, ways of perceiving it and accepting it for what it is. I'm far from Nirvana. Hell, I don't know if I'll ever get there, but the fact that I want to create more openness and acceptance in our family for Maks is proof I've made quantum changes in my thinking." Jan dragged Maks to his feet. Somewhere in his defence he'd started crying and didn't want Ema to see.

It was Ema who'd wished for a child. Jan agreed believing that family life could calm her endless search for satisfaction and reinvention. But she'd fallen even further into the search since conceiving. He was often told, "We have to live outside the box, Jan, in everything we do," as Ema started to read the next article on *Reaching Ultimate Happiness and Tranquillity In Life* or some similarly ambitious title. He was sick of it.

Jan composed himself. "If we never set boundaries for Maks, all we do is teach him that he can do whatever he wants with his life and that he doesn't have to commit to anything. We teach him stupid things, like not making the world better is okay. We teach him that he can be nothing and it doesn't matter. That being nothing is fine."

Ema took Maks from Jan and cradled him in her lap. They played, and she found some calm in his tiny body. As she rubbed his cheeks, she said, "New issues keep popping up. And I know they will for the rest of my life. Overcoming them means I'm growing, that I'm changing myself and my surroundings. I am moving in the right direction."

She can only look at herself in this. Jan thought. He put on a hoodie as air-con coldness filled his body. He remembered the years of torture and disappointment for them both when trying to conceive. He never said no to any of the crazy treatments. He never said it was time to stop trying because he knew how much she wanted a baby. He thought about the day Maks was born and Ema saying, "If I survive and the child survives, then we'll have an ordinary, boring life. I swear." She'd forgotten her promise soon after. There would be no ordinary and no boring.

"It's not possible to raise a child without some structure, Ema. Maybe it's time to admit that you actually liked some of the things your family provided for you rather than trying to do everything differently to them. You might be surprised." She said nothing. "Honestly," Jan laboured home his point, "this was not the best vacation for me: backpacking with an infant."

She agreed to herself. *It was the worst. Not our cup of tea at all.* But she wasn't ready to let go of the rebel that shouted inside her, demanding she be different to her mother, demanding adventure. So she said, "I think it was nice. We learnt a lot about us, our child, Morocco..."

Jan stretched out on the floor. His back ached and his legs were tense. He felt annoyed with Ema but also wanted to poke her playfully and break the tension. Unable to carry on in stony silence, he said, "You know, the apple doesn't fall far from the tree, Ema."

Ema wasn't good at letting go, so when she set her mind to something it had to be realised. She wanted to prove to everybody that she was different from her parents, her friends, her society, that she was more adventurous, that she was more. But she hadn't found this to be true yet and that hurt her.

She retorted, "Well, this apple did. The tree was on a hill and I rolled far, far away." Jan left her to her victory and carried on stretching and breathing through his tension. Maks played with Ema's fingers, sucking and pulling at them.

She sat there, wrapped in Jan's jacket, thinking, *The same things that annoyed my mother are starting to annoy me.* She closed her eyes and breathed. She tried to breathe slowly. *Inhale fully.* She told herself. *Slowly exhale.* She guided. *Calm down.*

Jan observed from the floor. In the safety of her closed eyes, he allowed himself to be honest. *I don't know how much longer I can do this. She needs professional help. I have to remove the blindfold from my eyes: I'm not Jesus. I couldn't save my mum. I can't save Ema. I've tried, but I know I can't. But what about Maks?*

"How have we come to this?" Ema asked, eyes still shut. "Where did the excitement go? Why isn't this fun?" Her deep breaths stopped. "I feel like I'm being choked all the time. We have everything, Jan. We are healthy. We finally got our little miracle." She opened her eyes, and they both watched Maks who was now playing on the floor with an empty plastic bottle. "Seven years we waited for him. Seven years of yearning, doctors, and appointments in clinics. Time passed as we waited and wished."

Jan knew what she was talking about for the first time in a long time: they were momentarily on the same page. *How can I give up hope after so many years?*

"How can I fill the void inside me now, Jan?" Ema had tears in her eyes. "I should be the happiest person in the world."

"I'm happy." Jan said, raising himself to the seat next to her and taking her hand. "I think I'm happy, not with this vacation but..." he tried to laugh and comfort her. "I would've preferred a resort and all you can eat. But, all in all, I am happy. When I wake up, I feel content." He wasn't being entirely honest, but it felt like the right thing to say.

Ema was angry now and not sure why. She leaned back on her chair and closed her eyes again. *Inhale fully. Slowly exhale. Calm down.*

Jan let go of her hand.

What's missing? Why isn't she happy? Is this my lot in life, balancing out Ema? He watched her chest rise and fall, watched her try to be okay, stable, balanced. *But we are blessed. Why doesn't she feel it? She has a void. How can I fill that? We have a child.* Maks made his way back to his parents and started bumbling about at Jan's feet. *How is it possible that she doesn't feel the fulfilment of Maks being here?*

Jan also tried to breathe and allow his mind time to problem solve. He had no idea how to tackle this. Ema was getting worse. As a couple, they were getting worse.

The thing he found the most challenging was the dramatic shifts in Ema's outlook. One moment she'd be hopeful and positive, praising her latest god, guru, or diet, and the next she'd be disappointed and searching, again, for a theory, a way to eat, a workout routine, a new way to open chakras.

Since they'd become parents, Ema's dislike for her own family intensified. Jan couldn't understand the need to do everything in opposition to their values. *What happened there? They're decent people, a bit stiff, yes, but good people. They like to do things in their old way, but they've got good intentions. They always help us, despite Ema's rejection. Could they really have hurt her so much?*

Jan's mind jumped on. *I want a normal Christmas tree. I want a fucking traditional, green Christmas tree with lots of lights and colourful decorations. And I don't want the decorations to match. Who wants a pink tree with one colour of lights?*

Closing his eyes too, Jan asked, "Ema, what do you need to be happy?" No response. "We have good family, friends, good jobs. We have two cars, a couple of bikes, a house, and a holiday cottage in the mountains. What more do you need?" Frustration crept into his voice.

Jan loved Ema and always tried to understand her: how she was feeling; what she needed or wanted; what theories she was following. He felt it his duty, as the husband of a new-age woman on the search for spiritual awakening, to invest in her searches, but everyone has a breaking point.

"I do not know, Jan. If I knew, we wouldn't be having this conversation. Something is missing. I am not happy. Something is missing." She spoke frantically in between deep breaths. "I promise I'll tell you as soon as I figure it out."

Jan opened his eyes and looked at Ema in silence. Maks was asleep on her lap. He observed the scene as if a passer by, like all his feelings had shut down with the flick of a switch and he wasn't really there at all.

He'd tried hard. *Every higher power that watches over the human struggle knows I've tried to be a supportive husband.* But his goodwill had run out. The final drops of passion that wanted to fight for them and wait for her peace had run dry. He'd given years. Now, he'd sacrificed a much needed relaxing vacation for a backpacking trip where he felt more exhausted at the end than when they'd started and was being fed anger and closed eyes. He was done.

"I need a break." He said suddenly.

The only thing Ema liked in her life was her reliable husband, Jan. Hot waves travelled through her stomach to her face. The heat forced her to open her closed lids. "What do you mean?!" She didn't mean to but she screamed her question and woke Maks who started crying. Passengers turned to see where the trouble was and looked on at the crumbling family. Ema composed herself and lowered her voice. "What do you mean by a break, Jan?"

"Just that, Ema. I need a break to find myself in all of this. For the past ten years, I've followed you on your search for inner peace.

I've sat in meditation classes, gone to astrology therapies, attended regression treatments, and revisited my family traumas with that weird old fart you told me to talk to." Ema never knew Jan felt he followed her rather than travelled with her. But then again, she hadn't asked him how he felt for a long time.

"I just don't want this anymore." He continued. "I don't want to try another new thing. I want a calm life, to wake up, read the news, go to work, and then to cycle or camp on the weekend, something easy. I want to focus on Maks, our son, growing up into a healthy young man with his priorities set properly. And I want to have a real fucking Christmas tree that I've cut down, brought home, and decorated with cheesy, flashy decorations. I want a home-cooked meal for Christmas with all the traditional trimmings and mulled wine." Jan had never said 'I want' so many times before.

Neither of them knew what to say next, and so they sat in silence and absorbed the newness of their situation.

Jan felt light as the burdens he'd carried for so long began to fall away. Unintentionally, that weight shifted onto Ema, who's void quickly began to fill with panic and worry. They sat silently, facing each other, seeing one another clearly after years spent out of focus.

It was unpleasant to know that they were done and made worse by the fact they still had some way to travel before they would be home.

* * *

A young lady approached. "Sorry to bother you guys. Do you maybe have a lighter?"

Ema broke eye contact with Jan, remembering that I was in her bag, fished me out, and gave me away.

The young lady headed to the bathroom and unpacked small scented cubes into her hand. She burned them, releasing an intense smell, and fanned the scent towards her face.

116

It seemed as though something unpleasant returned to her here, on the floor of the ferry bathroom. Bad memories erupted. She was disturbed and unsettled by a face similar to one she didn't want to remember.

Six: LEA

Like me, she hadn't lost her fire, but she definitely found herself broken and in need of repair.

"Open the door." Patrik screamed.

Lea sat in the corner of her apartment shivering. She held me tight in her hand. I'd become a symbol of safety since she procured me on the ferry from Morocco. She used me to burn herbs and flowers for meditation. She would play Tibetan bowls and listen to throat singing, gongs, affirmation, anything that had relaxation at its centre.

Now, we waited in her Slovenian apartment for real protection to come and save her.

"Lea, you can't stay in your apartment forever. I'll find you." Patrik's voice boomed through the walls. "You belong to me, Lea."

She heard her neighbour come out of their flat and ask him to calm down or they'd call the police.

"Sir, mind your own business. I'm talking to my girlfriend. Lea, open the door!" He roared.

Patrik started knocking on the door, then beating at it. He pressed his face close the crack in between the door and the frame so Lea could hear his breath.

"Lea, honey." He implored, "You've had your get away, your time to go wild and get everything out of your system. Now it's time to come back home. Okay? I miss you so much. I bought you a cat." He paused. "I know you love them and always wanted one. I would pull stars from the sky for you, Lea." His voice became a soft, intimate whisper. It was the voice she'd fallen madly in love with. Now she felt mad for completely different reasons. But today, she would not become soft and willing for him.

"Babe. Come on babe." He purred.

Lea tried to breathe in the way she'd been taught at Vipassana Meditation, but she couldn't focus. The banging on the door had started again and it was too intrusive. She comforted herself with the knowledge that sooner or later some neighbour would actually call the police or, at least, threaten to do so again. She tapped me against her forehead and shook.

"Dude, I'm going to call the police. It's clear you're not welcome here." Another neighbour had returned home and the growing crowd made him too visible to carry on.

"My love," He whispered again. "I see you need more time. I'll be back for you. I love you to the end of the universe."

As he moved away from the door, Lea sent panicked texts to her friends and family. *Why couldn't I write to them when he was here? I'm pathetic.*

* * *

Honey, where are you?
Hey, I want to come over.
Why don't you reply to me? I always reply.
Are you cheating on me, cunt?
You fucked up.
Call me now.

I forgot my phone at home. All good. Stop texting me.
We broke up. Don't want to be rude. Just stop. L

Bitch. You should always keep your phone with you.
I love you so much. I was worried.
I'll come over now.
I miss you so much.
I love you so much.

Not now. I'm going to bed. So tired.
Leave me alone. Please. L

I just want to see that you're okay.
I can bring you something.
Hello? Don't be rude, Lea. We have history.
Fucking bitch.
Hope you get some kind of disease that kills you slowly.
I know you're there. Open the fucking door.
Can't you hear I'm buzzing you?
Ding. Dong. Ding. Dong.

Stop. I will call the police. L

I will be back for you, Lea.
You are mine.
You can't escape my love.
P.

* * *

"You can't live without me, Lea. You'd die." Patrik said with his lips pressed against her ear and her body held against the wall. His weight gently threatened her. He panted, almost intimately, but his eyes told the real story.

"I can and I will live without you." She said quietly. "Now let me go." She didn't move but waited to be released.

"Hello?" A voice called from the front door.

They came. Lea smiled with relief.

"Who's that?" He asked, pushing harder into her hips.

"My parents. I called them."

"I will never let you go, Lea. You're mine." She could feel his hot breath against her neck.

Lea managed to break away and run into her parents' arms. She cried euphorically, overcome with relief.

Her parents waited, never letting her out of their sight, until everything she wanted was packed. She gathered a few personal belongings but left most of her things behind.

As Lea filtered through the life she was ready to walk away from, Patrik paced up and down the hallway outside their apartment. He was mute in front of her parents, but his anger was felt through the walls that divided them. *How could I think that he loved me? Naïve, stupid me. My king, gentle and good, is dead.*

They left the apartment, and Lea vowed never to look back.

* * *

Lea was excited to spot her friends in the shopping centre. It had been months since they'd seen each other and she'd missed them. Her friends, however, did not feel the same way.

"Hey, long time no see." Lea welcomed them eagerly, albeit a little shy because of the looks they were giving her. "How are you guys? What's up?"

After a pause, one friend replied. "Book Club. You know? The one we started because of you? The one you never made time for. You don't seem to have any time for us any more."

"Oh," Lea was embarrassed. "I know. That was lame of me to ditch you guys for the first one, but you could've invited me to others. I didn't know you were carrying it on. The first one was months ago. Why didn't you ask me again?" She blushed afraid of their answer.

"We did, but you stopped replying to texts, social media, everything." It was the other friend's turn to be angry. "We're fed up of hunting you down to hang out. You just delete everything. So we decided not to bother inviting you to ditch us again."

Lea was confused. "What are you talking about? I haven't had a text from either of you in months. In fact, I haven't heard from you since the day I stood you up. In my defence, I only ditched to have wild sex. You understand that, right?" She giggled thinking they'd approve. They didn't. "The time just flew away from me. You know?"

"You should have at least written back to tell us you're sorry or something." She could see her friends were softening, but now, Lea grew more confused.

"I did write to you. I sent it in our chat. What do you mean?" *How is this possible? I know I wrote to them as soon as I read their angry messages.*

One friend opened their chat on her phone and showed Lea a string of deleted messages that comprised the last conversation. Lea checked on her own account and read out loud while showing them:

Girls, I'm so sorry. I know I'm lame.
But I'm addicted to him. I love him so much.
We just had sex against the wall and on the floor.
It was so exciting.

HAHAHAHAHAAH

Now the trio were confused. They agreed to sit in a nearby bar and work this out over whiskeys.

"How is this possible?" Lea asked. "If I'd deleted them, I should see that on my phone too?"

"It's totally possible. Look." Lea's friend demonstrated on her phone, "I just press this and click 'Delete for others'. So I can still see what I've written, but you can't anymore."

Lea looked at her in horror. "I don't understand. I didn't do that. I didn't even know I could do that."

Lea's friends had met Patrik after their second date. They did not see what Lea saw in him.

"I understand. It's simple. He managed to see our messages before you and erase them. Does he have the passwords for your phone?"

Lea didn't compute.

"I think he caught our messages, maybe even blocked the notifications from us, so you couldn't see anything new coming in."

"Who? Are you talking about Patrik? I know you don't like him, but this is a serious allegation." Lea defended, unable to believe Patrik was capable of something like that.

But her friends weren't letting it go. They showed her weeks' worth of messages and missed calls.

They questioned her about where she was at these times and what could have happened that she didn't see any of them. As circumstances had it, she had always been near Patrik when they'd tried to contact her.

Now they were looking together, Lea could almost remember every situation. She'd hear her phone ring and at that time Patrik would ask her to get something from another room. When she'd check who the call was from, there'd be nothing on the screen.

He'd convince her there was no call and that she'd imagined hearing it ring. He'd tell her, "It's a thing. You know? People often imagine phantom messages and calls."

Lea had confided in Patrik about how she missed her friends and was sad that they ignored her, that they'd disappeared. He would comfort her with, "You don't need anyone except me, babe. I'll never leave you, never ignore you."

Lea's phone rang next to an empty glass on the bar table, intruding the circle of friends. Lea didn't pick up. She wanted to hear everything her friends could tell her and needed more solid answers.

They called someone who explained that with very little technical knowledge someone could monitor her social media on their own phone and intervene from a distance. Lea listened in distress; she didn't know how to react; she couldn't move, couldn't talk, couldn't think. The illusion of her love was forming cracks like a glass ceiling being smashed by something heavy. Soon it would shatter and shower her in shards of pain.

Her phone lit up.

Where are you, babe? Dinner is ready.
You should have been back hours ago.
Is everything ok, my love?
Miss you so much.
P.

Reading the text, Lea felt sick to her stomach. She covered her mouth with her left hand and scrolled the phone with her right. Acid boiled inside her. She wanted to vomit.

"What do I do?" Lea gasped. "What can I do? I still can't believe this is possible? How?"

Both friends leaned forward and held her in a human shield. They looked at each other over Lea's hunched body and their eyes told each other, *It's going to be okay.*

We have to stand by her and help her grasp the situation. They held her tighter, letting her know she was safe.

"It's hard to discover you've been tricked by someone, but you'll be okay." They promised her.

She felt tears escape down her cheeks. They united on her chin as bigger drops that periodically fell on her lap and marked her clothes.

Sweetheart, I'm worried about you.
You should be home by now.
Please call me as soon as possible.
I'm going to call my friends at the police station,
so they can find you.
P.

"What do I do?" Lea whispered.

It was time to encourage her. "If this was me, I'd leave him." One said in a calm voice.

The other added. "Be smart, Lea. If he's really doing this, soon he'll have you locked up in the apartment. He'll want you to leave your job and everything so he can have you to himself."

Lea's tears kept silently falling. She didn't want to tell them Patrik had already proposed to her, that she'd said yes, and that he already suggested she leave her job. He'd agreed that, if she didn't want to quit now, it would be right to do it when they had a baby. He'd started encouraging her to go off the pill and taken to calling her, "The mother of my children." It all seemed romantic at the time, normal.

Lea found her voice. "I have to think."

"What is there to think about?" One nervously asked. It was hard to empathise as an outsider.

"I have to go back." Lea said in shock and got to her feet.

"Stay at my place."

126

She thought about the offer for a second before agreeing. It was a relief to know she had more time to process and plan. She texted Patrik.

> I met a friend. We're going to have a girls' night. Too much gin and tonic. I'll spend the night with her. All good. L XOXO

* * *

"Where are you going, love of my life, my queen, future mother of my children?"

Lea giggled. *How lucky am I to be showered with such affection?*

"I have Book Club." She giggled again as he nuzzled into her neck. "I put it on the calendar. I know you like to know where I am."

He kissed her neck and slowly pulled her dress up. He found his way into the elastic waistband of her panties and slowly teased them down.

"I told you, the calendar is just in case something happens to you." He said in a loving purr. "So I know who to call and where to find you if you don't come home. There's a lot of crazy people out there." Patrik joked. He lifted Lea's dress over her head and pressed her against the wall. He pulled her up to his waist so that her legs wrapped around him. She was aroused and didn't want him to stop.

"I have to go..." she moaned unconvincingly.

Patrik carried on touching and kissing until Lea was so aroused that she couldn't talk. They played for hours and Book Club was forgotten.

When she finally picked up her phone, she had ten missed calls and five messages.

L, where are you?

Hey, we're going into the cinema now. Your ticket is at info.

Fuck, L. You promised you're coming.

This is so uncool. You never have time for us. WTF!

This is the last text you'll get from me. When you have time, call, or not. It's up to you.

Lea's guilt made cry. How could she let her friend down, again? It was the fifth time in a row. Patrik hugged her and tried to comfort her with kisses.

"They're just jealous, Lea, that we have such an amazing connection. Hey, love, don't cry. They're not worth it."

* * *

It was moving day.

Lea's friends and family voiced their scepticism about moving in with Patrik so soon, but she ignored their concerns. Over the past months, they had tried time and again to talk her down from her delirium but it didn't make a jot of difference. Lea was head over heels in love and not in the right state to discuss being sensible and going steady. They warned her against the move but nobody had the balls to tell her they didn't like Patrik, that there was something psychopathic about his cold, icy eyes and impeccable manners.

Lea packed and chatted away to her silent parents about how perfect her boyfriend was and how happy they were going to be living together.

Patrik coordinated a van and movers so that there was no need for Lea's loved ones to ride to the other side of the city and help her unpack. The two of them would be just fine moving without anyone's help.

* * *

They watched television, snuggled together under a blanket. Lea inhaled Patrik's delicious smell and wanted to pinch herself. She couldn't believe she was with the man of her dreams and that he truly wanted her.

"Hey, I love you." Patrik said and kissed her on the forehead.

She turned. "I love you more." He smiled now, with glass eyes that she mistook as being full of adoration.

"We should move in together." He proposed. "I can't stand being apart from you. Plus, you could save what you're paying on rent, and maybe we could even start thinking about a mini me and you." Patrik combed her hair with his fingers and spoke with utter sincerity.

They had been together for less than a month. They'd had, maybe, ten dates and spent four nights together. Lea knew it was too fast.

"Wow." She said. "Wow. I love the way you think. But babies and moving in together? I mean, yes, but maybe in, I don't know, in some time. I've got a three-month notice period with my apartment, and I just don't think I can make such quick changes in my life. So maybe in three months?"

"Honey, I feel sad every night that I have to go to bed without you and even sadder when I wake up and you're not there." Patrik rested his head on her shoulder as if in pain. "You can cancel the apartment already and move to me now, before the three months is up. This way, you have time to think about it, and we can see if we match living together. If we don't, you still have your place and you can move back." He tapped her nose with a finger, making the conversation feel playful. His suggestion relaxed her and seemed to make a lot of sense.

"You're right. Why should we wait? We're not fifteen. Let's do this." Lea said smiling. He pulled her close and kissed her passionately. She could feel his joy and excitement as he brought her closer.

"We'll stay together forever, amazing love of my life. I don't want to be away from you, not even for a second."

* * *

A card read, "You are the love of my life."

It was the sentence that everyone waits expectantly to hear from their partner, and it was tucked inside a box of expensive Belgian chocolates that Patrik had given to Lea just one week after their first date.

* * *

Patrik and Lea met in the city centre and hugged. They rented bikes, rode around the city, and finished the date by sharing a muffin. It was a lovely evening, where they laughed and trusted each other with personal histories.

As they parted ways, Patrik shouted, "Call me when you get home or text me. Okay?"

Lea blushed, thinking him caring and sweet for wanting to know she was safe. She went on from the date to meet with friends and dissect every gesture and word spoken. She was in heaven retelling the details and overcome with pride that she had finally found someone great.

A message flashed and Lea showed her friends, squeaking like an excited little girl.

Where are you?
Is everything ok? You should be home by now.
P.

Her friends commented that the message seemed possessive rather than sweet, but she wouldn't let them burst her bubble. She was ecstatic. "It's cute. He's worried about me."

Lea replied:

Hey, all good. I am with friends for a coffee.
Still not home. L

130

To which Patrik instantly responded:

Oh, which friends?
You didn't tell me you had other plans.
I was worried.
Xoxo. P

Lea felt blessed, despite her friends' looks of horror and reproach.

"Isn't he cute? He cares so much, and we just started dating."

"Yeah, just started dating and you have to report back about where you are. Cute."

Lea acted mock shocked. "Oh, don't be so mean. This is adorable."

The friends bit their lips and said nothing.

> **Oh, sorry. It was a spur of the moment thing.**
> **They called me, and we were close so we met.**
> **All good. :)**

Another message lit up her phone.

Well, text me when you're home.
I need to know you're safe. P.

* * *

Lea received a message ten minutes after entering her apartment.

We have to repeat that.
We didn't share a muffin :)
P. Xoxo

She couldn't stop smiling. *How did I find such a sweet man, and so out of my league? Lucky Lea!*

* * *

Lea called in her troops, who arrived with the necessities that mark an important event: sexy outfits and make-up. Preparing for her first date was like the production of a great romantic musical. Her friends dressed her in red elegance and helped her apply the perfect mask. They talked through how to flirt with someone handsome and charming. They instructed that she be close and make her body language suggestive. It promised to be a brilliant evening.

Lea hated waiting because she always had to for the people in her life: friends, family, exes. Patrik picked her at 8 p.m. sharp, like they'd agreed, and she relished his punctuality.

"You look like a dream come true." He said, standing next to an impressively new and fancy looking car. Patrik kissed Lea's palm, which she loved. He opened the door for her and guided her in. She wasn't used to that.

The king of attention. Lea thought. *What does he see in me? He could have anyone.* Patrik took his seat behind the wheel and smiled. *He's amazing.*

Their first date was a fairy tale. Lea's mind couldn't have created a more perfect evening. They ate in a posh restaurant that made Lea feel sophisticated and beautiful. Patrik was clever, witty, and full of interesting information. He listened as Lea told him about herself and her life. She drifted on a cloud towards a parallel universe of love. After the meal, they walked around the city centre, got ice cream in a trendy ice cream bar that Lea had never visited before, and walked out of the centre towards the river. Patrik bought her a red heart balloon, which then floated in the corner of her bedroom after the date. He was the perfect gentleman from beginning to end.

* * *

Lea waited a few days after getting his number before texting.

132

After much discussion with her best friends about what to write, whether to be funny or cute, and with their eventual united approval, she typed:

Hi. Would love to share a muffin with you.
Ponytail/red sweater

They unanimously agreed it was fun and flirty.

Lea stared at her phone for half an hour after sending it. She was nervous.

"Lea, stop it! If he remembers you, he'll text back."

She put her phone in a draw and tried to forget about it. A voice in Lea's head chipped away at her brutally as she waited, so she left her phone in the draw and went out for a walk.

Lea found that she could leave the problem at home, but she couldn't shut away the mean voice in her head. It lived within her. *Don't kid yourself. You think he likes you?* It taunted her as she walked in the fresh air. *His photo could be next to the word 'handsome' in the dictionary. What words would define you? Have you looked at yourself lately? He's a catch; he could get anyone. And you?* She felt her inner critic laugh. *Why do you search out of your league, Lea? What's wrong with you?*

She started running to shut the voice down, but the more she ran, the louder the voice screamed. *You're ugly. Face it. You should lose weight. Why do you think anyone would want you, would love you?* She ran until she had no breath left and then walked the last stretch back to her apartment.

Lea tentatively took her phone from the draw and pressed the home screen. Nothing. It was blank except for her normal background and the time. She felt seeds of truth from her inner voice settle in and take root. A disappointed message was dispatched to her friends who replied with loving, positive encouragement to be patient.

She locked her phone away again and watched a sad, romantic movie that she knew would send her crying to sleep.

As the sun rose so did Lea, and she immediately checked her phone. *A MESSAGE!* Her heart pounded as she opened it and read:

Dear ponytail,
I would love to share more than a muffin with you.
Tonight at 8?
Where can I pick you up?
P.

Lea jumped in the air and sang out loud. She ran in circles around her living room typing:

I'd love to!

She replied in a state of such ecstasy that she forgot to give her address and so had to send an immediate follow-up. A nervous fear grabbed at her stomach and made her consider all the ways she could screw this up.

* * *

Lea sat with friends, drinking coffee in a local bakery come cafe. They talked about life, TV shows, personal updates, and then she noticed him. They all noticed him. His beauty stood out: tall, black hair, green eyes, Mediterranean, gorgeous.

When Lea caught his gaze she felt butterflies all over her body. It was an amazing sensation, like being tickled intimately by their wings as they fluttered around her. She blushed and giggled. Lea wasn't used to being the centre of attention, especially from someone so handsome. He saw her. She could tell. Something drew him to her, and before leaving, he sent chocolates to their table with a business card carrying a note on the back.

Hey ponytail/red sweater,
If you're single, call me.

Patrik.

The friends looked at each other to see who the chocolates were for. All three had ponytails but only Lea had a red sweater.

"Oh my god, he means you, Lea!" Her friends squealed hysterically.

Lea turned to him, blushing, as he left the shop. The blood from her body moved to her cheeks, and she felt them sizzle. He smiled a charming smile and left.

"OMG! OMG! You have to text him! But not yet. You have to wait, Lea. Aah, he's so hot. Lea!" The friends yelled over one another and revelled in excitement.

* * *

Lea sat in her lawyers' office. She played with me nervously and tried to breathe. Like me, she hadn't lost her fire, but she definitely found herself broken and in need of repair.

There was a long discussion about what Lea had been through and what action could be taken now to keep Patrik away. Lea felt lighter by the end of it, almost delirious. She hadn't experienced the feeling of clarity in an eternity, and in this bubble of safety, she accidentally left me on the chair of her lawyer's office.

The next day, Lea's lawyer picked me up and away we went. She poured gas in me and took me to her grandparents. Here they smiled and celebrated. She lit candles. They talked until it was dark, and then, she left me behind as quickly as she'd picked me up. I stayed, poised by the candlesticks.

Seven: JANEZ and PETRA

For people your age everything is now, now, now, now, and me, me, me, me. But if you live like this, there's no chance to gather cherries from the forest.

The grandfather of Lea's lawyer was called Janez. He lit a candle with a freckled, shaky hand and smiled at his wife, Petra. They raised their glasses to fifty years of marriage and took small sips of celebration. It would be a lie to say they had married for love or went on to live an idyllic life in each other's company. The younger members of their family wished to hear this version of their story, but it was fiction. Janez had been without a wife at thirty after his first love and fiancé had tragically died. He was left a singleton, destined to live out his days alone if he didn't act soon.

Petra came from a good family and had what people called golden hands. She was fair looking and healthy but still childish. As a young woman of seventeen, she understood life was economically safer with a husband. Being the youngest of five children, she couldn't risk waiting to marry last, or worse, become the spinster sister left behind. So Janez proposed and they were quickly married.

Their marriage was founded on mutual convenience and respect; love came much later.
After receiving some scars from life, they began to look at each other with tenderness and this feeling grew over the years together.

On their toast to fifty years of companionship, Janez gently embraced Petra, feeling her large breasts against his chest, and kissed her. He knew now as an old man that marrying her was the best decision he'd ever made.

Janez overheard her speaking with their granddaughter one day and explaining, "Life's all about focus. Obstacles challenge us for more than just one day. Some of them are hard to overcome. When faced with something tricky, I try to calm myself down and then I tell myself, 'Just do the best you can.' There's nothing more you can do than that." He'd smiled hearing Petra talk about life so confidently. "Sometimes it's best to step away from the problem altogether. You should never react with a hothead. When your Papa angers me, I go to the forest and scream. Then, I pick fruits in the forest, feel nature in my hands, and come home. We have a golden rule, me and your Papa: never, never go to bed angry. Once, we stayed up all night to reconcile an argument. For people your age, everything is now, now, now, now, and me, me, me, me. But if you live like this, there's no chance to gather cherries from the forest."

* * *

The day after their fiftieth anniversary, the old couple woke and had breakfast. Petra inspected her plants, while Janez read his newspapers. They said blessings before lunch and enjoyed their meal, listened to the usual radio show in the afternoon, and walked for an hour to the end of the village and back in the evening. They walked holding hands and admiring each other. They were lucky to have come this far together and aware of it.

At home, under a dark sky, they prepared for bed. Janez's body crashed to the floor and his soul was gone before the ambulance could arrive.
He stayed long enough to tell Petra, "You prepare the best coffee in the world, my wife." His voice was very small.

"And I'm grateful for every egg you cooked. You always made them exactly how I like them. Every single one was perfect."

He fell a few days shy of his eightieth birthday which was a tragedy to everyone in the family.

* * *

Petra lit candles at the cemetery. It was a gloomy event, with everyone dressed in black. The attendees held good memories of Janez in their mind and tried not to think about his flaws or his now permanent absence.

After the funeral, the widow Petra began mourning. She was confused. For fifty years she'd been directed by her husband and didn't know how to be without him, how to think as one and not two. Her family, especially her granddaughter, distracted her with information about workshops and books. They shrouded her in activities, covering the time that could be left to consider loss. But the distractions confused her further to the point where she wanted to cry and say, "I'm too old to start again." Which was quickly followed by a panicked, "But I'm too young to roll over and die. What do I do?"

So Petra did what many grieving people do. She cleaned. After much wading through a closet of long forgotten clothes and shoes, she found a small black notebook. It was her diary from the time just before her wedding, 1969. She opened it and was intrigued by the notes of an impressive, innocent young woman.

19th July, 1969

I have decided to marry Janez. I don't know what I should feel, but I know that he is a good catch. He is older, but he is not ugly.

I can still finish school and there is much more that I intend to learn. I'm really excited about looking after a house of my own. I tried to cook a one-pot with mushrooms today. I still can't cook it like my granny. There is something missing. I hope I will master it next time.

Petra looked at the words and knew she'd lived the life her seventeen-year old self imagined: she was a wife, housewife, mother, grandmother, and soon to be great-grandmother. But for the first time, she felt without purpose or direction.

When her children became adults and formed relationships, she vowed to leave them to it and never be an imposition. Petra was particularly respectful of their partners as her own mother-in-law had been a nightmare, and she had no plans to reenact that role. She didn't want to bother her children and would never force herself on them. So Petra faced her this emptiness alone and read on.

5th September, 1969

I had my first night contact with Janez. I bled. I have to admit, I was afraid. Mama did not explain the act to me well and everything came as a kind of unpleasant surprise. I closed my eyes, but the time did not pass faster.

Old Petra blushed and giggled. *Oh, how ignorant I was. And how times have changed. Everybody's so relaxed about sex now.* She remembered a shocking time when her granddaughter asked her if she ever gave grandpa oral. She'd had no idea how to answer that question.

The black notebook unravelled before Petra's eyes until she found a list.

140

15ᵗʰ October, 1969

What I want to accomplish:

- Be a good wife and mother
- Be a good cook
- Visit the Vatican
- Learn photography (First, must collect money and
  buy a good photo camera)
- Read books

She reread the list. *I set such low goals for myself, and even worse, I didn't achieve them.* Petra never visited the Vatican; she never learned photography; she did carefully save money for her camera but it got used time and again for the children, and so there was no camera. *This won't do.*

Petra found a large piece of paper and wrote:

23ʳᵈ May, 2019

TO DO:

- Finally buy a camera
- Sign up for photography workshop
- Sign up for computer workshop
- Open Instagram
  (ask someone to explain what Instagram is)
- Visit the Vatican
- Read books

She decorated her list with colours, small hearts, and flowers. It was reviewed and then taped to the fridge. *I spend so much time in the kitchen, I won't be able to ignore my plans here.*

Petra continued cleaning the house and reflected. *How many experiences have I missed?* An old song played on the radio and Petra swayed as she worked. *I loved to dance, but Janez liked to be home. He liked to vacation at the same apartment every year, while I wanted to travel. But we never travelled.* Petra wanted to dance in a room outside of the house. She wanted to learn new skills and new stories.

"Now is the time to catch up." She declared to the solitary room.

The next day, Petra signed up for a free computer workshop and went to town to buy her first semi-professional camera. She explored the world around her and found joy in her new decision making. In a frenzied excitement, Petra added to her to-do list:

- Learn the tango
- Learn to meditate

Her granddaughter cheered and provided everything needed for her journey. As a lawyer and a fiercely independent woman, who had just witnessed the harm of being trapped by your partner, she understood her grandmother's current path. Petra never felt trapped in her marriage, but she could see now that she'd sacrificed many things for the happiness of her husband and this needed to change. *No more sacrificing myself.* She promised.

Other family members were less accepting of Petra's new outgoing life, almost jealous. They missed having her around and began to realise they needed her. She had been a dedicated mother and grandmother after all.

With the blessing of her granddaughter, Petra joined a senior travel society and finally ventured to Italy and the Vatican City. She joined a book club for widows at the local Serenity Club but quit after reading five depressing Russian classics in a row.

It was a hard decision. For a moment, she felt she'd abandoned her intentions but then started to read for herself, romances with women at the centre of the story, and found she loved reading again. She attended Zumba classes, as there was no local tango teacher, and shook her hips and waved her arms around joyously. Petra was living for herself, and it felt great.

* * *

Petra's granddaughter picked her up for a clothes shopping trip. The mourning time had passed, and Petra had lost so much weight enjoying and adventuring that she needed an updated wardrobe.

"Granny, I have to tell you something amazing." She said excitedly.

"What's the news?" Petra asked, always interested in amazing things.

Her granddaughter smiled at Petra's genuine intrigue. "One of my clients told me about this camp where they meditate every day. It's called the 8-Day Experiment. I don't know how or why they're doing it, but it sounds interesting. You have meditation on your bucket list, so what do you think? Are you interested? I would join you but I can't take eight days off work at the moment. We've got cases piling up."
Petra was instantly enthused and pushed to hear more. She mentally signed herself up then and there before even seeing the application form.

Eight: 8-DAY EXPERIMENT RETREAT

I am extra, and I am ordinary. I can be all or nothing, and that depends on me.

An amazing sunrise burst from the Alps. From Petra's village in Slovenia, she could see mountain peaks running through both Italy and Austria. *Slovenia you true, green beauty.* She thought as the sun warmed her.

The sun continued its ascent. Petra lit candles for Janez at the cemetery and was then driven by her granddaughter to the 8-Day Experiment Retreat. The retreat was no more than half an hour away from Petra's village which surprised her. *How have I never heard about this place when it sits right under my nose?* Petra and her granddaughter hugged goodbye, and she suddenly wished that they'd been able to do the retreat together. It made her sad to see her granddaughter drive away but that wouldn't stop the new nervous excitement growing in her stomach. The setting was idyllic, lying on the edge of a forest and decorated with artwork made entirely from natural materials. *This is going to be a great week.*

"Hello," A stranger greeted her. "I'm Gregor. What's your name?"

Petra, not used to meeting new people, took a moment to see if she recognised the stranger and then realised that, no, she did not. He was in fact an instructor at the retreat. She felt he didn't label her as anything, not a mother or granny or neighbour. He saw a person, human, and participant. *I can be who I want here.* Petra smiled. This was the first time entirely separated from a community that knew her. "Petra." She announced with a grin. *How exciting.*

Gregor directed Petra to her room for the week. She sat on the bed and began to reflect on the past year spent trying to catch up. In doing so, and because she felt far from home despite only having travelled a few kilometres, she contemplated whether she'd actually mourned Janez. She lit a candle for the departed and searched inside herself. After some time with no conclusion reached about her feelings, Petra shoved me in the pocket of her baggy fisherman pants that had been bought especially for the retreat. *Everyone at meditation camps in the movies wear fisherman pants, and so I should too.* Then, she inspected a fabric gift bag, which Gregor had given her on arrival. She pulled out a pencil with the 8-Day Experiment logo and a notebook made from recycled paper. She boiled the kettle for tea and waited to be told what to do.

* * *

In the evening, Petra was invited to sit in a field with pillows laid on the floor. She had her gift bag in one hand and me in her pocket.

Petra took a seat close to the stage, which was like an altar decorated with potted flowers and large candles. She watched Gregor attempting to light candles with matches and fail more than once. Standing up, Petra handed me over. "Take this lighter." She smiled. "It looks in a poor state but works well."

Gregor gladly accepted the gift and carried on his work. When every candle was glistening and lighting the space, he placed me on a shelf overlooking the stage. I had a stunning view of the Alps and the lavishing fields of flowers below. And, then, I saw them.

Kara and Tina came in together and took pillows next to each other. Jacopo was next. Then Storm, who had taken me from Paris to Fuerteventura, looking tranquil. Nick arrived, unhealthy and distressed, just like in London. Brave Petra started talking to people next to her and one of them was Jan. Finally, Lea came running to the space, her energy low. They were all here, and I could once again provide light for their journeys.

Gregor took his place on the stage next to seven other teachers and, without demanding attention, started the first meditation. Petra tried to follow but her thoughts wondered and she became distracted by surrounding bird songs. She tried harder to focus. The wind played with her scarf and teased her. *Come on, this is important.*

Lea was also unsettled. She couldn't keep her eyes closed, as instructed, for fear Patrik would run out from some corner or shadow. Nowadays, Lea unwillingly pulled him into her thoughts about everything. She didn't apply for the 8-Day Experiment under her real name and took the longest possible route to get there, including an hour-long detour to a nearby town and then a public bus, for fear he would find her. She mentally left Lea in that town and arrived at the retreat as Jane Doe.

Storm, on the other hand, melted into breathing and becoming one with the sounds around him. He'd been invited by one of the teachers after they'd met on Fuerteventura. He gave her surf lessons and in return she instructed him on advanced tantric breathing. She then extended an invitation to the 8-Day Experiment Retreat so he could, "Reflect on his recent loss."

Jacopo didn't hear any of the first meditation. Instead he replayed Rocco's betrayal. When they returned from their honeymoon, Jacopo found new messages on Rocco's tablet. "Well, if you wanted to cheat, Rocco, you shouldn't have connected all the smart devices should you?!" Jacopo relived the moment he saw Rocco and Ted together. Every time the group was instructed to breathe, the vision came to him. Inhale; he saw them. Exhale; there they were again.

Jan thought of the custody dispute that had arrived by post just days before. Ema seemed intent on ruining this reflection time for him. He'd asked for space and really needed it, needed time-off. Now he found himself sitting in a field of people he judged to be very different from himself. *How will this help me? What was I thinking coming here?* Jan repeated in his head.

Nick had problems relaxing in general and it was the same here. He felt drops of sweat trickle down his body. *How did I let myself get sweet talked into coming here? This is the first and last time I take advice from randomers on holiday in Spain.*

Kara looked content as she closed her eyes and listened attentively. She'd lost weight and seemed calmer. She even managed to find a few seconds of happiness between the inhale and exhale. She seemed on a firm path to something.

Tina, however, did not look happy. Her mind jumped, searching for answers without any peace or direction. She'd been advised about what could help her a million times, what actions could be positive, but it seemed she needed to hear it a million more times before anything would sink in. Before following Kara uninvited to the retreat, Tina was in a state of intentionally doing nothing for work, family, friends, health, nothing at all. She had hit the pause button.

Gaya, a teacher with long golden hair, greeted the group after meditation.

148

"Welcome, dear explorers into the depths of your well. In the next eight days, you will meet yourself. You will make peace with the patterns you have cradled since birth and others that you have created along your path so far. You will meet anger, self-pity, hate, and envy. But remember: When you are angry, try to look at it and understand why and how it can help you; When you pity yourself, ask if you should feel pity or whether it's blocking your power; When you hate something or someone, analyse the hate to find where it reminds you of your own flows and how it mirrors you; When I say flows, remember, I am addressing what you call flaws, but I don't see them like that because they can make you stronger; Finally, when you envy someone and wish to switch places with them, ask yourself, 'Do I also want to carry their burdens?'"

Gaya looked around the gathered crowd. Sixty-four people sat before her, listening. Some with focus, some with scepticism, others visibly overwhelmed.

"Call this time your experiment. It is close to your being, your existence. It is your homework, task, goal. You could think of it as a game to conquer, a game with varying levels of difficulty. I like to look at these experiments as games that can't be lost, ones where you gain a lot.

Before any resistance finds you, I would like you to know that I have tried all these practices. I have experienced what I invite you to experience." She smiled at the group, easing them. "Maybe, you will have a eureka moment in each game. Maybe, it will only happen once. This week may not be enough time to get you there, but try to be open to the possibility of enlightenment. You should not expect every day to be pleasant but know moments will bring you comfort. Give yourself time to understand what is happening. Try to see the way you feel and accept your reality. When you find yourself experiencing discomfort or negativity, try to dig into it and ask yourself, 'Why is this uncomfortable?'"

"You will discover your beliefs are rooted in the cells of your body. You will feel them being disrupted while you're here. But these beliefs come from your upbringing, things you've heard your family say over and over again, from traumas experienced in the passage of life, and those beliefs do not actually belong to you. They have been given to you but are not the core of your soul. They are not your essence. Try to react to them like a child: question them in your childhood mind and ask, 'I am young and interested. How should I respond?'"

A different teacher started to play Tibetan bowls, mixing natural sounds with those from the bowls.

Gaya continued, "Tonight is a time to blend, meet people, and share your expectations for the week. For the rest of the week, we encourage you to take your own space." Paused.

"Phones and computers have been removed to avoid external distractions. You may find yourself searching for distraction elsewhere, but try not to take other people's drama as your own. What you hear from other participants are stories. Try not to empathise with those stories. We have also removed watches. Conventional time is irrelevant here. Let the sound of the gong guide you between spaces. When you hear it, you know it is time to come together. If you miss the gong, don't worry; you are still on time.

"We are here." Gaya rested her hands on the floor. "You are in nature. Spaces for meditation and walking are all around you. Experiment with tools and practices to discover what helps you create calm and find the roots of neglected internal pain. We encourage you to keep practices private, where possible.
They are stories. You do not need to share the story because it is for you alone, and you are in control of it."

A teacher stood up, took a wooden drum, and started playing. A new melody mixed in with the existing sounds.

"If you have come here because you think we can save you, you should leave now. Only you can save yourself and you must know this. We are simply tools available for insight and explanation." She looked around and paused to see if anyone would move.

Another teacher stood and moved to the gong, joining the orchestra.

"On this day, you will lack patience and that is okay. Nothing good comes overnight. This is hard to accept because our modern world teaches us to expect everything in an instant. But while you're here, your aim is to look past the instant and relax."

Three more teachers stood and embraced their musical instruments. The orchestra grew powerful and caressed the participants like welcome waves.

"This week, be still. Stay present. Enjoy the path ahead. Feel and observe your feelings. Do not judge. It's hard because we judge every day. We think the same thoughts every day. We repeat. Any person has between fifteen thousand and sixty thousand thoughts a day. The majority of these are negative. It's suggested that only five percent of our daily thoughts are original." Gaya looked up to the clouds.

Petra followed her gaze but was disappointed when she didn't feel anything special.

"Ask yourself, 'What is emotionally eating me? What do I seek? What makes me eat my feelings? Why am I sick?' Everything between your mind and health is connected. We must be healthy inside and outside. When we are not at peace, we poison ourselves."

Lea's eyes hectically searched the space and hoped not to see him. She felt the pain that Gaya mentioned rooted inside her. She understood.

"We choose poison by denying peace. Poison comes from our food, especially junk food composed of E-numbers and low energy. It comes from alcohol and smoking. They are socially acceptable but do not help us accept ourselves. And it comes from relationships that we allow to pull us down."

Gaya's words sank into the group and a new stillness took the space. People let out mumblings of agreement as they recognised a sentence for themselves.

Nick cradled his head in his hands, something in him already unlocking.

Lea continued in the same distressed manner, replaying seeing Patrik at a coffee shop a week before. She'd changed every place to hang out, but he always found her. He came close behind her as she paid and whispered, 'I'll always find you. Always, Lea. You're mine." She wanted to cry.

Petra thought about the moments she'd prioritised others, cooking the food Janez preferred, vacationing in the same spot every year. *Is it too late to catch up? I must add 'learn gong' to my list.*

"And do you know why you are poisoning yourself?" Gaya questioned and allowed silence to follow. "Because you want to satisfy everyone else before yourself: your family, society, neighbours, peers. You are always last because you don't want to be hated. But it's good to have a few haters and to be at peace with that." Gaya smiled a broad, good-humoured smile.

"People that hate you are not vital to you. If someone focuses on you, they send you energy. If that energy is loving, accept it.

152

If it isn't, tell yourself, 'I am attractive and good. This person has problems with me, but I can't help them with their hate. Their hate is their own, not mine. I send back their bad energy.'"

Kara followed Gaya's breath, floating in a state of perfect harmony. For the past year, she'd sent bad energy back. She'd tried ayahuasca and now embraced experimentation and new paths. On this experiment, she'd ended up taking Tina with her, although that was not her intention. In the past, Kara wouldn't have minded, but now she registered Tina's imposition as an invasion. Kara didn't want to share her space and energy, but she also couldn't say no.

As Kara gained balance, Tina struggled to stay sane while detoxing from her chosen poisons. She'd cut all connection with her lover, so they hadn't been alone together since the girls' trip. And though she knew the affair was wrong, she missed the intimacy. Tom had grounded her. Now, she felt herself slowly losing her grip. Her husband worked overtime or escaped being present at home by constantly entertaining. Tina was utterly empty and alone.

Storm sat free and at ease, breathing and opening his mind.

"Some of you are here because you feel lost. You are working hard. You are kind. And you do not understand why good things aren't happening for you. You are unhappy because you're forcing a life that can not be forced. Life will not bend for you. Everything happens for a reason and at the right time. But sometimes we insist on forcing it, pushing and abusing our very nature.
We pen animals for mass food production and play with the planet until it's climate is irrevocably changed. Mother Earth could wipe us out, like the parasites we are, but she has not yet. So try not to force life. Stop forcing it.

Money, relationships, happiness, will be lost if you take them before you are ready. Everything will come when you are poised, working, directed, loving, and appreciating the path you're on. When the time and place is right, everything will synchronise. When you are ready, it will be easy. Everything will follow your flow."

The wind blew Gaya's blonde hair and sunlight fell upon her making it glisten. Jan thought she looked like an illustration of a god and nervously lusted after her. He couldn't wrap his mind around all the points she presented but tried to stay open-minded. His logical nature resisted.

Jacopo listened very confused. He also found Gaya attractive, which had never happened to him before. Her composed, calm presence inspired him. He absorbed every word, and they made him want to stand up, clap, and cheer. *Yes, I have to find myself first. Yes, synchronicity. When I'm ready, I will meet a new love. Yes. Yes. Yes. Stop forcing it.*

"I am extra, and I am ordinary." Gaya said. "I can be all or nothing, and that depends on me.
Every one of you that listens to my words could also speak them, possibly with better eloquence and examples. Who I am is not vital. I, like you, initially resisted this path, but a brutal headache would not leave me at peace until I started to walk in the right direction."

"The 8-Day Experiment came into being in October 2016, when I started to conscientiously write this programme.
I found notes full of scribbled thoughts all over my apartment and at my family house, and I skimmed all my journals and notebooks to discover short sentences from different times in my life were coming together and creating new meaning. In 2016, they finally made sense. I seemed to reach some kind of equilibrium.

Nothing terrible happened in my life. I can't talk about horrific experiences that haunted me, as some other writers, teachers, or gurus can. Some of the teachers here will speak of experiences like this, but I cannot. There was no extreme. I am, at my core, a very positive and lively person, always happy and excited about life. But, still, I managed to internalise a fear. The fear came from my environment, perspective, and from programmes imposed upon me. I have had a wonderful life. I was a wanted, loved child. I grew up in a small village surrounded by family, nature, and animals. I have a wild, colourful imagination. I was ambitious, set to become an actor or writer. But I was told that it wasn't possible for a girl from the countryside. I believed this." She paused.

"I stopped writing because I feared the cost of getting published. I stopped acting because I would not move to the city. But my passion for reading never died. Today, I eat books. It's my great passion. But I did give up some very important things because of fear and a belief that was passed on to me. A belief which I did not form.

Society is shifting. Changes are constantly happening around us, and we are told to be focused and alert to them. We are told that if we sleep, we are not living. But we need to wake up. We embrace the fluctuating world and its realities, beliefs, and circumstances. They soak into us, and they affect us.

Eventually, I awoke and realised I do not need to exist as the society that was set for me. I am a creator, as are you. Now, I am in constant search of light, happiness, peace, and love. But to find all of the above, I had to become all of the above.
And that is how the 8-Day Experiment came to be." Gaya's words hypnotised her audience. A fusion of sounds and energy connected them harmoniously.

"I have read and listened to many gurus and teachers.

At the end of every teaching, the conclusion I come to is always the same: we are one connected body composed of a series of links. Some are stronger links than others but we coexist in one life. Our aim this week is to become a link in that chain that will not break at a single pull, to become a strong part of the chain of life, a link that is formed by our individual journey. Tomorrow, we start. Tonight, talk and sleep well."

DAY ONE: PREPARATION

Enjoy the pallet of emotions: love, fear, happiness, doubt. But don't take it too seriously.

The meditation space was prepared in a semicircle. All eight teachers sat quietly on the stage wearing colourful dresses that acted as a balsam, like sunshine, for the eyes.

After meditation, Gaya addressed the group for a second time. "Good morning. I hope you slept well and are ready to dive into the week. We will begin by opening and exploring the sealed boxes of our core. We will question them and uncover their secrets.

The programme is simple. After breakfast, take time for yourself. You may not know what to do with yourself, but try to feel the time that is yours. Feel your thoughts and the vibrations of your body. Later, you will need the notebooks we gave you on arrival. I hope no one has lost them." Gaya smiled. "We will come together after your time, and I will give you pointers for activities and games you can find around the estate. You will decide where to go. We will give you written tips as well, so if you need a reference point, you will have everything you need.

Throughout history, wise people have highlighted the relativity of life experience. Everything is relative.
In our case, this week, relative is how we manage to focus on our inner world. We each live in an individual world of stories.

When I talk to my people about a movie I've seen or book I've read, even an event that we experienced side by side, each of us has different realities and ideas. We do not experience the same story, feel the same words, remember the event in the same way. This week is about your unique response to being here and perception of experiences you have here. Your version, your reality that is important. Try not to think how your family and friends would feel here. Try not to guess what the person next to you is experiencing. Try not to compare this with other institutions you have learnt from. Try to focus solely on your inner world and your presence.

I do not promote permissive upbringing and education. I believe in boundaries, but I believe they should provide the opportunity to personally explore society and the world around us. This is easier once we introduce ourselves to new people and cultures because they encourage us to question and explore. If you cannot travel to explore, you should explore with reading and talking. Life is a multi-layered experience. The world is a group of shared cultures and societies. You must try to know your own culture and its surrounding layers intimately. And you should try to explore other cultures to better understand your own."

With this image of unity in the air, the group were released from the semicircle and invited to the dining area. They moved around beautiful white tents which lay under trees. They ate vegan food and drank tea or barley coffee. They were informed that simple food allows the blood to go more freely to the head, since the body spends less time digesting, and helps with focus.

Tina followed Kara to every food station, tea pot, and coffee table, possessively glued to her. She was evidently uncomfortable in this setting. Kara inhaled loudly, trying to remove the building hate within.

Conscious breathing, yoga, meditation, and chanting normally helped Kara find balance, but she was starting to understand no amount of breathing would rid herself of the suffocating and unwelcome presence of her friend. *An explosion is on the horizon if I don't do something.*

"Can you please give me some space to breathe, Tina." Kara announced, less controlled than she would have liked. "I am here for myself. For me, this retreat is not about you. I have a lot of things to reflect on, so I need to be alone, at least for a day," She paused, "But maybe for the week." Tina was visibly hurt. "I have to focus on myself, Tina. You know that."

Kara was Tina's best friend and had always supported her. *Now she's abandoning me,* thought Tina as she swallowed her tears, too proud to show them to the outside world.

Kara could see what she'd done so continued in a softer voice. "Look. I am searching for something in myself. You're searching too. We're here to jump into our problems, Tina, not to distract ourselves with each other. That's not the point. Let's make a deal." She took Tina's hand. "We have freedom from each other during the day. But in the evening, we'll sit together for dinner and talk about how we are feeling. Okay?"

Tina didn't look convinced but was comforted by the clarity.

"I need this, Tina. I have to look at the feelings I have uncovered and make peace with my past, with my patterns. And you do too." Tina looked down. She found Kara's honesty hard to embrace. "You have to focus on yours, by yourself, Tina. It's the only way. Nobody else can save you. Remember? I love you. But I want to love myself first." Kara walked away and took a seat without Tina.

Feeling rejected and abandoned, Tina sat on the stairs. She ate with her tray on her knees and swallowed food mixed with salty tears.

Jacopo stood next to Petra in the line for food. Unable to resist the temptation to meet someone knew, Petra asked, "How are you, child?"

Jacopo smiled and blushed. "I am good." He was craving attention, craving love and kindness. Jacopo hadn't spoken to his family for a long time, and since leaving Rocco, he felt he'd lost all his friends as well. Petra's motherly spirit warmed his soul. He wanted to hug her, but controlled himself. "How are you? What brings you here?"

They had a sweet, instant connection and recognised themselves in each other, like friends from a past life.

"Same as you, dear." Petra said wisely. "I'm here to find my voice. But you'll find yours at the beginning, and me, five minutes before the end of the game." She laughed. They automatically walked together to a table and talked with ease.

Lea looked nervously at Nick, who sat across from her. She didn't want to look at him, but he made her unreasonably suspicious. She tried to focus on her plate and think about something else. When their eyes locked, Lea jumped and spilt food on her dress. She'd forgotten a napkin and frantically searched for one around the tent. Nick gave her one from his tray and tried to offer a welcoming smile. Cleaning her dress, Lea looked up intent on reprimanding him for startling her, even though she knew he hadn't done anything intentionally, but when she looked deeper into his eyes, she saw kindness.

"Thank you." She whispered.

Jan watched Gaya and Storm sitting together and laughing. He didn't understand how the child, Storm, could be so relaxed beside goddess Gaya. *In some moments,* he thought, *they even look like lovers. But that can't be. She's the teacher. That's probably not allowed, especially with a student so young. Or is it?*

After an hour, a gong sounded and the meal was over. Participants were directed to their circle and Gaya stood in front of them again.

"I want you to ask yourself some questions." She glanced around the space and steadily delivered one question after another. "What do you want to achieve with this experiment? Do you want to find focus? Are you trying to test yourself? Do you want this to be the beginning of something? Did you come here because you want to experience the world differently? Do you plan to set goals?" She allowed the questions to grow roots.

"As you consider these questions, calm your inner voice. Ask yourself to stop thinking about what has not been achieved and start thinking about what you want." She was silent for a long time as participants sat with closed eyes and searched their desires, their purpose in coming here. When silence felt natural, she gave them another question. "How would you feel if you achieved the thing you want?" A new silence was gifted to them.

"Life gives us various challenges that we have to tackle. Approaching and overcoming these challenges is a process. Sometimes, in the process, we manage to have that 'aha' or 'eureka' moment, where we feel satisfaction, like we've finally conquered and won, solved a trauma, or figured something out. When you take rest, there it is: you're new knowledge, like opening a door. It's a fresh breeze of understanding.

"Then, new challenges appear, new obstacles. There are new lessons to be learnt, and the process continues.

163

The journey begins again, and you are restless for a while. You have to start back at square one; this is a new journey. But these processes are pit stops from which we must carry on. Our goals are not end points, instead they are beginnings. There is no end to the process. It rejuvenates.

"Another challenge for you, is to enjoy the process, the journey, the path, the sailing in life's changing waters. Enjoy the pallet of emotions: love, fear, happiness, doubt. But don't take it too seriously. Don't overthink it. And remind yourself, if you manage to overcome one challenge, you can overcome more.

Take a moment, just a few seconds -- well, maybe a minute." Gaya was having fun. "Take the whole day if you want. Take the whole of your life to keep asking yourself: What processes are repeating in my life? What keeps coming back that I don't overcome? Is it a type of person that takes my energy and then leaves? Is it dieting? Is it work, unhappiness, health? If you can answer these questions, you will experience magic. If you cannot ask yourself these questions, you will fall back again and again. The process will fill you and take your power."

The energy around the circle grew heavy with fear. Sensing this, Gaya lightened the mood. "Does your car keep breaking down? Has it happened multiple times with different cars? Do you find yourself with the same problems at your job? Are you irritated by your colleagues?
Ask yourself, 'Is the problem them or me?'" She guided them. "We are well-conditioned creatures of habit. If you take control and change your behaviour, the circumstances could change as well."

She was nearly ready to let the group go and could feel the shift to a more positive place; they were energised. "In this experiment, you should face your fears and insecurities. When I release you, I want you to find a spot alone in the resort.

As you have seen, we have more than enough space to spread out and focus on ourselves. Try not to wander into the village. This is a time to quieten external noise. When you find your place, settle and consider the things that scare you at the moment. Let them come into your mind and pass out again."

Petra wrote down Gaya's instructions. She never finished school so now she seized the opportunity to be a good student

"Then, consider what your ideal world looks like. A world that does not judge you. How would that feel?" Gaya searched the circle and sent her energy around the group.

"You will be given a sheet before you wander, and on this are a number of techniques you can use to find your answers. If you have questions, we are here. Do not hesitate to ask us anything you want. When you hear the gong, slowly return, and we will come together before lunch."

Teachers handed sheets to participants, and everyone took their own direction. Some carried a kit bag, others grabbed pillows and yoga mats to help them get comfortable once they found their place. No one person took the same things as another.

* * *

Jan sceptically wandered to a nearby tree and sat down to read his instructions. Petra took a spot near him and carefully prepared her surroundings. For Petra, everything had to be perfect. She organised her pens and pencils by colour before starting to read.

∞ ∞ ∞

Dear participants,

We welcome you to this beautiful Infinity Estate and to our 8-Day Experiment. Take your time to find yourself here.
The purpose while here is to look inside. All eight of us are ready to help you answer questions or debate things that are blocking you.

Dear participant, I hope the tools you find here will prompt the change you desire. At the very least, I hope they provide you with information about the type of change you want. The material world will not alter because you wish it, so try to see that your relationships can shift and the world can be viewed with a different perspective.

Nowadays, because of the internet, we can read, hear, and discover wise words from many authors, gurus, teachers, and everyday people. No matter their age, status, or knowledge, they are there for all to see. This should help us understand that, in the end, we are all teachers. Every person can teach something, just as every person can learn. You will find something to teach yourself here, something that perhaps others could also learn from.

DAY ONE'S TASK:

Today is a preparation day. You have two focus goals. You may discover other goals along the way. The first of your focus goals is:

> Relaxation - You have been asked to consider what scares you. Once you welcome and release these ideas, use the tools around you to calm yourself. You have access to the studio and workshops, as well as a small library.

There are manual tools, art kits, fabrics and beads, paint, paper, and much more. Look at your map to find a location that feels good to you. Be creative. Think about what you already have.

On the next page, you will find some basic terms that we use at the retreat and techniques for relaxation. Be infinite in your creation, search, and play. Enjoy the process. It is a story. It is your story.

Bliss. Love. Magic.
Your 8 teachers

Basic terms of the 8-Day Experiment:

My people – The group of people we let into our inner circle, our chosen family. They say a lot about us. If you are unhappy with them, it is an expression of something wrong within you. Your search for flaws in others is actually a refusal to look at the flaws in yourself. You must accept your people as beautiful, perfect, and majestic. Change them and you change yourself. They are your pupils, teachers, and companions. If you don't like them, you don't like yourself and should question this.

Path – The journey through life and the decisions that lead you to your goals.

Pit stops – Fantastic moments in life when you feel at one with the world, at peace within yourself, and happy with the results you see around you. This normally happens after reaching a goal that you have worked hard for.

Goals – A place and time that you work toward. This goal is a perfect version of yourself: a healthy, adored, successful version that is loved by yourself, thus loved by the world.

Techniques

There are many techniques to create calm and gradually promote change. No single method helps in every situation. You must find which ones lift you to climb out of darkness and into light.

Some suggestions:
- Listen to music.
- Paint.
- Do physical work (my preference is working with wood).
- Walk.
- Talk with calm, happy people.
- Write down frustrations. Burn the paper, and throw the remains into water. It can be a river, a lake, or even your toilet. Symbolically, you burn and wash the problem away.
- Write down why you are extraordinary.
- Sit in complete silence.
- Clean and throw out clutter.
- Shout in the forest or somewhere you are alone (this is recommended by all 8-Day teachers).
- Sleep.
- Watch the clouds, sunset, stars, moon, trees, whatever you find compelling.
- Read.
- Meditate.
- Play with a child or pet to bring out your inner innocence.
- Write a list of your gifts and blessings.
- Find activities you enjoy.
- Stop dreaming. Start realising your goals and write steps to achieve them.

These are ideas, not solutions. Find what suits you. If you don't enjoy something, don't proceed with it. Nobody has the answers for you. No guide can take you back to your source. Read, listen, talk, think, be with an open mind.

Everything you need is on the premises.

Bliss. Love. Magic.

Your 8 teachers

∞ ∞ ∞

Storm moved to the stage near the gong. After reading his instructions, he smiled and lay down to watch the clouds. His mind was empty of thoughts, and he felt intensely calm.

From under the tree, Jan could see Storm and rolled his eyes. *That guy.* He turned to find a happy looking Petra. *I wonder what she's doing here?*

"Hello." He decided to find out. "I'm Jan."

Petra smiled. "Hi, I am Petra."

"If I may ask, Petra, why are you here?"

"You may ask, dear Jan." Petra offered Jan her most open and friendly energy. "I want to focus on myself. Until recently I was married. We were together for fifty years, and now I'm widowed. When Janez died, I felt lost and without direction." Jan knew about being untethered since leaving Ema. "Now, I want to find me; I didn't know who I was without Janez, but I intend to find out." Petra smiled and looked down at her sheet, finishing the conversation.

Jan understood and gave her space. He couldn't figure out why she picked a spot next to him, but he let her be. Leaning against the tree, Jan tried to meditate.

Petra questioned, *Should I walk? Should I talk to this man? Maybe that was the purpose of us sitting by each other.* For now, she stayed put.

Kara practically ran away from Tina when the group was released and delved into the woods. She walked around and around, focusing on trees and bushes, taking in the different shapes and colours. In the past months, she'd found great mental escape in walking. Her daily goal was ten thousand steps. On this day, she walked in circles until she heard the gong and so achieved over thirty-four thousand.

While Kara walked, Tina took shelter in her room, curled up in a ball, and cried. Since she had decided to try and stop being a repressed person who told lies she cried a lot. After what felt like a long time, Tina dragged herself up, wiped her tears with the back of her hand, and declared, "ENOUGH!" She shouted it. "Enough crying. I take my power back." A small voice repeated, "Enough."

Tina moved to the art room and searched for markers and coloured pencils. She took a poster-sized piece of paper and tucked herself away in a corner so no one would see her. Without specific intention, she started drawing, colouring, cutting out images found around the room and tapping them to the paper. By lunch time, she'd created a beautiful focus wheel. At its core was everything she wanted. The word peace in the centre identified her purpose for the week.

Nick was the only one who walked far away from the meditation area and settled near a renovated old cottage. Unbeknownst to Nick, the staff lived there and Gaya snuck inside unnoticed to lie down and sleep.

Nick found peace between wild bushes and flowers. He'd cut contact with Linda since she got pregnant and asked him to be the godfather of her child.

170

He couldn't face having a deeper relationship than he already had and knew spiritually caring for her child would destroy him. Sitting in nature and contemplating his fears, he tried to write her a letter. But every time words formed he crossed them out. He started many times, repeating himself and crossing it through. *I can't force myself on her. She's not mine to explain to.*

Taking in his surroundings, Nick noticed leaves scattered around the courtyard of the cottage. There was a wheelbarrow and rake that called to him. He gathered the foliage and piled it in the wheelbarrow. He hadn't done anything like gardening since visiting a distant relative's farm and that was years ago. He took great pleasure in his chore and managed to clean the whole courtyard. *I'm ready to stop. Linda will never make me happy.*

Jacopo, driven by a desire for homeliness and comfort, took himself to the dining area. He collected a selection of pots and objects from the adjacent kitchen and started to drum. He was alone and thought about his Nona's kitchen as he played. He felt love in abundance there with her, and the memory brought a pang of longing for his family and Rocco. He wanted to see the new family he'd gained at Rocco's side and the friends they'd shared. *I've been forgotten by everyone.* Jacopo stopped drumming and looked around the empty space.

Lea followed some teachers to sit in the shadows near a lake. She felt safer as part of their crowd. She dipped her feet into the water and stared at it's glistening surface. Lea had heard that showering cleanses bad energy, and she thought about this with her feet in the water. At home, she would stay in the shower for hours.

After some time, the teachers left Lea with her feet in the chilled lake and moved towards the meditation area.

They played the gong and participants gradually regrouped, appearing from all directions. Gaya waited until all sixty-four had returned. Nick, the last to return, was sweaty, dirty, and happy.

"Welcome back." Gaya announced. "I hope you had an excellent first half of your first day. Now, we will divide into eight groups of eight people. Together you will evaluate or, let's say, talk it out. If you struggled this morning, do not worry. That's normal. New things are hard and require practice to make them work for you. This is called training." She smiled a broad challenging smile. "The work never ends. Think about yourself as an old city, like Rome, London, or Athens. They are beautiful, mysterious places filled with buildings of each era. They grow and evolve and work themselves out to function perfectly for each generation, and the development never ends. Isn't that amazing? You are an old city, a never-ending creation, a developing masterpiece.

In your games, your challenges, your evolutions, listen to your guts and your intuition, whatever you call the inner voice that pushes you to travel further in your journey. Take your time and follow the flow of that voice. Try to look past the sneaky, little judging voice that undermines you. That judgemental voice will not guide you to your goals. You postpone your life by listening to that voice."

The group was more still than they had been the night before. There were still disruptions and movement, but already, they were easing into the process.

"Listen to the kind voice that tells you what is right for you, the one that is encouraging and interested. We call ourselves teachers here." Gaya gestured to her colleagues on the stage.

"But we are all teachers, and we are all students. Between us, we have explored many paths. In the end, we all discovered the only person we should dedicate ourselves to is our inner voices.

Gurus help, but they do not help as much as our inner voice. We have taken pearls of wisdom from many places and adapted them to our own lifestyles, views, and values. This selection and adaptation is what makes a lesson strong and lasting. Try to do the same with your time here. Read, try, think, feel, and take what you want to incorporate to help you improve. Do not take everything or you will fail. Take only what feels good.

I believe our work is never finished, that reaching Nirvana will take a long time, but you must continue trying to get there. Nothing will happen if you don't invest and believe in it. There is no action without belief. With focus, thought, small steps, and time, you can and will create change. If you learn to enjoy each step towards your goal, you will be even more successful. Goals achieved are markers of your success. Pit stops are to be enjoyed and part of the course of life." Gaya seemed to take much joy in sharing and that joy filled the air.

"After the group session," She said, clapping her hands together, "Is lunch. Relax during this time, and in the afternoon, we start writing in our notebooks."

Gaya gestured for participants to rise, and people were led to their group areas. My searching souls were placed together in one group of eight and so continued on a shared path. Gregor was their guide and lit candles around the area to create hope and calm during the time to share.

"Welcome to our first circle. If you have any questions, now is the time to ask. There are no stupid questions, so feel welcome to speak. If you don't have a question, perhaps you can share an experience from this morning."

The group looked at each other in silence. Then Jan took the first turn. "Why did you take our phones away? I think I'd be more relaxed if I could watch videos when we have free time. "

He didn't look relaxed at all. The group gave him their attention, which he found a little disturbing. *What am I doing here? How will this shit help me?*

Gregor smiled warmly. "Thank you for your question. We live in a world of chaos and noise. Because of this, we enjoy other people's dramas. This pulls us away from our soul. The information, the stories on our phones are endless, and it makes us feel we know everything about everything. Despite this, we are often unable to say what we like and don't.

We struggle to know what is good for us, for our physical and mental health. We coverup these uncertainties with information and pictures because it makes us feel in control. We avoid dedicating time for ourselves to learn what we like. We search for solutions but intoxicate ourselves with options and stories. Boredom is hard. But sometimes, we have to be bored. We have to be annoyed. We have to feel our emotions fully and engage with them rather than turning away from them to a screen: hate, disappointment, sadness, anger, everything. If we do this, we can go from feeling to motion and motion to change. That is why we removed your phones; so you can feel and ultimately step into motion."

Jan was annoyed. He didn't want to be rude but couldn't help questioning. *How will that help me?*

Nick was next. "I really tried, just now, to write a letter to someone important, but I couldn't." He didn't mean to open up like this so early on but the words escaped from him. "I feel deep sadness. It's like something is pressing on my lungs, and I wanted to put that in the letter. But I couldn't describe it to this person. They pull me down, and I don't want them in my life anymore. But I couldn't write it. So I started to work in the garden, cleaning leaves. I still feel sad, but it's mellowed. I felt better for a moment."

Gregor nodded but said nothing. Instead, he looked around to the other participants and waited for the next one to speak up.

"I walked the whole time." Said Kara. "My feet are a bit sore now, actually. Walking helps me, so I continued that practice. I looked at the nature around me and it helped keep my thoughts under control."

Gregor smiled at Kara, briefly closed his eyes, and bowed his head in acknowledgement of her contribution. He looked around again.

Petra took a big breath. "I realised before coming here that I missed a lot of what I wanted from life because my husband wasn't interested in the same things as me. Sitting here today, I embraced a wish to try as many new things as possible, including playing the gong. I want to care for myself, prioritise myself, and enjoy what's left of my life. But I don't know what can calm me and bring me back to myself yet."

Tina felt empty listening to Petra. *Is this me in thirty years? Will I lose myself for my husband?* She spoke. "So ..." Tina took a deep breath. "I feel lost. I feel like a huge hypocrite because I have everything I wished for. But I'm not happy. Nothing fulfils me. I'm unable to be alone but often left alone." She looked around the space. Everyone was with her. "Half of the time, for that exercise, I just lay in bed and cried. For the other half, I tried to do art. I started a collage but scrapped it in the end. I wasn't satisfied with it."

Now Gregor did speak. "The question is not: did you create something perfect? But rather: have you enjoyed the process?"

"I did," replied Tina quickly. "But, the result wasn't good."

"We are obsessed with results." Said Gregor softly. "We can get so obsessed with them that we stop doing things all together. Which is worse?

175

The path is the important thing and finding enjoyment in the process. With practice, everything gets better." Tina tried to take these words on board.

Storm shifted in his seat and said, "I just looked at the sky. Since I was a child, it's been the most effective form of meditation for me."

Jan grew more annoyed by this young man and his piercing blue eyes. Storm smiled presenting snow-white teeth.
The wind played with his blonde hair, making him look like the Little Prince. And Jan couldn't help himself. "You are still a child." He spat.

Storm laughed. "When you judge others, you are judging yourself." He smiled at Jan, unoffended and undeterred. "I think something's bothering you, but it's nothing to do with me. I have no bad feeling for you. You should focus on what's annoying you and why. Yes, I'm still a child, but I'm also a man. I can also be a woman or girl if I decide. It's all an illusion." Storm held Jan's gaze.

How can that child be so eloquent? What does he know?

Gregor waited for a reply which furthered Jan's discomfort. No reply came. Jacopo couldn't stand the silence and so shared, "So I'm also in distress. The love of my life cheated on me. And I don't know how to shake the frustration I feel. I tried drumming on pots and pans in the kitchen today. It helped me for a while, but then I came to the same thoughts I always come to. I'm searching for solutions."

Lea coughed to introduce herself as the next speaker. "I watched the water. I'm here as an escape from the real world." She spoke quickly and quietly.

Gregor took a deep breath which some of the group followed. "I see you had an interesting morning. Congratulations. This is only the first half of the first day. There are lots of interesting revelations to come. You can go to lunch now, and we will meet again before dinner for a sum up of the day." He lifted his hands, guiding them to stand and leave.

In the dining area, Tina filled her tray and sat in a corner away from the main crowd. A pinching headache plagued her as a result of not drinking a drop of alcohol for the past few days. She'd always considered herself to be super healthy, but now, an evil voice inside said it had been the alcohol deluding her all along, tricking and numbing her true health. *Fucking Kara, why did I listen to her about changing myself. This isn't liberating at all. And she's not evening speaking to me.*

Kara noticed Tina sitting on her own and contemplated joining her. She knew they needed space but wanted to hug her friend after hearing Tina's confession in the group. They had always been connected, but now, they were divided. In the end, she opted to maintain the space and joined Storm. *It's better like this for now.* She recognised Storm and nodded as she sat. "I remember you from Fuerte." She said. "You helped us with ... hmm ... natural products."

Storm laughed as Gaya and Gregor joined them. The quartet chatted and Kara took great joy in the experience and satisfaction in her choice.

Jacopo, Nick, and Jan sat at the same table, gravitating towards each other after sharing something personal.

Nick ate in silence, occupied with his thoughts. He knew he couldn't wait for Linda anymore. *I don't want to be her bell boy. Enough. Enough. Enough.*

Jan pierced his sweet potato with a fork, unexcited by the small, vegan meals. "I don't get it." He announced. "I think Gaya and that surfer kid have something going on. How can a woman like her be interested in that child?" His frustration on display.

Jacopo licked his fork. "I would totally do him. He's gorgeous, though I doubt he's single."

Jan's fork dropped to the table. This was his first interaction with an openly gay person.
Well, that explains why he ignores all the looks from adoring women around here. Five women had checked Jacopo out in the brief time they'd been sat down to lunch.

"You're gay?" Jan tried to ask as if this was a totally normal conversation for him. *He looks like an athlete ...* Jan had assumed all gay men were scrawny, talked like girls, and wore pink. He assessed Jacopo closely and noticed he was very carefully maintained. Initially, Jan assumed that was an Italian thing but was starting to see all his prejudices were off.

"Yes, a total queen." Jacopo smiled and pouted his lips.

Lea took a seat next to the solo Tina. They stared at their plates and played with food. One could see, feel, smell the bad vibes at their table, but Petra couldn't help herself and joined them, her nature implored her to help. She tucked into her food and was surprised by how tasty the vegan dish was. Today, she'd taken a one-pot and a small wholegrain roll.

"I have to get the recipe for this." She informed Tina and Lea. "It's so good. Don't you think? Well, I'd add some sausage on the side, but I think that's still okay." No response. When she finished, she looked at Lea, and then at Tina. They were both in visible pain. One swam in mental distress and the other physical.

"Ladies," She tried again. "How do you like the programme so far? I'm very excited about the week."

Tina looked up from her plate and they locked eyes. She smiled and felt seen for the first time in an age. They started to talk and explain what led them to the retreat. Tina found she was indeed looking at her future self if she didn't make changes. Petra was different because she was happy and had a happy marriage. But she was lost, dissatisfied, unaccomplished like Tina.

Lea moved two chairs away.

As the meal came to a close, one teacher spoke to the collected participants. "Now we begin the second half of our day, and you begin your second focus goal. Your first was to relax and explore your thoughts. Now, I want you to find your perfect spot on the estate. Be wherever feels comfortable. We encourage you to stay in nature, but if you wish, you can retire to your room. When you settle, take out your notebook and write down your goals for this week. Why did you come here? What was the motive? What do you want to achieve? Try to focus on yourself here and give others space. Connect with the earth. Walk barefoot. Enjoy. Try to be the best company for yourself. You can draw, write, combine skills, collage. Make a focus wheel. Find a way to express yourself. Try to continue expressing yourself as time passes."

The teacher raised their hands and off everyone went.

* * *

Nick sped back to his spot at the cottage and was relieved to find it equally abandoned. He took a seat under a large tree, opened his notebook, and wrote.

My goals – 8-day experiment
- I want to forget Linda.
- I want to be able to see other women.
- I want to express myself better.

Nick closed the notebook, lay down on the earth, and watched the tree branches and leaves dance with the wind.

Lea stayed by the lake but walked further away from the teachers this time. She kept people in view and found comfort in their closeness. Taking a black marker in hand, she wrote frantically.

I want peace. I need to quieten my mind. I want to sleep through the night without nightmares. I NEED to feel SAFE again. I want everything to be over. I cannot carry this fear anymore. I need to find relief. The feeling that someone is following me, stalking me, has to go away.
I want to feel safe. I need to walk down the street and not look at people in paranoia.
NO MORE FEAR. NO more HATE.
No more feeling I won't survive. I want to feel like me again. I want to find passion again.

She didn't know what else to write so started doodling. She ran circles over **FEAR** again and again indenting the page with deep marks.

Storm stayed at the table in the dining room. He watched panicky participants run and try to find the perfect place. Storm felt he could create the perfect place anywhere. He opened his notebook and started to draw a beach, waves, seagulls, windsurfers, and a smiling sun. He dedicated his focus to small details. If you took the smiling sun away, it was very realistic. Then he took a blue marker and wrote **BLISS. LOVE. MAGIC.** across the middle of his work. When he was done, Storm lay down on his bench and closed his eyes. He smiled and felt peaceful.

Petra walked to her bungalow and sat at a table in it's porch. She felt more comfortable sitting.

Day 1 – 8-day challenge

My goal on this journey is to find out what I like and what I don't like.
I want to learn how to meditate. I think I am on the right path to meditation.
I want to meet new friends and learn as many new things as possible.
I want to become an independent woman that enjoys life.
I want to find my own voice.
I want to know when it's time to interfere and when it is time to let go.
I want to learn all the techniques that can help me and to give myself to this process.

I want to meet people without prejudices.
Thank you, Lord, for answers.

Jan walked to the morning meditation spot and opened his notebook. He hated writing about his feelings. *I don't know what I expect from this experiment. Solutions to my problems? That would be great, although it's pretty far fetched. I hope I'll find a method that helps me speak to my soon-to-be ex-wife. I want to be the best father for my son.* He tried to think of anything else, but it made him want to go home and scream. *How can this bullshit help me? I don't know what I'm doing here. Why did I come?* He took a big breath and tried to be positive. *Well, I've paid, so I might as well try and stick it out. I would definitely go home if I could get my money back.*

Kara went directly to the forest. She walked until she found a big rock to settle on and take lotus position.

She closed her eyes and tried to meditate but soon stopped. Her chosen stone was horrendously uncomfortable. *Far from perfect.* She got up and settled under the shade of a tree but soon realised meditation wasn't possible. She couldn't focus. Every whoosh of wind or shaking branch kicked her out of her Zen mode. Giving up meditation, Kara opened her notebook and started to write.

My painful spots or long-term goals:
- I want to change my appearance and to keep it the way I want it.
- I want to learn how to love myself.
- I want to change how I talk to myself.

My goals this week are to:
- focus on me
- learn how to say no
- learn how to set boundaries
- learn different tools that can help me every day
- meet new people
- be less annoyed by Tina
- talk to as many people as possible
- write down new food combinations so I can eat them when I get home
- wake up early and walk (ask how many km around the estate)
- try all techniques from the sheet
- get to know the teacher called Sun (super cute, reserved, charming)
- give 100% every day
- see a significant change at the end of the week
- be loving
- smile a lot

Tina roamed the estate like a woman possessed. She felt out of place. Her headache was getting worse and when she asked for something to help with the pain a teacher brewed herbs and flowers for her that were, so far, not having any effect. The tea tasted so bitter that Tina swallowed it in one great hesitant gulp. Walking, the pressure built on her eyes and manipulated her vision. She finally came to rest on a bench. She opened her notebook and stared at blank pages. *Why am I here? What is my goal?* She laughed out loud. *This is insane.*

Tina couldn't think straight and closed the book. She massaged her temples and opened the notebook again. She had no words so drew instead. First, she drew a heart, then a couple holding hands, a cloud made out of small hearts. Finally, at the bottom of the page, she wrote:

I want to be happy and satisfied.

Jacopo headed to the forest and found comfort under a tree. He inhaled and exhaled. He acknowledged the pain moving inside his body. *It's toxic. Look at it or it will eat you alive.* A few more breaths, and he opened his notebook.

I came here to forget my first love. I still feel betrayed and all the emotions that come with that. I don't want the anger and hate. Yes, I was deeply hurt, but I want to move on.

Rocco cheated on me. He was my first love. I would have done anything for him. I assumed he wanted to settle down ... but, in the end, he didn't want to with me.

My goals for this experiment:
- I want to move on from heartbreak.
- I want to feel joy, love, and happiness again.
- I hope to find new friends and confidants.

- I don't want to feel alone anymore.
- I want to learn how to listen to myself.
- I want to learn to express myself clearly.

For some the time flew, while for others it moved slowly and painfully.

A teacher struck the gong, signalling the start of evening meditation. After a short reflection, groups were dispersed to their small groups and teachers. Gregor waited for his group to be seated and still before asking, "How was it?"

A series of mumbles filled the air and then silence. Some time passed until Petra took her book out and read what she wrote. She ended with the comment, "I hope I was clear in my writing. I just want to find a way to be happy and to catch up on the opportunities I missed."

The others admired her bravery for going first. Gregor soothed Petra by assuring her, "It's never too late or too early. It is always the right time. Learn from our diverse group. Everyone has something to tell and something to learn."

Storm went next. He presented his picture and explained the scene. "And for the **BLISS. LOVE. MAGIC.** I believe you have to find bliss in order to find love. And when you find love, it's **MAGIC.** Simple." Storm smiled proudly.

Jan, fed up, exploded. "What do you know about love, about bliss, about magic? Why are you even here if you know so much?"

Gregor gave Storm a look to check he was okay. Storm smiled, so Gregor turned to Jan and waited.

"I am here because I want to learn." Storm replied coolly.

"I think you can never be too happy and that it's important to discover new paths to happiness, satisfaction, and peace. For me, I always found those things in surfing or just sitting on a board on the waves and watching the sea life. But I think there could be more. And as our teacher has just said, it's never too early or late."

Jan became more enraged by Storm's ability to react maturely and he wanted to punch him. Instead, he grabbed fistfuls of grass and pulled strands from the ground.

To cut the tension, Tina showed her work while delivering her generic 'everything is perfect' synopsis.

Gregor raised an eyebrow. "So you're telling us that you have everything figured out and that this is a waste of your time?" Tina tried to smile in agreement but couldn't because she didn't agree. That wasn't what she meant at all. "You are wasting your time by repeating this story. We will learn something from this. I hope you will too. " Tina blushed.

Kara couldn't believe she'd just heard Tina's, "I have a perfect life, perfect children, perfect husband. I shit perfect golden nuggets," routine again. She rolled her eyes and looked away.

Tina was aware she had to accept her path, but her ego wouldn't let the mask go. "Well, I guess I need more time to share. But some of it is true. I want to be happy in the end. I guess I am not at the moment, although I feel I should be."

"We know." Gregor confirmed. "We support you. When you're ready, you can share. Just remember, when you tell this story, you're not lying to us. You're lying to yourself. It's hard to look at the things we don't like, but it is liberating when you finally do. Try to let go of your ego. Release your rebellion, and accept yourself."

Next, Jacopo read with unexpected tears tracing his cheeks. "I loved him from the moment I saw him." He said between heavy breaths. "I feel a void without him. But I love myself too much to let this go, to forgive him. I want to." He said, voice breaking. "But I will never be able to forget. I want to share my life with someone who loves me unconditionally and only me."

Jacopo's pain seeped into the group. They could all connect with the emptiness of loss. They struggled not to let empathy set in, as they'd been instructed, but the heaviness was there. Jacopo composed himself and took a big breath. He smiled to the group and felt some hate wash away through his tears.

Kara was next. She read her intentions to the group and added honestly, "I've been hiding my whole life. I want to uncover myself, enjoy myself. And I want to appreciate the things I've worked hard for. I want to feel free. There's so much I wanted to try and never did. Now is going to be the time."

The energy of the group shifted with Kara's focus and they saw that they could all aspire to try.

"We are connected. You see?" Gregor brought the group and their thoughts back together. "We are part of one universe. All problems created in this world are universal and become part of a collective memory."

Jan experienced his first glimpse of recognition in Gregor's words and looked at Storm again. *Does he annoy me because he's calm and free? Do I envy him? Now's my turn, I guess.* Jan read from his notebook.

"It's hard. I'm struggling." Jan had never admitted this before. He'd thought the words but never said them. "My whole body resists me. My head's telling me this is stupid, but I think I've tried everything else and nothing's helped me save my wife." He corrected himself. "Ex-wife. I'm confused."

The grass that had stayed clenched in Jan's fists was released. "My wife lost it after we split up. It was hard. It is hard. But I have to become better for myself and my son. I guess, I also feel I have to do it for Ema. But, more than anything, I know I have to change for me. "

Gregor nodded in appreciation of Jan's honest contribution.

The session would soon come to a close, so Nick read next. "I followed an illusion for a good five years. I was madly in love and waited and waited for something to happen. I waited for five years for Linda to realise we were meant to be together. It was stupid." He felt ashamed hearing himself aloud. "It shows my lack of inner belief, my lack of power. I have to start looking around and meeting new people."

Gregor was content with his group. He could see some still battled their egos, but they were opening up. He turned to Lea, the only one left to share.
She seems alienated. He thought, but as she met his eyes, she immediately opened her notebook and read in a whispering voice which made his thoughts about her travel on. She didn't raise her eyes from the floor and seemed to physically restrain herself from engaging with the others. *She's wounded.*

"Do you want to add anything," Gregor offered, "Now that you've heard the others?"

Lea shook her head without taking her focus from the floor.

"Then, thank you for sharing." He nodded to Lea and moved on to address the whole group. "I'm glad you had a good first day. Remember, there are no miracles. There is only work and games. I encourage you to go to bed early tonight. Your mind needs time to process, and tomorrow will be an early start.

After dinner, try to end conversations and go for a walk, observe nature, and observe yourself, and then rest. You can slowly move to dinner now. Good night, and well done."

The group sat at one table for their meal but did not speak.

DAY TWO: A DAY FREE OF GUILT. *NO, I AM NOT SORRY.*

I discovered that letting go of negative emotions is in fact the first step towards better health.

The gong woke everyone early. I travelled with teachers to light candles and incense as participants dressed.

The day started with meditation and healing sounds. Afterwards, an older teacher with a white beard addressed them.

"Good morning, dear participants. You have spent more than twenty-four hours without mobile phones now. How do you feel?" He cast his eyes over the group and noticed some unsettled seats. Participants looked to each other questioningly to see if they were alone in their experience of separation. They weren't.

"I see conflicted feelings amongst you. Nowadays, we are overloaded by information being constantly streamed to our hands. It comes from the media and social media, even from our family and friends. This creates a continuous practice of comparing goals and successes. We are overloaded by an expectation to live like those on TV and social media. Most people experience guilt because of these expectations.
When we don't meet the expectations of our family, bosses, friends, society, we feel shame, but most importantly and most worryingly, we feel we have failed ourselves.

It's vital that you accept your path, that you let go of childhood dreams, and don't criticise yourself for them not being realised and the path changing. It's okay. You should try to appreciate the journey towards goals, the knowledge gained from moving towards them, and the moments you experienced along the way. We are on this beautiful planet to play, not compete. The only person you should compete with is in the mirror."

Kara saw her reflection in this lesson. She had turned towards others for too long and now it was vital that she start looking at herself.

"You are not guilty if your partner didn't get the raise they wanted, if someone is feeling angry or out of control, if your mother expects you to call her every day and is disappointed when you don't. You are not responsible for other people's expectations."

Jan took a big breath in and tried to let go of his feelings of responsibility for Ema.

"The goal for today is to start letting guilt fall from your shoulders. Breathe away the guilt from your boss, society, family, friends, and most importantly, from yourself." The bearded teacher placed his hands on his shoulders and breathed deeply in and out, demonstrating how to release guilt and let its tension fall.

"You are the most important component to your happiness. Failure and feelings close to failure affect us. It does not matter how they affect others. Listen to how they affect you. I do not encourage you, beautiful souls, to be uncaring, but there is a difference between being aware of another's feelings and carrying their problems yourself. The weight on your shoulders is enough. You don't need to take extra. We often put others before ourselves and our needs.

If you feel you are not reaching your goals, forgive yourself. Be proud of the work you put into your plans, even if you are only dreaming and not proactive. Be proud and ready to take motion. You have all the time before you, until your soul leaves this body. And even then, who cares if you reach your goals? You must just enjoy and be proud of what you are doing. Do you think you will care when you take your last breath? Do you believe a rich dead person is happier than a poor dead person? Do you think either of them care about upcoming goals that will be left unfinished?" The old man smiled at the absurdity of his questions and enjoyed bringing some humour to the morning.

"We came here to play." He continued, looking like the epitome of playfulness. "Our western society trains us to stop playing and to take everything seriously, but this is the biggest problem in life. In the modern world anxiety, burnout, and depression are on the rise because we have forgotten that we are here to play. We try to help ourselves with drugs, sex, smoking, drinking, spending money, and impressing people because it feels like an attempt at play. But do these things bring us long-lasting happiness?" The group looked to their hands and surroundings for an answer. All of them could connect with something from the list and all were listening intently.

"Try to remember, the path is more important than the goal. Stop waiting for perfect timing. Enjoy now with an imperfect body, unpredictable relationships, a lack of money, and everything else that isn't what your goal looked like. Perfection and completeness are subjective ideas. You can decide what is perfect for you. Problems are there and always will be; it's up to you how you approach them and make them part of your journey." He took a small pause and looked at the group before him. He smiled at their focus and carried on.

"Imagine you have planned the perfect getaway. It's meant to be a paradise. You booked the ideal hotel and room. It's going to be what you always wanted.

192

Then you arrive at this beautiful place and see a welcome basket waiting for you on an indulgent bed. You're excited. But you open the basket and see a pineapple inside. 'But I hate pineapple.' You shout into your heaven, and now, your whole vacation is ruined." He made them wait for a beat. "Everything ruined by a pineapple. Do you see? We focus on the pineapples of life without looking to see if there is also chocolate, our favourite nuts, or tickets to an adventure park." He gave the group a mischievous grin.

"By focusing on the things that are missing or that which we hate, we fail to see the whole picture before us: chocolate and nuts, the lavish bed, the beautiful setting, the people around us that are amazing and worthy." The old man spoke with such humour and warmth that he could see smiles spreading across the crowd.

"So today," he instructed, "Try to focus on those things that bring you guilt. In the first part of the day, write down everything you feel guilty about, and I mean everything, even the things you think are irrelevant, like, 'I ate all my younger brother's sweets when we were in the third grade.' Shame transforms into guilt, and I want you to explore where this comes from for you. You see, shame comes from not following social norms. When we don't adhere to the norms, our shame tells us we aren't doing what is expected. 'Bad, bad you,' says Shame. And then it burns inside to become guilt, weighing us down like a fireplace full of soot. Guilt is stored in the heart and brings you heartache, heart attack, even arrhythmia. We have to take care of our physical body and our mental health together."

Tina thought about her headaches, whilst Jan contemplated the tension that would take over his body when he and Ema argued. *It's all connected.* He thought, as the old man got carried away with his theory.

"And you can pinpoint feelings connected to guilt, like feeling lost, angry, and helpless."

The teacher directed his hands to different parts of his body as he explained. "Anger nestles itself in the liver." He placed his hands on his lower ribs. "Grief affects the lungs, so when you are mourning," he said, taking his hands to his chest and inhaling deeply, "You can't breathe. Worry burrows in the stomach. Stress weakens the heart and brain. Fear stores itself in the kidneys. Shock meddles with the heart too." He took some deep pleasant breaths.

"Guilt can manifest as physical back pain. It teaches us we deserve pain and punishment, but this is not true. Holding on to this feeling is self-sabotage. If guilt is left unchecked, it can result in long-term hip problems, sinusitis, dramatic weight change, anxiety, venereal disease, migraines, insomnia, impotence, heart diseases, depression, hernias, even Parkinson's." A nervous energy gathered as participants' aches became a condition induced by intoxicating guilt and stress.

"Be my guests. When you get home, research it. Read. Your ego needs that. But also know, I am a medically trained doctor who has practiced medicine for half my life. But when my son experienced burnout, the medicine I had dedicated years to didn't help him. So I started to research alternative solutions. During this research, I discovered that letting go of negative emotions is in fact the first step towards better health."

"Parents, society, and even we teach ourselves to suppress feelings. This is a mostly unconscious, protective mechanism. At some unspecified time, we teach ourselves that we can't handle the pain and intensity of our feelings, so we hide them, bury them within. But these emotions are destructive and suppressing them makes them stronger.

Migraines and headaches show we put too much pressure on ourselves. Allergies can in fact be a reaction to something in your mind. Obesity can come from insufficient self-love. But why don't you love yourself? What kind of protection do you think you need? What's making you insecure? Why do you need to eat your feelings? Do you feel protected by your size? Are you filling an emptiness?" Time was given for participants to reflect, but the bearded teacher kept reflection momentary.

"Cancer can grow from resentment, hopelessness, and disappointment. Resentment breeds when we cannot express ourselves. It grows stronger and becomes anger. And we feel resentment from many sources: family, partners, friends, or bosses. It's that feeling that you are being treated unfairly or used. But, if you don't let it go, resentment can cause back pain, tumours, even osteoporosis."

"Arthritis can be a result of seeking perfection and criticism. Constipation and bladder problems come from holding on to old, illogical beliefs. They mean you are blocked, stuck. If you feel stuck, you can't change. You might replay old scenarios and ask yourself, 'What should I have done? What would have made it better? Did I take the wrong path?' This type of block can result in repetitive strain injury, varicose veins, mouth ulcers, obesity, kidney problems, sciatica, rheumatoid arthritis, and paralysis." The participants worried for their health and listened intently to their bodies.

"Try to remember you can't take anything with you when you leave this earth except your soul. So why hold on to all that baggage?" A smile to relieve tension.

"Society wants us to behave in certain ways but these ways lead to feeling rejected. Rejection stays within us for years and ruins our relationships and wellbeing. Rejection is always too personal, and we reflect it on ourselves with horrible thoughts. 'I'm not good enough. Something's wrong with me. Nobody wants me.' But these statements are not true. You are beautiful."

Jacopo repeated this to himself and tried to believe it. *I am beautiful. I am good enough.*

"Instead of saying thank you for life continuing before us, instead of changing or trying to find a new job, love interest, passion, and instead of trying harder to achieve our goals, many of us just roll on our backs and feel sorry for ourselves. Rejection is reflected in our habits and diseases: cold sores, frigidity, stress, tension, anxiety, numbness, paralysis, anorexia, bulimia, obesity, mental breakdown, arthritis, multiple sclerosis, endometriosis."

Kara's personal rejection tugged at her. She had faced it and confronted it for long enough to be in control, but it wasn't gone from her entirely.

"Low self-esteem creates depression and fatigue. The idea that you're unable to do anything valuable manifests physically in the limbs and eats at your energy stores. People with low self-esteem are quick to judge themselves which makes the body feel worthless. It breaks down, becomes weaker, and they feel more and more worthless all the time. It can lead to acne, warts, weight problems, ovarian cancer, and in some cases, memory loss."

Kara touched the smooth skin of her face and reassured herself that she was recovering.

"I know I'm repeating some ideas, but this programme aims to reconstruct the way you think about repressed feelings. You can find charts, books, and other robust tools in our library to help lay strong foundations for your understanding of the connections between your emotions and your body. Research and be curious. Dive into Eastern Medicine."

Some participants whispered to themselves, piqued by the ease with which their teacher explored complex ideas.

"So, dear participants, a reminder. After breakfast, write down every moment you feel guilty about. Be honest with yourself.

When you hear the gong, come back together for a group session before lunch. For now, spread over the estate. Find a place where you feel safe, and start writing."

With that, he raised his hands, and they moved off quietly to the dining area. Participants ate a light meal and drank tea, then quickly spread themselves around the estate. The energy for this challenge was focused and eager.

Nick automatically walked towards his cottage, but this time, Jacopo and Storm followed him. He'd agreed to share his spot after accidentally telling them how calm he felt there. Each found a private space around the cabin where they became invisible to each other.

Storm put pencil to paper and started drawing. He drew a car crash. Underneath were the words:

NO MORE GUILT FOR THE ACCIDENT. IT WAS NOT MY FAULT. I DIDN'T STOP THEM, BUT I CAN'T CHANGE THE PAST BY BLAMING MYSELF FOR NOT TAKING AWAY THE KEYS. THERE WAS NO WAY TO KNOW THIS WOULD HAPPEN. IF I COULD, I WOULD STOP IT. I FEEL DEEP SADNESS.

For the first time, Storm's barrier fractured. He looked up from his writing and surveyed the area to check he was still hidden. Then continued:

I HATE MYSELF. I FEEL GUILTY FOR RUNNING AWAY FROM MY FEELINGS AND BURYING THEM BEHIND A MASK. I FEEL ANNOYED BECAUSE I CAN'T FALL ASLEEP WITHOUT BEING COMPLETELY HIGH.

Storm's body became very still, acknowledging and embracing the thoughts.

Jacopo, out of sight, sat in lotus position and leant against a shack. He breathed deeply, calmly, with purpose. The moment was utter perfection. When ready, he took a pen in his hand and wrote:

I feel guilty for disappointing my family, church, and community, especially my mother. I miss her profoundly. I would love to hug her again.

A burning pain travelled through his body.

It devastates me that they don't understand I am not rebelling; this is who I am. They don't see me and that fills me with anger. They've erased me because of who I find attractive and who I want to share my life with. Can't they see I'm the same person they knew and loved?

Jacopo gasped for air as his family flashed through his mind like a distant memory.

I'm angry. They talked about love and acceptance, and healing the world, but they won't accept me.

I feel guilty that I couldn't express myself with them. I feel guilty because I couldn't fall in love with Vanessa and I fooled her for so long. I knew she was in love. But I couldn't tell her. I'm sad she's not in my life now. But I'm also angry that she rejected my attempts to explain.
I feel guilty for reading Ted's letters. I feel ashamed for crossing the line with Rocco's privacy. I feel hurt that Rocco cheated on me after the honeymoon. I feel guilty for betraying the trust of Rocco's mother after all the kindness she showed me. I feel guilty that we keep in touch behind Rocco's back.

I feel sad Rocco didn't try harder to start over. I feel angry that he didn't fight for me and instead chose Ted.

I feel guilty because, deep down, I wish that something terrible will happen to Ted.

Jacopo lay down his pen, drained, and rested his head against the shack.

Nick returned to his tree, where he nestled in shade. He rubbed factor fifty onto his pale skin and then challenged the blank page. For half an hour he sat there and willed words to form but none did. He stood up, jumped with both legs up and down, sat again, applied cream one more time. He was ready.

I feel guilty – 8-day experiment

- for not telling Linda how I feel
- for thinking I am less than others
- for using girls for intimacy while knowing I'll never love them
- for promising Amanda we'd move in together and lying to her over and over again about my feelings for Linda
- for putting a virus on Mike's computer
- for not visiting my granny more when she was alive and for never visiting her grave
- for feeling unmanly
- for wanting to be some alpha man
- for declining social calls from friends
- for not wanting the potential 'great on a paper' partners (I can't force myself to like someone)
- for hating all Linda's boyfriends

I feel angry and sad that I became obsessed with Linda

And that was that. The words were out. Nick had said them all.

After breakfast, Lea had followed the teachers to the woods' edge, totally away from the dining room and cottage. The teachers sat in a circle and meditated, while Lea rested nearby. They were always visible but far enough away that she couldn't hear them. She didn't hesitate to start writing.

I feel guilty about my naivety and for not trusting my friends and family when they warned me about Patrik. I feel guilty for not finding the power to get out of that relationship with him. I feel guilty because I believed he was good. I feel guilty for not loving myself and choosing him over me.

I feel disappointed that I didn't cherish myself, that I could become so small under his 'love' and attention. I feel guilty for my credit card debt. I feel guilty for not working and being on sick leave.

I feel sad that I can't find joy in life and that I don't feel safe.

Petra had wandered back to her cottage and sat on the terrace. She made herself comfortable on a chair and poured tea. She inhaled and slowly began.

Day 2, 8-day challenge

I feel guilty about:
- Not being well educated; I always felt I couldn't help my children study.
- This need to search for myself in my old age.
- Not focusing on my grandchildren.
- Ignoring friends after Janez's death.
- Not missing Janez more.
- Feeling relief soon after his death.
- Not finishing all the tasks I want to do in a day.

- Not keeping up my photography project.
- Not being there for my children.

She took a sip of tea and laid her pen down. The liquid was warm and soothed her throat.

Kara walked to the other side of the lake and revisited a bench she'd found the day before. Opening the notebook to it's blank pages, she felt overwhelmed. She stood up and started pacing along the beach of the lake, twenty meters right, and then left, back and forth, until finally she was ready.

I feel guilty:
- Giving in to cravings when I'm completely full
- Falling out of diet plans and sabotaging the process
- Paying for trainers and fitness instructors and then not attending sessions
- Gossiping and focusing on other people's lives instead of my own
- Staying in and eating in my pyjamas while binge-watching TV series over the weekends
- Lying about eating and not writing honestly in my food journal
- Lying to my personal trainer
- Faking in front of friends
- Not trying harder with love
- Always putting myself last
- For journeys abandoned when I was losing weight
- Because of my job and friends
- For my relationship status
I feel remorse:
- Because I never focused on myself
- Because I said 'yes' when I actually wanted to do something else

- For not setting boundaries with others
- For not trying more activities

I feel angry:
- At my friends that took advantage of me
- At myself for not loving me first

She put her notebook away and marched on to the forest and the sounds of nature.

Jan stayed near the meditation area and let words pour out of him.

I feel guilty I couldn't stop Ema's delusions. I regret that I couldn't stay with her.
And I feel guilty that I have a problem with Storm. I understand this anger isn't caused by him; it's me. It's my issue.
I feel guilty that I didn't lend money to an old friend going through hard times.
I feel guilty when I pick Maks up late - my poor boy.

Tina kept away from Kara, deciding she would not be the first to talk, but it didn't feel good. In today's task, she had a chance to explore her protest.

I feel guilty for: falling in love with my husband's best friend, for not being focused when I am with my children, for not keeping in contact with friends that moved abroad, for rejecting their calls, for not replying to an email when I should, for my marriage, for not knowing where we stand, and even more, for not knowing where we should go, for saying embarrassing things when drunk, especially for shaming friends when drunk.

I am angry at Kara because she ignores me and is passive-aggressive, and I don't know what is wrong.

The gong announced it was time for groups to gather. Tina packed her stuff and questioned how honest the last phrase was. *Do I know what's wrong?* But before she could linger on the thought, she saw Gregor, who waited and smiled at his group until all were seated.

The last to return were Nick, Jacopo, and Storm, who hadn't heard the gong. The wind carried its sound off in another direction and isolated them with their thoughts for a little longer.

Gregor invited everyone to share, and each bravely confessed the sources of their guilt.

"So, now we have a break for lunch." He said rewardingly. "After, we will meet here again and you will work in pairs. The pairs will be: Jan and Storm, Lea and Petra, Jacopo and Tina, and Nick and Kara. I'll tell you more once you are full and with renewed energy. As you eat, remind yourself that everything happens as a result of your thoughts, actions, and feelings."

Gregor raised his hands, and they moved off in a trance to the dining area. Each was brimming with information about themselves that they'd never processed before.

The group ate in silence, and each vibrated in their own way. Some hummed with answers and the power that they can influence their lives, while others shook in resistance, refusing to accept that everything is a result of their actions and effort. Occasional whispers could be heard from a table, but otherwise only the scrape of forks on plates and chewing filled the area. An emotional transformation was happening. Relief, frustration, and annoyance was painted on alternate faces. One nervous participant searched for a ghost phone in their pocket.

Another thought about what they'd missed in the outside world: news, social media updates, messages from loved ones.

The old bearded teacher observed these twitches and recognised their discomfort.
He thought, *To connect with their fears and emotions, they must learn to look inside and start resolving their habitual processes. Everyone is alone in their process.*

Lunch was finished and groups reunited. Gregor directed his group to take their places in pairs. Each pair sat facing each other and awaited instruction.

"To start off with, you must decide who will share and who will listen first." There was a series of nodding and gesturing amongst pairs. "Now, you will each have five minutes to explore your emotions. One will talk, while the other listens. Listen but do not discuss. Listen and offer eye contact. After both have explored their feelings, you will be given a short time for reflection, but don't fill this space saying things you think you're supposed to. Talk from the heart. And remember, whatever you hear is not your story or your feelings. Do not attach to their pain."

A drum sounded to mark the start of five minutes. Petra began and Lea, feeling uncomfortable and close to imploding, tried to maintain eye contact.

"I've been a housewife my whole life. It was a life I chose. Yet, as I watched my children and grandchildren grow up, I felt a building sensation of missing out on something. Sometimes, I hate to admit it," Petra broke eye contact for a second and gathered her strength, "And I feel ashamed, but I envy my children for the opportunities they've had." She composed herself. "Now, I'm trying to catch up with time because I don't want my life to finish feeling like this.

My whole life, I thought I had problems, but now I realise it's because I could never fully express myself. I had a good husband, Janez. He was kind, attentive, and a good provider, but he never really heard my voice, my wishes. They weren't even grand wishes."

Petra took a moment and stroked the palm of her hand. "I feel guilty that I resent Janez. I should be thankful, but I'm not. I could have had a bad life with a disrespectful husband. Although my children gave me a lot of joy, it's not enough." Petra didn't feel any better for saying these things out loud. "I hope to find answers to these feelings."

Lea resented Petra's confession. The only thing Lea wanted was a good partner, but instead, she caught the biggest psychopath around. She struggled to keep her emotions level, and grabbed at grass in an attempt to direct her resentment into the ground and not towards Petra.

Beside them were Jacopo and Tina. Jacopo appreciated the chance to speak first. Tina watched him with focus and kindness.

"I grew up in an amazing family, influenced by the Roman Catholic Church. I was an altar boy. I was good in school and played sports. Yet, I always felt different. I couldn't live as myself. I never understood why the church talked about being a good person while rejecting good people that were like me. I feel hurt by my family, and I'm angry at them. Because of them, I felt ashamed when I realised I was gay. Because of them, I tried to pray for a cure. I stayed with a girl I could never love, Vanessa, and lied to her repeatedly in order to follow what others told me was right. But I couldn't spend my life with a woman, or share a bed with a woman. I considered becoming a priest or even a monk and closing myself off from the world." Jacopo knew these thoughts long before the exercise, but they felt weightier said out loud.

"When I eventually put myself first, all hell broke loose. Nobody from my family talks to me any more, not even my siblings. They broke my heart. Sometimes, I can't breathe." A tightness pressed into Jacopo's chest, making his lungs small and his courage falter.

"Recently my partner cheated on me, so I feel like the only person I did trust has betrayed me too. I started to feel angry, which isn't normal for me, and wallowed in depression for a long time. I know, now, the betrayal was as much my fault as Rocco's. I wanted so desperately to be loved that I became obsessed with the threat of the past and created this whole awful situation. I pushed Rocco back to his ex by acting crazy and not communicating. I should've said something when I found their old letters, but I didn't."

Jan, frustrated, and Storm, tranquil, stared at each other. *I hate him. I hate him for no reason.* Thought Jan in a tornado of emotions. He'd previously prided himself on being a calm person but was questioning that now.

After staring at each other for some minutes, Storm broke the silence.

"I had a different upbringing to most. My parents exposed me to the colourful world of art, surfing, free spirits, meditation, and crafting. I grew up in the most perfect place and family anyone could ask for. But even people living in perfect environments experience challenges. For one school year, we left my paradise and lived in Paris. Being in that city was very hard for me. But, when there, I met a girl I really liked, Jacqueline. She made it bearable. We've lost touch now."

Jan followed instructions, maintained eye contact, and bit his tongue.

"I present myself as someone that is happy, but it's a mask. When we moved back to our island there were lots of parties.

206

One was on the beach next to our old trailer, and some friends got wasted. I went off with a girl that was on holiday and left the party. When they ran out of beer, a friend decided to drive to the city to buy more. My younger brother, Rider, joined them. My drunk friend drove straight off the cliff road leading to the city. That was the end for them. Rider was dead."

The resentment that had previously consumed Jan melted away. His shocked heart beat heavy in his chest.

"My parents never blamed me, not for a second. Nobody blamed me. But I can't shake the feeling that if I'd stayed it wouldn't have happened. I can't change the past, but still, I can't help thinking that. After the accident, I started smoking to escape the world. That's when I met Gaya. With her help, I saw beauty in the world again and did things to respect Rider's memory. My brother wouldn't want me to wallow. He loved life, and he was a person of his own decisions. Nobody could stop him riding off like that."

Jan had to remind himself that this story and these feelings were not his, that he shouldn't attach to Storm's words, should not engage in his drama. But he found that very hard.

Kara and Nick felt warm sitting together and looking into each others' eyes. Normally, they lived invisibly, overseen, especially by those they wanted to love, so it felt incredible to just see each other. They agreed Kara would speak first.

"I have felt fat and ugly for as long as I can remember. Historically, I self-sabotaged: I didn't try new things, especially not connected to moving; I did everything I could to avoid funny looks from people; I dreaded fit people judging me in a bathing suit, skiing, or at the gym; I connected everything to my looks and never understood how skinny people could be unhappy. But now I know that not everyone is judging me. I also know that happiness is more complicated than being skinny.

In past months, I observed myself and paid attention to when I need or want to eat. I looked for my triggers and then tried to focus on the source of wanting, rather than the wanting to eat. I've lost ten kilos now, and for the first time, I feel a bit stable. I have a long way to go. But I'm trying hard to appreciate my body and focus on the fact that my stomach and kidneys aren't in pain." Kara smiled at her accomplishments.

"I can see I've stored negative feelings in my body and so my body reacted. It gave me back pain, breathing problems, and pain in my bowels. I covered my shame and guilt by always being there for my friends and family while ignoring myself. At least they love me for being useful." She joked. "Giving them everything made me feel a bit worthy. You know?"

Nick nodded. He knew very well.

"It is so hard being hungry when you know you've just had a healthy meal. I think this could be an everlasting problem for me, but at least I can try to recognise why I want to eat, to look at how my body feels and question it. I eat when I'm under stress. I love to eat in company, and I have problems stopping when I'm full. I eat when I'm sad. I feel love when I'm full from pizza, chips, chocolate, and ice cream. I feel safe and happy when I'm stuffed and binge watching movies and daydreaming about being skinny. I'm changing these habits, but it's hard to let go of the old comforts. And it is real work." Kara said smiling. "It's hard to talk kindly to myself, to not judge myself for bad days or bad meals. I was avoiding my feelings before, and it's time to change all that."

Gregor struck the drum, and everyone took a moment to inhale and exhale, release the negative emotions spilling out. He reminded them not to attach to each others' feelings and began the second round.

Nick transmitted all the kindness he could through his eyes to Kara and then took his turn.

"I always wanted to be a nice guy. I had a modest upbringing and was warned about arrogance and egos. And so I was always nice. When I met Linda, we were at uni and the world stopped. The connection I feel with her is intense, even now that I hate her.

For the past nine years, it became my goal to make her happy. I would do anything she said, go anywhere she wanted. I was there no matter what. I was her best friend and confidant, but I never had the balls to ask her out, to light a spark between us. I stupidly thought she'd just realise one day that I was the perfect person for her. But she never did." Nick felt, for once, that he could genuinely laugh at this idea. It wasn't a sneer of self-pity but an understanding of his mistake.

"She changed boyfriends one after another. I had some relationships, but Linda was always in my heart. When she broke off a relationship, I would too and wait, again, for her to see me.

And what do I feel now? Fed up. Now she's pregnant, and it made me realise, finally, that it's over. It was over years ago, but I could never let her go before. The dream, that one day she would come to me open and loving, was dead. It was never going to happen. She'll only ever run to me for comfort. And she always knew how I felt, so I'm angry with her too. I know she's not guilty of misleading me. But she kept me hanging around, waiting on her.

Ultimately, my hurt is on me. I devoted myself to her as her best friend, her safety net, her shoulder to cry on. Her husband, Mike, calls me her bell boy, and he's not wrong. I never did anything because I was scared to ruin what I had with the perfect woman. Now, I feel hate and anger, and I don't like this side of me. There's an aggression that I've never felt before. I just want to put everything behind me and find someone special. But I can't do that until I let her and all of my feelings for her go."

Across the circle, Tina decided to be honest, one to one with Jacopo who had demonstrated such bravery during his turn. "I do not know what to tell you or how to start." This was true; she was totally dumbfounded. "I lived by the rules, following the high school to-do list: finish school - check, find job - check, find a boyfriend with good husband potential - check, get married - check, have children - check three times, travel - check, buy expensive clothes, go to concerts, visit the theatre - all checked.

But a few years ago, I realised I was living between expensive things I don't use and definitely don't need, that I have no connection with my husband, and that I don't enjoy being a mother. I realised that I needed affection, and so I took a lover for a short period. I feel guilty about it now, and I'm still unhappy. I don't love my husband. I hate school shows and parent meetings. I feel guilty that my children bore me, that I don't feel a special connection to them. I feel guilty about hurting my ex-lover. I don't think we have enough time to go through my whole list." Tina said, attempting a joke. "I started to search for different solutions to my problems and none were successful. There is no quick fix. But I hope I can find some peace this week."

Tina cried, wiped her tears, and hoped her make up was still okay.

Lea tried painstakingly to look at Petra as she talked, but her eyes flitted constantly between somewhere vaguely on Petra and the grass. Lea wasn't able to look at her, didn't want to speak, and struggled to control her breath. After some time, she took the plunge.

"I feel stupid. I wanted someone to love me and start a family with. I had little experience with relationships. No boys ever liked me in school, and that didn't change much as I got older. All my friends had boyfriends but not me."

Lea mostly watched the grass now. Petra gave her all the encouragement she could when Lea did occasionally pluck her eyes from the ground.

"I never dreamed someone as beautiful as Patrik would find me interesting because I feel totally average. So when he showed interest, I fell head over heels for him." Lea chanced a look to see if she was being listened to. "When friends and family told me something about our relationship was abnormal, I thought they were jealous. Now, after all the drama, I feel shame and guilt because I didn't listen to them." Lea's voice became very small.

"I never knew what a normal relationship was. So I blinded myself, and I stayed. If he hadn't started to be physical, I'd probably still be with him now.

I don't love myself enough. I kept telling myself, I couldn't get anyone better. He told me that too. So I stayed. Now, because of him, I feel like I don't deserve love. I'm scared. I look over my shoulder all the time." Lea pulled grass from the earth and stared at her feet. She leaned her chin on her knees and cradled herself.

Jan had a problem expressing himself. It was like his throat closed up and choked his voice. But today he persisted.

"I loved her." He forced out. "I still love her. I love my soon to be ex-wife." He worked through thoughts by expanding definitions. As he did, the chokehold loosened and his voice came back. "But I couldn't have that home as my life anymore. I just want peace. We tried so hard to live side by side, and I tried to be the best partner I could be. But something was always missing for Ema. And I couldn't help her.

I started to worry that our child would grow up without structure or comfort from his parents.

Ema wouldn't go to therapy or accept offers of help. I tried to get her to see the doctor, but she'd only engage with alternative solutions. She was obsessed with them. It was always the same cycle: 'This will help me. This will be the answer. This will make us happy, Jan'. But she grew more and more depressed. It's ironic that I came here, really. It's totally her kind of thing. But when I read the 8-Day pamphlet, I felt for a second that I could find some answers here."

Gregor circled the group and used me to burn sage, cleansing the accumulated energy bursting from sharing couples. The drum signalled the end of another five minutes, and with that, Gregor said, "Now, reflect. Try to remain detached from the other person's feelings. Go with the flow. Don't force anything. Do what you feel."

Light chatter filled the room, and with it, a blanket of tension floated off.

Jacopo and Tina hugged and giggled in relief. She took Jacopo's face in her hands and said, "You are an amazing, beautiful man. You do deserve the best, and you are powerful. You chose not to live a lie. That's incredible."

He smiled and felt her loving attention rain upon him.

"And you don't have to feel ashamed of your feelings. They are yours, and they are legitimate." Jacopo placed his hands on top of Tina's and they stayed like this, sharing warmth and love.

"I'm sorry for how I behaved towards you," said Jan.

Storm extended his hand, smiling. "It's all good."

Petra tried to get Lea's eyes away from the ground, telling her, "Your experience in that relationship is not your fault.

You have to find self-love and try to see the light at the end of this dark tunnel. I've heard group therapy can be really helpful. You never know, maybe group support is just what you need."

Lea looked up with tears in her eyes. She felt validated by Petra even though she'd resisted her during their time to share. Feeling seen and forgiven, she moved closer to Petra and hugged her. "You are an amazing woman." She whispered. "You will be able to give more to your family when you're happy and working on yourself."

Nick and Kara held hands and embraced each other with their eyes. They didn't need any words but felt ultimate comfort in each other's gaze.

The group moved around the space and shared in other pairs, all of them feeling open and soulful, happy and united.

Gregor then called the group together and congratulated them. He gave them free time before evening meditation to be wherever they felt relaxed and calm. As they left his session, Gregor lit a small rolled-up cigarette and turned me over in his free hand. His group spread across the premises and wandered around in their thoughts.

The only pair blocked from each other, despite the unity amongst the group, was Kara and Tina. They did, however, gravitate towards each other now.

"I feel like you resent me." Tina cast their no talking during the day rule aside. "And I don't know what I've done wrong. Not speaking with you is tough for me. I miss my best friend."

"I know." Kara admitted. "I miss you too. But I've always been there for everyone else, and I was never there for myself.
And, yes, you encouraged me with dieting and you supported me, but I have to find my own way to get better.

Your solutions weren't helpful for me. My body is different. My motivations are different. It's tough for me. And just like I can't help you in your marriage, you can't help me fix how I feel about my body."

It was the first time Kara managed to clearly define her needs and it felt good. "I know I've started this journey many times before, but now I don't want to stop. I'm fighting my thoughts every day. I have good days, but they can be ruined in an instant and become terrible ones. I have to be focused all the time, and it's hard, but it's something I need to do. Life's passed me by somehow. I love you, Tina. But now I need space and understanding from you."

Tina hugged her friend and was comforted by being together like this, like never before. "I love you too. You're my best friend on the planet." She whispered in Kara's ear.

After dinner, participants sat by a fire and listened to the teachers create music which seemed to emanate directly from their souls.

DAY THREE: NOBODY IS IMPORTANT, YET I AM.

Do not place your burden on the shoulders of others. Doing that does not help. That burden is your lesson, your challenge.

Tina was late to morning meditation. She'd paced up and down her room for half the night trying to release her guilt and then couldn't drag herself out of bed in the morning. *It's easier to forgive others than yourself,* she thought as she raced from her room. She joined the group as one of the teachers, a woman with a bald head, stood up.

"We are all haunted by titles."

Don't I know it. Tina told herself sarcastically.

The teacher continued. "We question people constantly. Who are they? And why are they important? But, in reality, importance is relative. The people we are supposed to consider important are often irrelevant in comparison to the ones we actually care about. It's easy to lose perspective on what is genuinely important. You must adjust your perspective, put yourself at the centre of importance, and heal yourself before you can heal your view of the world.

Today's primary focus is yourself. Say, 'I think. I feel. I see. I want.'" Participants repeated in a chorus of willingness to be important. "On this day, you are the most important person. Focus all your energy on yourself, and find a way to express it.

You can write, build, paint, or walk. The only thing that matters is that you do something personally invigorating. You can start something, leave it, and come back to it later. Don't force any processes. Focus on feeling joy and the beating of your heart.

There are no group sessions today. Every minute is dedicated to your needs. Approach a teacher if you want to discuss anything. You can, of course, talk with other participants, but make sure they are willing to share their time with you. It's important to understand that it's not egotistic to focus on yourself. If you choose to work with another member of the community today, it is of your choosing, and it is a pure gesture. If you feel reluctant to share your time, tell that person, 'Today, I put myself first. I am important, and I choose solitude and reflection.' This is okay.

In life, we meet people who appear dedicated to society or seem to donate all their time to charity. We might judge ourselves against them and feel bad because we believe we are not giving enough. These actions can be genuine and good. But they can also be a means to feel better about themselves, to get social validation, or to feel worthy. When this is the case, a person is acting from ego. Do not compare yourself with others casually because you can never know their motives. Comparing yourself with others will never bring happiness.

"We often confuse the path to happiness with the desire to be good. Our wish to be entitled Good People can quietly consume us. And so we confuse ego with self-love. We confuse sticking our noses in other people's business with being caring. But if you focus on yourself first, you arrive at divine peace without confusion. Here you can tackle your fears, patterns, and bad habits, and after tackling them, you can consider sharing your energy and helping others.

And we begin today. As you clear through your fears and patterns, you will find there is a mountain before you.

216

There are levels, and peaks ahead. You should embrace them. For as long as you live, you will have to look inside and clear out unwelcome fears and negative patterns.

At the first level, you see everyone gets exactly what they can handle and nothing more. This is their path. You learn obstacles are part of it all. You become aware of your obstacles and begin to understand you can't help anyone else: you must help yourself.

If someone asks for help when you're on this level, offer your opinion or solution. Inform them your words come without strings attached. Do not include your feelings in their drama. You could offer tangible support like money, time, or an opinion. But ensure that you, figuratively, walk away from their drama once the conversation is finished. Their problem is not yours. Their life is not your life. Do not drown yourself in good deeds as that only prolongs drama.

Similarly, do not place your burden on the shoulders of others. Doing that does not help. That burden is your lesson, your challenge."

Tina listened intently and embraced her guilt as a personal burden. *How do I overcome that challenge?*

"Ask yourself honestly, 'Do I question the repeating burdens in my life?'" Tina looked up, feeling the question was hers alone. The teacher continued. "Until you challenge your burdens and find answers, you will continue to fall into the same situations.

A poem by Portia Nelson teaches, 'There's a hole in my sidewalk: The romance of self-discovery?' Consider this line. She explores the idea of falling in the same hole on the same street time and again. The speaker of the poem falls even when she knows the hole is there, and she continues to fall until she changes her path.

In life, she repeats the same patterns, hoping for different results. Her patterns cannot change, until she starts to walk a new path.

Today, think about when you put others before yourself. Consider how you feel when you don't receive respect or gratitude for your sacrifices. Think about all the times you felt ignored and question why that hurt you. Is it because you gave away your time, attention, money? Is it because you wanted the same in return? And then stop yourself and ask, can you force anyone to replicate your behaviours, your sacrifices? No. So what needs to change, them or you? What fears do you need to tackle? What patterns must you break?" She left these questions lingering over their heads.

"Our energy omits vibrations to those around us. When you give from a place of self-pity, a place of need, you pass on uncomfortable, even aggressive vibrations. You pass on the feeling of rejection and absence. If you belittle yourself, you also transmit that feeling. Why do you want to make yourself small? Try not to let yourself feel small.

If someone hurt you or broke up with you, and you are still thinking about them, who has the power?" Jacopo's ears rang with recognition. "Are you still alive and breathing?"

Yes, he thought.

"Are you safe?"

Yes.

"That's no accident. You made sure of your safety." A small smile appeared on Lea's face when she heard this. "You made sure this person can't touch you anymore." The teacher talked softly but with conviction. "Why would you give them power by thinking about them now?

218

Why allow yourself to believe this person is more important than you?" Sunlight created a halo around the teacher's bald head, making her saint like.

This was the first voice to intrigue Lea since Patrik had fractured her life. At this point in time, Lea was Patrik's victim; that was her identity. And while she was happy to be free from him, she also wasn't ready to move forward. There was a dark part of her that felt threatened by the teacher who wanted to take her victim status away.

"Are you heartbroken?"

Tina released a silent, "Yes," from her lips. Lea's head hung down and her eyes clenched shut.

"Of course, your heart needs time. Mourning is important. But, eventually, we must ask ourselves, what am I holding on to? Is it the feeling of being with that person? Is it the love they once gave me? Is it anger? Is it my ego? Do I know why they broke up with me? Do I know why they chose not to fight for me? If you ended the relationship, would they fight for you? Would that feel different?" Many participants embraced these questions and found reflection in the sky above them.

"Ultimately, that person was not good for you." The saint declared earnestly. "That person was not your twin flame, not your soul-mate." She stared at the crowd and strengthened her statement with her eyes.

Jacopo watched, worried that she was about to take away his last connection to Rocco. In Jan hate multiplied.
And Nick waited, hopeful, to hear that sometimes people are scared of their emotions, that they can still come around, that Linda could still love him.

"If the person that hurt you is not in your life anymore, or they don't exist in the way you want them to, be real with yourself. They are not your soul-mate." Nick's head dropped. "You do not share vibrations. Maybe, one day, they could be your soul-mate, but a switch in energy has to happen first."

Nick swam in confusion.

"When a flame burns with self-love, security, and confidence, it is healthy. When two healthy flames join, they create a bigger one, with double the energy. Each one develops a brighter inner light that can be shared and enjoyed together." The teacher dipped a candle into a bucket of water. She joined two candles together, letting the flame of one light the other. But as one lit candle touched the wet one all flames went out.

"See? You can have a healthy flame, but you cannot ignite another that lacks inner light. And it is not your domain to do so. The fire must be balanced."

Which one am I? Questioned Tina.

I am an extinguished flame in a bucket of water. Answered Lea.

Did I destroy the flame or was Rocco always on a different vibration? Jacopo asked, facing the mountain ahead of him.

"A friend cried to me recently because his fiancée left him." The teacher set down the candles from her hands. "He wept like a child, saying, 'I planned a life together. I built a house for her. I wanted to give her everything. I love her. I hope she'll come back.' It was pathetic." The word fell like a stone on Jacopo.
"When someone ends a relationship, the time you had together is not important anymore. What's important is whether the relationship is still romantic or if it's platonic. Is it a partnership or a friendship? I told my friend, 'You should hug her and say thank you.'

220

Because, if someone is unable to give the same affection as you, and they tell you so, they have released you to find your balanced flame."

Looking around the group, she could feel the energy becoming heavy. "We crave external confirmation. Think about when you enter a new social situation. Do you ask yourself: Will I like the people? Do I like you? Do I want them? Or do you ask: Will they like me? Will they accept me?" Nick knew his answer before the questions were finished.

"When you are at peace with yourself, you do not ask these questions. They are a reflection of your uncertain energy. Few people believe they are birds or trees, yet many fail to believe in themselves. It is better to stand alone than be crowded by the wrong people: those who make you feel the need to hide your true, crazy, beautiful self. Live your vibe." She willed them. "Live your truth. When your body screams, 'Retreat! retreat!' Follow your instincts and just say, 'No, thank you. I chose myself.'" The energy was building again and focus gathered in participants.

"Now, we think about today." The teacher said, bringing her hands together. "How can you make time for you?" She asked in an almost whisper. "If you are burned out, annoyed, filled with disappointment at coming last, rejected, what kind of energy can you give to your family and friends? Your children, partners, parents, friends will understand the space you take for yourself. Maybe not straight away, but when you are happier, more full of love and attention, they will understand. Quality over quantity." She said baring her hands out like scales. "Everyone in your life will manage without you for a few hours. They will."

Tina smiled.

"Breakfast is almost ready. Eat, and then it's time to go off on your path. Ask yourself what you need. And if you feel bored, excellent! The best ideas are born out of boredom and need.

Venture out of the box. Rethink your life. It's not the end until you pass into the other dimension. Find your inner child and play, be creative. We came here to have fun, to have a fantastic adventure, so enjoy."

She smiled and left the stage, her halo slipping away with her into the forest. Lea followed quickly after her, filled with something but unsure what.

Storm grabbed me from the altar and headed to the dining room. He sat at a table where the rest of his group, except Lea, were already gathered.

Kara was the first to comment on the morning's speech. "I need a smoke; that was some intense shit. Storm, do you have anything with you?"

Jan, Petra, Nick, and Jacopo turned to Storm confused. He also didn't understand the question straight away and sent a puzzled expression to Kara as his answer.

Tina smiled. "You sold us hash on Fuerteventura. You don't remember because you spoke with another friend from our group, but we remember you." She couldn't help but flirt a bit. "Do you have some?"

"Yeah, I do. The teacher said we should do whatever we want. Who's in?"

Lea joined them, got the update, and the united group agreed to go to the lake.

* * *

Sitting under the shadow of a tree at the lake's edge, away from other participants, the group of eight buzzed. Kara and Tina were excited.

Petra found herself in an internal debate about the danger of meddling with drugs; she'd heard bad things about the slippery path to addiction and ruin. Nick contemplated whether to try or to just be there with them as was his way in the past. Jan, who had bad experiences in his youth, decided it was time to try something different. Jacopo stopped smoking to recover from Rocco and missed the sensation of inhaling and relaxing. He was ecstatic someone else suggested it now. Lea decided to stop dwelling on the past and this felt like a good way to move on.

Storm rolled eight joints. "For me, smoking was never about getting high. I can be relaxed and happy without it. But for me the purpose was to quieten my mind, to listen to the soul. Here we go." He looked up smiling and lit the first joint. It started to travel around the circle of nervous rebels.

When Petra took it in her shaking hand she asked, "How do I do this, just inhale and exhale? I've never smoked in my life." She laughed.

Storm smiled, remembering Jacqueline. "Just relax and inhale. Count to five, and then exhale."

Petra listened, inhaled, counted to five, and exhaled. As soon as she did, an intense tickling sensation covered her body and brought giggles with it. "Who would think, smoking at my age?" She laughed from the bottom of her belly.

"Age is a concept." Storm replied. "A person that is one hundred years old can live less days than a thirty-year old, despite having spent more time on this planet."

Petra sank into those words and had to agree. She'd stepped out of her small world and was now in front of an open door looking into what could be.

Lea took me out of Storm's hand and lit the second joint, saying, "I followed the teacher after her session this morning. I was so angry that she said, 'We create our reality.' So I screamed at her." Lea inhaled and looked to the ground. "Then I broke down and cried." She exhaled and her shoulders seemed to become lighter. "She didn't try to calm me. She just stood there and looked at me, smiling a bit. When I managed to breathe again, I asked why she wasn't helping me. I told her I need help."

The group listened in anticipation.

"Then she said, 'I can give you my perspective, my reality, what is true in my world. But you have to decide what is real in yours. I won't try to calm you because I don't pity you. I believe in you. I trust you to be strong. If you want to walk in this beautiful world as a victim, I can't stop you. I don't want to stop you. It's your perspective, your choice." She passed the joint to Kara, and they saw each other for the first time.

Kara hadn't spoken with Lea before now and was made mute listening to her. She felt something about Lea in this moment that wasn't there before and tried to support her with a smile.

"I told her that I don't want to be a victim." Lea continued. "She smiled at me again and said, 'I know you don't. But for now you are, and it's nice. Right? Your friends and family give you special treatment and the attention you crave. But wanting something is different to needing it. You wanted a relationship and an amazing partner, but you weren't ready for it. Take care of yourself and your perspectives so you can avoid this person and be happy." Lea took a deep breath.
She said, "You should stop blaming yourself and start loving yourself. You should love yourself more than anyone in the world." Lea seemed light and overwhelmed.

Joint number three was lit and its journey started.

224

"Now I'm in a space between victim and something else." Lea worked through her understanding of this conversation, tried to make sense of the pieces. "I know it's best to let go. I don't want to doubt my worth."

The group floated in their heads and embraced Lea's words.

"Well, we all have to let go of things." Nick said. "It's easy to create an imaginary truth, but it's not good for us. I can relate to you. When I think about it now," he half laughed, "I made myself my own torturer. I waited, year after year, for bits of love to be thrown my way. I'd do anything to get the tiniest bit of affection from this one girl. And, in doing so, I created an untouchable love. I ridiculed myself for not being able to reach her and endlessly tried to prove I was worthy. But I never was." Nick paused for a moment. He finally understood and saw his pattern clearly. "I didn't see anyone else; it was only her. I guess I wasn't ready for love between equals." The shame in Nick's voice began to lift. "She did me a service, really, by not noticing me. Ironically, she's in the same kind of relationship now that I would've been in if we got together. Always putting someone else first. Always rejected."

Jacopo jumped up like a strike of lightning. "We're all connected. We all have the same problems." He pointed to each of them creating invisible threads and stitching them together.
"We put others before ourselves. I yearned desperately for love and ended up creating a horrific mess. I'm disappointed with my family and have to resolve it." His mind was racing. "I have to learn that I'm worthy of unconditional love." A huge, proud smile spread across Jacopo's face.
"My family always gave me conditions, and I followed them. The first time I refused, they let me go. They forgot me. I'm dead to them now." His smile faded and he took a seat.

Silence enveloped the group, and Storm lit a fourth joint. The sun travelled higher in the sky, and they remained together in their circle, each staring off in their own direction.

Jan spoke and a fifth joint was lit. "I still don't know what I'm meant to learn. I was always happy in my skin. I didn't question life, it's meaning, or self-discovery, until I met my wife. Gradually, she made me feel like a simpleton, that I wasn't living enough, that I should be proactive and soul-searching, but it didn't bring me joy."

Petra understood. "Jan, I had simple wishes and they were never met. Now I just want to enjoy. Joy is everything. I want to take what I wish from life and to include others in that. But maybe that will only happen when I'm really ready. "

A sixth joint was lit. They began to slow down and finish one before lighting the next.

"It's fucked up." Kara said. "We have to overcome so many things. Socially and in work, we can tackle tough stuff with relative ease. But when it comes to looking in our souls, in our hearts, it's so hard."

Everyone silently agreed, nodding their heads and staring at the sky. Petra lay on the floor, her body tingling and stuck in place.

Tina took joint number seven and closed her eyes. "We have to learn to break the expectations given to us by society. Nobody ever teaches us to love ourselves for being who we are. Why do we strive to be special, to be extra? In the end, we're all the same."

Storm lit the final eighth joint. By now, the inexperienced group were very stoned and floated in their thoughts. The gong sounded for lunch, prompting them to move towards the dining room, where they ate with big appetites and few words.

In the middle of lunch, the bald teacher stood on a chair to address her audience. "We see you found a good flow and encourage you to follow that flow and take your time. The afternoon is also yours, remember you are important, and this time is for you."

After eating as much as they could, the group dispersed. Petra walked off to her room and fell straight into bed. *I can tick smoking a joint from my list - if I'd put it on there in the first place.* She laughed and drifted off quickly. Storm and Tina went to the art room and started painting, while Kara walked and didn't stop until the evening gong called her back.

Nick returned to his spot by the cottage and felt at peace. He found a comfortable seat under what he now decided was his favourite tree and enjoyed the clouds above. As he watched the white puffs move freely in the sky, he asked himself, *What would make me happy?* It was the first time in years that Nick had considered this. He knew he preferred to focus on a few things rather than many, and with that mindset, he opened his notebook.

What would make me happy?

- *paragliding - never did it because Linda is afraid of heights*
- *learning to fence*

He closed the book again and returned to the free-floating clouds.

Lea and Jacopo walked in silence along a road that led to the village. As they travelled further, they talked and began to open up to each other. Lea quickly felt safe and close with Jacopo. Her visible trust in him made Jacopo want to hug her. Lea was happy but couldn't help ask herself, *How much pain must one take to learn a lesson and move on?*

After lunch, Jan needed answers and searched for Gregor. "How can I overcome the negative feelings I have for my wife? Is it still possible to fix our marriage for our child?"

Gregor was amused by the question and smiled his usual welcoming smile. "Only you can know the answer to that question. But before you search for the answers, ask yourself if you need to fix your relationship with yourself first. You and your wife were a couple before your child arrived. Now, the fruit of your love, your child, has become a burden."

Jan was furious. "I love my son," he interrupted, "Unconditionally. How could you call him a burden?"

Gregor raised his hands in a symbol of peace and waited patiently for Jan's fury to pass. "I have been misunderstood." He explained. "I never claimed that you do not love your child. I merely pointed out that you and your wife wished for a baby. You both believed your child would improve the energy in your relationship, but it did not. You both still feel something is missing, and when a person feels something is missing, they begin searching. I'm not talking about you but all people. So my question, again, is do you need to fix the relationship with your wife or the one with yourself?"

Jan listened and contemplated Gregor's advice. There was no anger left. Instead, a search settled in.

The evening gong called participants to an extended meditation. The combined energy exhilarated soul searchers, who were beginning to break free of attachments and constraints from their usual patterns.

After dinner, Storm and Gaya felt humbled watching stars from the meditation stage. Most retired to their rooms. Self-work is challenging work, and lots of sleep is needed.

DAY FOUR: I DON'T NEED YOUR DRAMA, THANK YOU. I HAVE ENOUGH OF MY OWN.

We are given the prologue at birth, but then, we write the scenes.

The morning routine repeated. Participants were familiar with the programme and moved with ease between spaces and instructions. After meditation, Gregor explained the practice of the day.

"Good morning." He welcomed them. "I hope you slept well. We know some of you had breakthroughs yesterday, and we celebrate your progress. Today is another day to focus on pain and to explore the source of your personal pain. In life, we ignore our own pain by helping others and getting involved with their drama. But today, we will turn the spotlight on events that caused us pain and are interfering with our personal progress. This will be a hard day.

Today, it's very important to remember to stay out of other people's business. Their life is not yours and you cannot influence them until you have cleared your own shelves of drama. You cannot save anyone." Gregor said seriously.

"At lunch, you will have an opportunity to come together and talk. If you find yourself talking to someone that is sharing their drama, politely stop them and change the topic to something positive. Talk phatically about a film, books, music, puppies.

If they persist, excuse yourself and walk away. You do not have time to live in the company of negativity. Of course this isn't always possible, but try.

The question of the day is this: Is this pain mine? Does it belong to me? If it isn't, you should release it from your body. You cannot save anyone." Gregor repeated this seriously and heavily. He said it with such conviction that participants couldn't help but listen and take in his words.

"Focusing on other people's drama causes us to forget our own. It convinces you that your problems are not significant. But your problems are the most significant. They are the only ones you can solve.

You might think you can save people, but you can't. Stop trying. Yes, you can offer help and provide a break, but you cannot save them. You can lend them money, but they will have to pay you back. In the end, you did nothing. It was a temporary kindness, but it will not save them.

My father always told me, if you can help a person then help. If it's beyond your capability, the very least you can do is not laugh because you don't know what baggage they carry.

Learn your true capabilities. Don't distract yourself by focusing on others. We love to escape our pain, relationship and job problems, and issues with friends. It's hard to look at our demons because we prefer to look out of ourselves. But in order to change, we have to look in. You might have to end some relationships and break some patterns. You might lose people in the process: friends, lovers.
But if they are unable to understand your wish to change, they were dead weight and bad influences anyway. Wish them well and release them onto their separate journey. People that don't want you to change are burdens you should set free.

Let go of the ones that come solely to teach you. Do not cling to them, to that job, to their comfort.

In life, we take comfort in playing the same role. We like doing things that are familiar because it's easier than change. Every change means work, breaking patterns, creating new routines. People change when shaken. Ask yourself if you've reached that moment yet.

Small changes will create significant, long-term differences in your life. If you want to lose weight, cut out evening meals. You will lose weight. Not quickly, but slowly you will lose it. Or start to work out. Start with walking one kilometre a day, then five, and progress it. Eventually, you will see you can run that distance. In time, your eating regime will change as your body needs different things, and you will start to lose weight faster. Your body will feel happier.

There are many paths to the same result and they vary from person to person. In the end, you have to find your own way to become who you want to be." Gregor's tone lightened and his voice became very soft with guidance.

"If you have negative people in your life, cut them off or limit the time you spend with them. If you choose to limit your time with them and keep them in your life, you can also try to influence them to be more positive: switch to small talk; try talking about culture and beauty; don't gossip with them. The energy you put into conversations comes back to you, and gossiping hurts the gossiper most."

Gregor was ready to conclude his lesson and release participants to their reflection.

"So when you come together at lunch, if you have to speak with each other, see what you can learn.

If you talk about solving problems, make plans and listen for advice that feels good to you. Do not listen to what blocks progress, what is frustrating. Instead, try to find a peaceful conversation. If you cannot find this, take yourself somewhere to be alone.

Now, we showed you how to breathe in meditation. This morning, you must try to use this breathing as a guide towards the defining moment of your pain, and while there, stay objective. Identify where your pain comes from and forgive yourself. Try to focus on what's holding you back, what you need to change to feel better in your skin. Breathe and let go of your drama." Gregor said, his chest visibly expanding and retracting.

"Ask yourself, is this problem mine? Is it helping me? Can I change it? Find the moment you hardened yourself. What was your trigger? When did you first feel abandoned or overheard? What moment defined how you look at yourself? Go deep. Find the moment that made you who you are. Was it a situation or something people said about you? Once you find this moment, write a letter to your childhood self and apologise for holding this pain. Doing this releases it.

After writing to your childhood self, write a letter to a person that you believe further defines your pain, someone you see at the root of it. I'm almost certain they didn't want to harm you, but even if their actions were malicious, forgive them. Write them a letter, and forgive them. Their reality and actions have nothing to do with you. Their patterns and defining moments are their own, not yours." Gregor took a few deep breaths to relax the space and release the thoughts of people that caused pain.

"Forgive yourself." He paused. "And then forgive others. Enjoy this beautiful day. And remember, we're here to assist if you want more guidance."

Breakfast was swift. Participants were eager to venture into their blockers, to spring open closed doors, and to embrace the adventure of life.

Kara took a few apples and practically ran to the forest. Under the branches of trees, she speed-walked for half an hour, tracking back through the times she felt ugly and fat. As her heart pumped, tears unknowingly trickled down her cheeks. She remembered adult friends encouraging her diets with phrases like, "Amazing transformation, Kara. Another ten kilos, and you'll be perfect!" She travelled back and remembered school 'friends' making fun of her appearance. She travelled further and found a moment where she felt disgraced by her father. It burnt red hot. Kara stopped.

Defining moment:
I felt like a princess in a beautiful dress for a school dance. It was the end of primary school. Before taking a photo of me, I overheard my father laughing, "We made one daughter with height and the other with width." My heart sank, and I didn't feel like a princess anymore. Every time I see that photo, it reminds me of his words and my size.

Kara wept so intensely she felt her life's supply of tears would run dry. She let them slide along her cheek unchecked and drop on her dress. Pain travelled around her body, but she didn't let it consume her. Kara breathed purposefully and consciously and tried to release the feeling of despair and hurt. She screamed into the air until she couldn't any more, until her stores of physical and spiritual pain were empty and she was calm.

Dear fifteen-year-old Kara,
You are perfect just as you are. You are a beautiful princess and shouldn't listen to anyone that tells you differently. You should feel impressive and unique.

You are perfect. I want to hug you and tell you that in the end everything is going to be okay - it's going to be great. I am so sorry I let you feel this way. I forgive you for everything. You are amazing and one of a kind. Never forget this. I love you. I accept you. I support you.

Kara felt better immediately. She imagined hugging her fifteen-year old self and saying these words, how they would feel. She took time to pause on this warmth and embrace immense love for herself.

Dear Father,
I know your words were meant as a joke. I know you did the best you could to raise me and that you couldn't predict the ways your words would hurt me. But they are still painful. I know you love me and accept me, but it would mean a lot if you could tell me how beautiful and unusual I am, that I am your princess. I never needed more than that from you. I just needed your unconditional acceptance and to know you saw me as someone special.

Kara set down the notebook.

Petra walked back to the terrace in front of her room. She prepared tea and stared at the trees. She always felt defined by being a housewife. She knew her role was to keep the house clean, and the children and husband fed. When she tried to learn about things she was interested in or wanted to form an opinion on, Janez reminded her she didn't know anything. Of course, he showed an interest in her learning but there were always small comments that hurt her.

At twenty, I told my husband I wanted to take a photography course. He made fun of the idea, stating that I don't need special skills to take holiday photos.

234

He even told me once, after developing a holiday film, that I don't take nice pictures. I think his words were, 'You just don't have the eye for it.' He told me I should relax after my hard housework and not run around with a camera. He never said I couldn't do it, but he made me feel like I wasn't talented or capable.

Small comments from a person you adore can make you feel so little. Thought Petra. They're the hardest to get over.

Dear twenty-year old Petra,
I think you are brilliant and full of unearthed talent! You shouldn't feel bad for wanting to explore your interests. No one should forbid it or tell you what you can and can't do. You should fly and explore wherever you wish. And if you find out something is not for you and you're not good at it, don't worry. Do the things that make you feel happy and fulfilled.

In Petra's letter, she gave herself permission to fully enjoy life. She qualified herself for the privilege of enjoyment and existence outside her role as carer to Janez and their children. Looking back, she began to see Janez was threatened by her wish to be expressive. He had made sure she stayed in line, playing the role of humble wife. Looking back, she started to think maybe that made him feel accomplished and manly.

Dear Janez,
I know you tried to be the best husband for me. And I couldn't imagine spending so many years with anyone else. But still, there were times you made me feel little and unimportant. I wish you had encouraged me to follow my passions.

But I also forgive you for every time you told me that something was 'not for me'. I forgive you for every time you suggested that my knowledge was limited to housekeeping. You were old fashioned and did not see the need for self-realisation because you were working and respected outside the family. I know you loved me deeply and gave me everything you thought I needed. I accept that you did the best you knew, and I am happy to tell you that I am chasing my passions now. I started a photography class and felt like the oldest and dumbest there, but by doing things like this, I will own my age and lack of experience. I felt terrible, like I'd forgotten you, when I started these classes but I don't let myself feel that anymore. I still miss you, and sometimes I miss our slow routine. But it is time to try everything I missed while you were here. I will try to take beautiful photos and enjoy the process.

I love you, my dear.

Jacopo walked around the lake and made himself comfortable on an empty beach. To his left, a young woman with dreadlocks wrote like a possessed person. On his right, an older man alternated between staring at the lake and jotting a quick something down. Jacopo hesitated. It was hard to challenge the painful moments he'd ignored.

When I was six years old, I overheard my parents talking about a friends' daughter who came out as gay. They called her behaviour 'disgusting' and 'unnatural'. When I played with my sister's dolls, my father made it clear dolls were not for boys. He said it was unnatural to play with them.

Dear six-year old Jacopo,
You are not weird, and you are not responsible for your parents' narrow-mindedness.

236

I remember the shame you felt wanting to play with boys and feel their human touch. I remember how much you disgusted yourself when growing up, and I am sorry. Someone loving should have been there to guide you. You were just a child, and you had to cover your true colours.

I'm sorry you were born into an old-fashioned family that didn't believe being homosexual is natural, that didn't understand it wasn't a choice but who you are. I'm sorry that you had to pretend to be something else. I'm sorry you felt you had to be like your peers. I'm sorry you played football when you wanted to do art.

Now, nobody can touch you.

You are loved, respected, and accepted by your new community.

Jacopo stopped, thinking about everything he went through: disappointment, lies, pretence. He had repressed his feelings to a point of numbness. He felt lighter knowing that point was in the past.

Dear parents and relatives,

I forgive you for everything you said and did against me. I forgive you for ignoring my needs. I forgive your unnecessary comments and for cutting contact with me. I know it's not your fault. You believe you are operating with good hearts and that you can heal me, change me, make me straight. You believe excluding me will make me change my mind.

But I can't change my mind because this is not about my mind. This is who I am. I never chose to be gay, but I do choose to own my identity and be the best, proudest version of myself. I choose to not conform to your beliefs.

All parental love has limitations, and I forgive you for not accepting my decisions. I hope you are happy and that one day we will meet again as friends. I hope it will be in person. I love you and will always love you, no matter what. You can't hurt me anymore.
If you want, my door and heart are always open to you.

Jacopo smiled at forgiving his family. Peace overcame his body as, finally, he let go. There were no more what ifs: What if I go back home and say I'm not gay anymore? What if I go to that church seminar that makes you straight again? They were gone. He lay down, observed the clouds, and whispered to himself, "I have found new friends and a new family that both cherish and accept me."

Nick found himself back at the cottage. He couldn't understand why he had no desire to adventure to a different spot, but he felt at home there, sitting under the trees.

Day 4
Dear Nick,

I forgive you for being so foolish and for following Linda like a stray dog. Your heart was in the right place. I forgive you for always choosing her before yourself. This was just part of your story and self education. You made it possible for me to accept myself, and now, I put my needs first. You embraced living with so much pain, yearning, and waiting. You hoped she'd recognise your worth and good heart. But you have to know her blindness is best for us both.

I am becoming a better person. I had a choice: to search for Linda in other women or to give up on her and start meeting new people.

238

I am finally open to finding the right partner for my path, my heart, and my lifestyle. She will be a woman that sees me as I am and finds me attractive and reliable.

"That was the easy part." Confessed Nick, knowing he'd already forgiven himself. Now he had to face the anger harboured towards Linda. It had been growing over the week. Nick was sure he was over his love for Linda, but new hot flashes overwhelmed him when he thought about her. He wanted to punch her. Hate and anger were new to him and he didn't know how to manage them.

The old teacher wandered by the lake and Nick went to him, waving for help. The teacher saw Nick's distress and greeted him with a calming smile. "What's on your mind?"

Nick gasped for air. "I need to write a letter to a person that hurt me more than anyone else." He couldn't catch his breath. "I feel such hate and rage and anger pouring out of me."

The teacher laughed open mouthed. Nick wondered what about his statement had been funny and felt momentarily stupid.

"Let's sit under our tree." Invited the teacher. "I noticed you like this place. It's my favourite too." They faced each other and connected eyes. "Anger is good. It's better than sadness or hopelessness. It is better than grief or depression. It's a long way from joy, but you will get there. What we want is for you to write what you really mean, to let go. This is a practice letter for real life. You may have to write many more of them.
But when you forgive this person, you will be able to move on. You will feel love and acceptance because you will finally know this person taught you something.

We are all teachers and all students. I have learnt from you, sitting here together. The search is never over. There is always a next level. We learn our entire life.

Forgiveness is a big part of this learning. Isn't that amazing? Life is a never-ending story, a journey into the depths of your soul. There will come a time to say thank you to this person, and you will be happy they are not important to you anymore. Forgive all, and claim your inner peace. Nothing is more important in life than feeling good."

Nick understood intellectually what the teacher wanted to impart, but he couldn't see himself forgiving Linda or feeling joy and acceptance when thinking of her.

"I hope what you say will happen, but right now, everything inside me is screaming. I feel like I'm being torn apart. What is this scale of emotions?"

The old teacher smiled. "We have to remind ourselves that there is only one lead actor in life. In my life, it is me. In yours, it is you. Everyone else is a supporting role. Even if you put your happiness in the hands of another, their role is no bigger. That actor is not responsible for the projections you transferred on to them. Yes, we are given the prologue at birth, but then, we write the scenes."

Nick felt surprised at his understanding of this analogy.

"The emotional scale presents your emotional engagement. The higher your emotional energy the stronger your vibrations and the healthier your emotions are. Even when you're low on the emotional scale, vibrating emotions are present inside. You should read into this.
Briefly, after hate comes impatience, then boredom, which presents itself as middle emotions that are neither bad nor good. Then comes feelings like hope, belief, passion, joy, and freedom, which are at the top of the scale. You can research how to recognise your feelings in order to slowly move higher up the scale."

Nick took notes as he listened. "You mean with affirmations?"

"Well, there is no one way. For some, affirmations aren't helpful. If you say to yourself, 'I have a lot of money,' when you are aware you do not, it cannot create good vibrations. All that does is grow fear. For me, I move up the scale with gardening. As a matter of fact, I wanted to do a bit of gardening now. Would you like to join me?"

Nick accepted and followed. As they worked, they talked about flowers, plants, trees, bees, and dirt. Nick got sweaty and happy, letting Linda slip from his mind. The hate and anger residing within him lifted as his muscles connected with the earth.

"Go with this vibration and set free negative feelings." The teacher instructed. "Write. And if your energy drops again, come back here."

Nick returned to his tree and started.

> Dear Linda,
> I would not be here, at this camp, if there was no you. I would never challenge the meaning of my feelings if you had been interested in me. Maybe you were a good thing to happen to me. Time will tell. I set you free from my heart.

Nick tried to write a few more sentences, but he felt there was nothing else to say. It wasn't about her anymore, so why place another word in her name?

Storm lay on the stage and thought about his amazing, crazy, dead brother, Rider. He missed him and felt anger growing since mentioning him to Jan. Storm couldn't forgive his brother. Twitchy, he stood up and paced around the stage a few times. As his muscles relaxed, he sat back down and took pen to paper.

DEAR STORM

THE ACCIDENT WAS NOT YOUR FAULT. YOU DID WHAT EVERY BOY YOUR AGE DOES AT A PARTY. RIDER WOULD DO THE SAME. I GUESS IT WAS MEANT TO HAPPEN. IT WAS RIDER'S TIME. YOU KNOW YOU TRUST THE UNIVERSE. TRY TO REMEMBER HIM WITH PEACE AND LOVE.

DEAR RIDER,

I AM SO ANGRY YOU SAT IN THAT CAR. WHY WERE YOU SO STUPID? OUR PARENTS WARNED US ABOUT TRAVELLING WITH DRUNK DRIVERS. THERE WAS NO NEED TO GO. I WANT TO PUNCH YOUR STUPID FACE ONE MORE TIME.

I WANT TO HUG YOU ONE MORE TIME. I WANT TO SURF WITH YOU. I HATE YOU FOR DYING.

I FORGIVE YOU FOR BEING A STUPID LITTLE KID.

Storm cried in silence. He still couldn't forgive Rider honestly or himself. He felt sick to his stomach and tried to suppress what wanted to come flooding out. He rocked in his seat and reminded himself of Gaya's promise, "Deep-rooted issues and emotional scars are not healed on the first try. You need to tackle them many times and take each attempt step by step."

Tina wandered to the lake, eventually sitting by a tree. She made sure she was far away from other participants in order to think clearly about whom she needed to apologise to: her husband or her lover.

Dear Tina,

I am sorry you need external validation. I forgive you for being silly. I hope it will get better after a while. I don't see any positive effects just yet.

Dear world,
I forgive you. I know it's not you, it's me and my inability
to please myself. It's my desperation to trick everyone else
into thinking I am happy and perfect.

Tina wanted a glass of wine. Her body ached from abstinence. She leaned her head on the tree and pounded it gently. She laughed and mocked herself, "I can't even beat my stupid head in case it leaves a mark." Her laugh came close to a cry. "I'm half living. I don't know who I am."

Jan stayed in the dining area after breakfast. He tried to think about his tipping point with Ema, but another memory came shining through above anything to do with her.

He was a child, and his unstable mother was demanding validation from him over and over. "Tell me you love your mother. Tell me I'm more important than anyone else. Tell me you don't want to go outside today, that you want to stay in with me." Her pain kept him away from the outside world and fun. She often talked about killing herself if he left her, and she made him solely responsible for her happiness.

Dear young Jan,
You were just a boy. It's normal to want to stay out and play.
Your mother told you many times she'd kill herself without
you, but she was unstable and that was wrong of her. It is
not your fault. You did your best to follow her obsessive
instructions, even though you knew they weren't normal.
You are not guilty. You are not guilty.

Dear Mum,
I forgive you for being a bad mother. I know, now, that you
were in fact my most pertinent teacher. I forgive you for
making me feel afraid of you killing yourself and for
making me think I had to live my life next to you.

I forgive you for the guilt you put on me as a child, and I'm sorry for wanting something you were unable to provide.

In a red flash, Jan struck through his writing, feeling it pointless and worthless. He didn't want to reread it so left the words as an angry retraction. Sadness dripped out of him, little by little, but with it he found a new kind of relief. There was no quick fix, but Jan was unknowingly experiencing the healing of therapy.

Lea walked. She made two circles around the lake but couldn't find a place of her own. She still didn't know what to do, where to settle. She was haunted. With each pause from walking, she would ask herself, "What's the moment that broke me?" When she didn't know the answer, she kept going. Until finally, she knew. Squatting in no intentional place she wrote.

Dear Lea,

I forgive you for letting Patrik in your life. I forgive you for not listening to your friends and family. I accept that it was a lesson I had to learn. I will try to find confidence in men again. It will be a long road, but it is time to let it go...

Lea stopped writing, interrupted by forgotten memories. She was with her uncle. There were sweets, movies, books, and toys she had wanted. All were given as gifts, but it wasn't her birthday. Her uncle took her neck in his hand and slid his palm down her back while she was distracted unwrapping presents. He always wanted to cuddle her and would grip her tightly when she tried to get away. He bathed with her once and insisted on washing her although she was old enough to do it herself. She remembered feeling this was inappropriate. When she said it out loud once, he told her, "Your mind's dirty, Lea. Don't try to manipulate your loving uncle." He told her multiple times it was natural for an uncle to take care of his little girl, to love his little girl. Before she could tell her parents what the uncle was doing, he died in a car crash. She buried the secret with him and tried to keep him from her thoughts.

244

Lea remembered her mother's heavy sobs, heartbroken by the death of her baby brother. Her mother missed him unbearably and constantly told stories about him, so even if Lea wanted to confess what he was really like, it felt like the wrong time.

Lea became hot with rage.

Dear Uncle,

I hate you, and I am glad you are dead. But I forgive you. I forgive you so I can let go and move on. It was you that had a dirty mind and what you did, touching and petting me like a doll, was wrong. None of that was my fault. Your behaviour and actions were yours alone and so, for my own happiness, I forgive you.

Lea wanted to cry but no tears came. *How could I have repressed that?* She revelled at the power of her protective mind. *I have to tell everyone. Maybe he molested other children.* She thought for a beat and made herself calm down. *Is this the source of my problems?* Lea smiled.

The gong announced lunch. Everyone returned looking exhausted. Some seemed to have survived a battle, while others had won a war.

Lea took food and went to sit alone under trees. Others followed the morning's instructions and used lunch to spread good vibrations, talking about movies, music, and positive news.

Gregor stepped on to a chair. "When you have finished eating, find an activity alone or with others. Choose the company you wish and find what feels suitable. But you must maintain focus on today's task. You can talk about your breakthrough or issues. You can explore how you want to tackle and conquer them."

Storm locked eyes with Jan, Kara, Nick, and Tina, and silently agreed to meet. Tina informed Petra, who was sitting next to her ignorant of the exchange.

Jan told Jacopo, who came late to the table. But no one could find Lea, who needed time to contemplate her revelation and had taken solitude without a second thought for anyone else.

* * *

When lunch was done, they walked towards the mountains that surrounded the estate. On reaching what felt like a suitable place at the foot of the mountain, they took seats and Storm pulled me from his pocket.

"I realised today," said Jan, "That my mother manipulated me into loving her. She did the best she could, but she was an awful mother. I need to find a good therapist after this week. Maybe once I tackle this, I can fix my problems with Ema.
I think she was reminding me of my mother too much, and that's why I couldn't take any more."

The six friends were aware Jan didn't need their insight, but they nodded all the same. They didn't include themselves in his drama, but offered support from their nods. A joint was lit and passed around.

After her third puff, Petra announced, "I'm going to do every silly thing I want to. Janez didn't encourage my hobbies but I'm not going to reject them anymore." Petra felt pleased with her new agency and for forgiving the man that loved her but held her back. Her forgiveness released a new wave of energy and excitement.

I travelled from hand to hand with the joint. This time they smoked slowly. Storm added a second when the first was finished. The tempo was easy and quiet.

"I have to forgive my father." Kara said after a while. "I trusted him, and he hurt me. The way he spoke about me when I was a child defined and moulded me.

246

But it's time to reshape the image I hold of myself. I'm going to keep walking and eating healthily. I'm going to make myself feel like a princess." She giggled. "I've got to awaken the idea that I am special." Kara hugged herself. "I'm going to be the best bloody version of myself I can be." She threw her arms in the air and shouted a, "Woo-hoo!" to the sky.

Kara's supporters cheered and screamed with her, all laughing and enjoying her energy.

Another joint was lit. Petra lay down, watching the clouds, and grabbed at the grass fearful to fall from the side of the mountain despite sitting far away from any edge. Tina saw her clenched hands and calmed her, reminded her she was safe.

"I want to remember my brother with love." Storm added to the confessions. "I want to do something for him, something that carries his memory on. I don't know what it's going to be, but I'll find a way."

Time passed slowly. Everyone lay down and hunted different shapes in the clouds.

Jacopo interrupted the search with an idea. "I'm going to write a long letter to my parents to explain who I am and how I live. I'm going to show them I'm still their son. What they do next is up to them. But I have to try and connect with them once more. I just want to live my life. I want to be free of these bad feelings."

The group clapped a quiet but meaningful clap of support.

Standing up to your family is never easy, thought Petra.

Tina, inspired, added, "I want to be true to myself. I don't really know who I am or how to start, but I'm going to find out."

Storm lit the last joint as the gong struck.

Nick smoked fast. "I want to move on with my life." He said. "I want to live, to enjoy. Everything else is commercial shit and doesn't matter. Things can't make you happy if you feel bad in your skin. And I want to feel great in mine." The group smiled and praised one another with warm glistening eyes. They could see themselves taking steps towards better places.

* * *

Participants settled into evening meditation, and six of the seven stoned friends fell asleep as soon as they were asked to close their eyes. Storm was the only one able to access the practice. After meditation, they met with Gregor, who realised instantly that everyone but Lea was totally high.

"I'm going to make this short. I have no objection to smoking. It can be helpful to relax and gain insight, but I do not condone getting stoned to the point of vegetation. You all need to go to dinner. Lea, you can stay if you'd like to share your experience. The rest of you, go. Enjoy your meal."

Petra felt like a little child. She'd never misbehaved and bit her lip to prevent bursting out in laughter. The seven stood and migrated to dinner. They were the only ones eating at this time as other participants reflected in their groups of eight. Lea joined soon after, eager to find out what had happened to them. After eating, they went straight to bed with the exception of Storm. He returned me to the stage and was met by Gaya.

"Storm, you cannot escape yourself." She said with a mixture of care and annoyance. "And it is not nice to include other participants in smoking in the middle of the day. You can do that before bed if you really need it to calm yourself. But it prevents you from processing everything and makes your time here, their time here, a waste. What will I do with you?" Her voice became full of affection. She could see he'd had a tough day. "Maybe they needed that experience.

248

Some people have problems letting go. But for you, it's important to stay present here, in this reality, and to face your feelings. Go to bed, Storm. Good night."

She turned away and walked to her cottage. Storm wasn't invited. He headed to his room and fell down exhausted.

DAY FIVE: I AM GRATEFUL FOR ALL THAT IS AND WILL BE. PRAISE YOURSELF AND OTHERS.

Being grateful is a magical remedy to feelings like anger. It may not seem so at first, but being grateful has healing qualities.

Petra felt like she'd died the night before and was now resurrected. Whereas, Nick had a big, foggy headache. The first time the group had smoked together, he took one puff each round to be safe. But after yesterday's pain exploration and his forgiveness of Linda, he'd let loose and paid for it now.

The morning routine followed its usual steps: breathing, meditation, relaxation. Afterwards, one teacher took the stage. Before this moment, she'd kept her face concealed under a cloak, even with her group of eight. Removing her hood revealed that she was an incredibly young woman. Her youthful face was framed by short dark hair and a marked maturity in spite of her lack of years.

Familiar with being judged for her age, she started by saying, "I know you're thinking, 'What does this child know about life?' So let me put your mind at ease. I'm twenty.

When I was a child, my stepfather regularly molested me, and my mother rejected me when I told her about this.

She took me to a psychiatric hospital at the age of ten, claiming I was a pathological liar and a thief. Eventually, I was raped, which led to a mental breakdown.

251

I trashed our house and tore apart everything I could get my hands on." The young woman took a moment's pause. Her strength astounded listeners.

"Almost a year after my breakdown and with my mother still in denial, he started molesting my younger sister. Eventually, I was proven to be reliable when my mother walked in on him and was forced to stop deceiving herself.

I never trusted my mother again and ended up leaving home at sixteen. After careful searching, I found my first teacher. You all met him on the second day." She smiled full of comfort. "I emancipated myself from my blood family, travelled to India and, after many hours of meditation, found the insight I needed. I discovered that I cannot escape the world or my problems, that I carry them with me everywhere I go. And so I came back.

Now, my focus is on staying sane and helping others who have had similar experiences."
She gazed at participants while speaking, as if protected by an emotional veil. The listeners were less controlled and stared with all their emotions exposed: interest, shock, disbelief, amazement.

Lea connected to this teacher instantly. *She can help me. She'll understand.* Her heart leapt at the promise of salvation.

Jan was also interested. He could not claim experiences like hers, but he felt akin to her disappointment in her mother. He admired her honesty and matter-of-factness. *She talks with ease about the terrors she's survived. If she can be this strong, maybe I can too.*

"Today, I ask you to be grateful for your blessings. Consider what they are, and write them down.

It's easy to start with apparent blessings: your family, friends, clothes, luxury possessions, coffee, the ability to read and write, the ability to speak - maybe even more than one language. Acknowledge them because appreciation creates abundance.

Personally, I am grateful for small things: drinking coffee with friends on a hill with a view, having a picnic next to a river, reading and drinking tea at my place, flowers. Small things are beautiful. Have you ever watched a spider at work? It is perfect."

The young woman left the air momentarily empty of words and watched the clouds. It was unclear if this was intended to be a moment of calm and tensions unintentionally formed amongst participants.

"I'm even grateful for my stepfather." She said, letting them feel whatever reaction possessed them. "Without him, I wouldn't have learnt what I know and I wouldn't be here now. I don't want to bring up vibrations associated with him. I don't want to be connected to him at all. In fact, I would say the emotions linked to him are gone now. And that is why I can be grateful for him.

But I still have emotions connected to my mother and because of this I have problems forgiving her. The scars from her need much longer to heal." She found little comfort in this acknowledgement. "I have written many notebooks and then burned them to release my feelings about her. I have meditated. I have shared. But an angry little girl still exists inside me. It's the girl whose mother didn't believe her." She stopped and waited.

"Being grateful is a magical remedy to feelings like anger. It may not seem so at first, but being grateful has healing qualities. Gratefulness raises your energy levels, keeps you focused on positive attributes of life, and allows you to smile at what you have rather than mourn what you do not.

"Today, write down these things. Some of you are already making notes about this, but today I want you to write down eight things you are grateful for. You are on our 8-Day Experiment; look for eight reasons to be grateful; keep the cycle of gratefulness flowing around the number eight like an infinite celebration. And engage with the emotions you get from things you are grateful for as you record them: happiness, lightness, fluffiness.

If you need, start by writing two things you are grateful for and then dig into those things. Make your appreciation of them more specific: How do they make you feel? Why? Are they shared? Are they private? Where did they come from? Is that important? When you discover the origin of their importance, they start to mean more and become completely free to you. Appreciation creates abundance. For example: I have access to education, and I can walk. Where do those things come from? How do they make me feel? Can I share them? And so on. I will discover more that I am grateful for as I answer these questions.

We encourage you to continue this writing for at least twenty-one days. Later, you can think about what you are grateful for without writing it down, but for now, make it concrete, solid, real.

At first, it might be hard to find what you are grateful for, but with practice, you will become a master of gratitude."

An uneasiness surrounded the group, exposing their discomfort listening to this teacher. Petra tried to zone in on her feelings and question them. *I don't know how to listen to her because she isn't the type of person I'm used to. I've seen this in my village with disability and homelessness. I need to look past my preconceptions.*

254

"Dear participants, we can all cry and talk about how sad our lives have been, but now's the time to do something else."

Lea tuned in to this address. *No more being talked down to. I am no less human, no less than the person I was before. This teacher doesn't pity herself, so I can be the same. I will find my power, like her.* She grabbed at the grass under her feet and found strength in her hands.

"Laugh as you look at the small gifts you have." The young teacher continued. "As always, the first part of the day is your own. Record the gifts in your life. Then we'll meet in groups before lunch. After lunch," She smiled, "We go for a walk through energy fields along a nearby hill. Here, we'll celebrate the amazing life we have ahead of us." She left the stage, signalling the end of the lesson and the start of breakfast.

After eating, Lea searched out the young teacher and asked to go for a walk together. They wandered through fields on the estate and shared time. Lea gradually formed her questions, picking the right words and utilising the time given to her.

"So I came out of a possessive relationship and since then I've been totally lost. I don't trust my feelings anymore because I missed every warning sign with that partner."

The young teacher walked silently, ensuring Lea finished exploring her ideas before taking the turn to speak.

"I based the value of our relationship on his beauty and convinced myself I didn't deserve someone that appeared so... out of my league. Somehow, I still miss sharing myself with him. I don't miss him watching my every move and making me think I depended on him, but I really miss something."

Lea finished and waited.

"We all have defining moments in our lives," said the young teacher. "And it's up to us how we tackle them. You and I have different stories. I never loved my stepfather.
Because I had no love for him, I could forgive him and he doesn't mean anything to me anymore. For me, I'm most grateful for the fact that my little sister will not experience the things I did."

The young teacher directed them to a place to sit.

"You are the only one that can find gratitude in your life. Consider the questions you ask yourself to uncover gratitude. Rather than focusing on your partner's betrayal, maybe you should ask, why don't I think I'm beautiful? Why do I tell myself I don't deserve a beautiful man who is attractive inside and out?"

Lea connected with the teacher's green eyes. *I put myself down from the moment he showed interest in me. I praised external beauty and so never saw the ugly within.* A darker thought settled in Lea's mind. *If I hadn't bumped into my friends in the mall, I'd still be with him, still confident he was the best thing to happen to me. We might have had a child, brought an innocent soul into his unreasonable world. I have so much work to do.*

They shared a natural, loving energy that only transmits between equal souls. The young teacher had nothing else to say and, knowing it was time to be alone, left Lea with her thoughts.

Lea opened her notebook and embraced what she now understood.

I am grateful for my beautiful apartment, my safe haven.
I am grateful for my parents, who always stood by me and helped with the loan I needed to rebuild my freedom.
I am grateful for my friends, who forgave me after ignoring them.
I am grateful that my eyes were opened before the relationship became more violent.

I am grateful for this beautiful day and that I can enjoy being here under the mountains.
I am grateful for the teachers in my life.
I am grateful for my health and for not going crazy, especially in the past months.
I am grateful that I miss Patrik less and less every day.

Storm felt blocked today. He had to pause because he kept coming back to the same points. Avoiding repetition stifled him for a while, but he soon realised repetition didn't matter. The aim was to be thankful, not to be perfect. After a long intense wait, he wrote:

GRATEFUL FOR:
- HEALTH: MY STRONG BODY THAT NEVER GETS SICK
- FAMILY: MY CRAZY PARENTS THAT ARE TOTALLY DIFFERENT TO OTHERS
- BROTHERS: I HOPE WE RIDE MANY WAVES TOGETHER
- RIDER: FOR EVERY SINGLE MOMENT I SPENT WITH HIM - I'LL NEVER FORGET HIM
- FRIENDS: I LOVE THEM AND THAT THEY ARE ALWAYS READY FOR ADVENTURES
- FUERTE: FOR WIND, SUN, SEA, SALT, DIRT, FOR IT'S ENDLESS PLAYGROUND, FOR SURFING, AND CLIMBING
- FOOD: I'M BLESSED TO HAVE GOOD FOOD IN ABUNDANCE.
- HAIR: I LOVE MY HAIR. IT'S PERFECT.
- JACQUELINE: FOR SHOWING ME HER WORLD AND MAKING SURE I SURVIVED PARIS
- FREEDOM: THAT I AM FREE AND HAVE SPACE

Tina returned to the smoking spot at the foot of the mountain.

She enjoyed the view up here and let it distract her from unveiling deep secrets and much needed change. Denial was easier than change, and all Tina wanted was a drink. After much procrastination, she focused on the task at hand.

I am grateful for my sons. They are a blessing, even though I don't appreciate them in the way I should. I am grateful for my husband, who financially supports us.
I am grateful for my high school friends and that we travel together.
I am grateful I can buy things I want.
I am grateful to have a job I don't hate.
I am grateful for my acupuncturist, who always relaxes me.
I am grateful for my body. It works efficiently, so I don't need a special regime to stay fit and skinny.
I am grateful for gin & tonics. They always support me.

Petra repeated her well-established routine of returning to her terrace and appreciating the comfort of the cabin and a chair. She prepared tea, cut an apple, closed her eyes, and breathed in the peaceful moment to create.

Day 5 – I am grateful for:
- *Janez, with whom I shared a wonderful life.*
- *My children and grandchildren. I have been blessed.*
- *My health that allows me to enjoy new, exciting things.*
- *My new friends that support me.*
- *Photography (and I will try to learn more).*
- *Smoking weed because it allowed me to fly.*
- *The opportunities ahead of me to travel and see the places I've dreamed of seeing.*
- *My flower garden, which is envied by neighbours.*

- *My new (super expensive) bed, which feels luxurious and energising.*
- *That my brain still allows me to read and learn.*

Jan wandered towards the stage and sat under a giant totem that loomed over participants in morning meditation. His thoughts ranged through memories, and he tried to put them aside and filter to the things he was grateful for.

Thankful for my son. He is my miracle and showed me love beyond bounds.

Jan paused. This was not a natural process for him. He looked up to the sky, stretched out his neck, arched his back and felt the tension in his muscles, took a few deep breaths, and then carried on.

I'm grateful for Ema. I wouldn't be the same without her. Grateful for my generally good life. Thankful for my successful career, which allows me to live comfortably. Thankful for all the people I met here. Grateful my upbringing didn't mess with my mental health. I'm grateful for the places I travelled to, even recently.

He stopped writing and continued stretching out the tension in his body.

Kara walked through the first hour and a half of the morning, not out of necessity but rather from determination to maintain her positive routine. For the first time in her life, Kara felt inner peace. She was ready to accept her body just as it was. She came to terms with the fact that others had 'good genes' and that she would always have to diet to manage her weight. Thinking like this made it easy for her to focus on the positive things she had and forget what was missing.

While walking, she considered all the good things that had just appeared at her feet lately: projects she loved, new amazing easy clients, jobs gained through word of mouth. She was feeling lucky.

A click from Kara's pedometer declared ten thousand steps were completed, so she found a spot and started writing.

I am grateful for my family. Yes, I know they gave me issues, but we spend time together and love each other.
I am grateful for my career, where I am successful and can organise time as I wish.
I am grateful for excellent business partners. It's good to work with fantastic people and see projects develop from an idea into something real.
I am grateful for my friends. I know they're crazy, but they've been with me for more than half my life and they fulfil me.
I am grateful for my body. I love that I can go on long walks. Until recently, I didn't know my body was so strong, and I'm enjoying it more and more every day.
I am grateful for my health. Again, thank you, dear body. You are so kind to me, despite how I've treated you.
I am grateful for my home. It's a beautiful space where I can rest and create. I especially enjoy my sofa, watching movies, reading, and enjoying my privacy.
I am grateful for my morning routine. I feel blessed every time I wake up and enjoy a quiet coffee before the day kicks off and gets hectic.

Nick walked to his cabin, wishing he had a place like that for himself at home. He wanted somewhere away from the busyness of London, somewhere in a village to escape to when needed. Today, he didn't sit down but went straight to the garden and cleared leaves.

He observed the cabin's structure and enjoyed its charm. After his arms were heavy with work and his mind at ease, he opened the notebook.

I am grateful for my job and the firm that always wants me to grow. They provide excellent opportunities to achieve more and this will help me. I am thankful for the friends that stayed with me through my obsession with Linda. I am grateful for letting go of my expectations and my crazy fantasy. I am grateful for the life I was born into, that my family gave me strong values so I can be a decent person.
I am thankful that I'm finally ready to find a special person to share my life with and that I'm open to meeting them. I am grateful for the time I can take for myself now. I am thankful for being healthy and able to go anywhere I want. I'm grateful for this cabin, where I feel at home. I am thankful for the fantastic people I've met here.

There's so much more to life than I realised before.

Jacopo returned to his room, tired but satisfied. He'd had his doubts about messing with repressed feelings, but those doubts were gone. Now, he was content with his decision to come on the 8-Day Experiment and could already see his inner light shining brighter.

I'm grateful for my new friends and for finding a new family that accepts me as I am.
I am grateful I came out to my family, even though I lost them.
I am grateful for Rocco, who showed me that love is possible and incredible.
I am grateful for this time to focus on myself and explore the things that pull me down.

I am grateful I earn enough to try things I want and that I'm not in the red at the end of each month.
I am grateful for the new information I'm learning. It's helping me deal with sadness and loneliness.
I'm grateful for music and the ability to dance my ass off.
I am grateful that I no longer care if somebody looks at me with disgust.

The gong sounded. Participants gathered for lunch and were then directed towards a bus and a van which would take them to the start of the promised walk. When they arrived, they were welcomed by a surprise: all eight teachers removed their shoes and encouraged others to do the same.

"Today we will embark on a barefoot walk." The young teacher told them with a broad grin. "We will pass through twelve energetic fields. Focus on yourself and your body as we walk. If this is your first time walking barefoot and your feet are soft like a baby's, step carefully and considerately. It can be painful but in the end it's incredibly fulfilling."

Some were on board with the idea and removed their shoes eagerly. Storm was the first, embracing a practice from home. Petra, on the other hand, was uncomfortable having never let her bare feet feel earth. Kara, who had always wanted to walk barefoot but felt too embarrassed alone, was excited.

Along the first hill, the close-knit group became an outstretched snake. Storm walked beside Gaya, leading. Petra took the rear, walking with the bearded teacher.

"I'm too old for this shit." She screamed in frustration as he encouraged her along the way. She'd stepped on many sharp stones, and her feet were becoming very sore.

The bearded teacher laughed. "You are too old when you're dead." This made Petra smile briefly, and his humour continued to distract her as they slowly moved up the hill and passed through energetic fields.

Some participants took their time to experience the fields and embrace their power. Others rushed on to get the barefoot torture over and done with. Jacopo was one of them.
He didn't want to admit that this was out of his comfort zone and that he was losing the ability to walk. He was supposed to be sporty. This should be natural for him, but the whole thing felt quite unnatural.

Nick often walked barefoot in his garden at home, but this was the first time through a forest and up a hill.
He struggled but enjoyed the path, walking and talking with a cute female participant the whole way. He'd seen her at breakfast and lunch but this was their first conversation. Nick found himself fancying her instantly. He had no expectation, no crazy story in his head. It was a comfortable, exciting, brisk, barefoot walk.

Lea assumed a place next to the young teacher, and they walked in silence. She intentionally tried to connect with the energy fields and jumped with excitement when she finally felt an electric tingle over her skin. Lea laughed and moved around like an elated child. The young teacher joined in her celebration.

"See." She cheered Lea. "Everything will be good. This field was for healing your heart."

They hugged, feeling the pounding of each other's hearts, and then quietly, happily carried on.

Kara's eagerness for this task quickly waned as each step brought a thousand needles stabbing into her feet.

A teacher with dreadlocks walked beside her for a while, encouraging and motivating her.

"There are different paths in life: some are hard, and some are easy. It's up to you how you walk the path. It's not just about the end goal but also how you feel along the way. Try to find the way that suits you." Kara listened and took solace in the words. She searched for leafy parts of the path to place her feet and tried to breathe away her discomfort.

Tina walked in a group in the middle of the snake. She talked about workout sessions with like-minded people and enjoyed the practice. Tina seemed made for walking barefoot; it brought an easy freedom she'd not discovered before.

Jan found no satisfaction walking without shoes. He also had a secret foot phobia, which made the experience much worse as seeing naked feet made him sick to his stomach. He tried to rush through the hike, desperate to be reunited with his shoes.

* * *

At the top, an immense view of the valley embraced the wanderers. Even the most uncomfortable members of the group felt happy looking down at the beauty they'd journeyed for.

The young teacher stepped onto a large stone. "So who loved it? Raise your hand." She smiled to see many hands in the air. "Look at the people who loved this." The group with raised hands looked around at each other and acknowledged their kindred barefoot spirits.

"Who hated it? Raise your hand." Her smile was even bigger, almost a laugh. "Now, look at the people who hated it." Similarly, there was a smile in the eyes of those who shared a dislike; it didn't matter whether they liked it or not; they withstood, completed, and learnt from the journey.

"Who feels indifferent, like it was something to get over and done with? Look at the hands." Shared souls saw each other again.

"Now, you are fifty-six people. Each of you will retell this story in your own way. Even if you were with someone throughout the journey, you cannot assume their feelings. Your feelings are yours alone. Embrace them.

Some of you had a wonderful time, and I can see that on your faces; you found harmony on this path. Others are annoyed because your feet hurt. Some of you still don't get the point. Eight people stayed behind and decided not to walk the path at all. Our feelings are ours alone. Our choices are also entirely our own. Never forget that.

Now, find eight things you are grateful for from this experience. Don't write anything, just think. I am grateful that I have feet, that I am fit, that I could breathe fresh air, that I could enjoy nature, that I could feel the energy of the forest, that I had a friendly conversation, that I massaged my feet for free." She started laughing with such passion that others joined in her infectious joy.

When the laughter subdued, each participant was left to their thoughts to count what they were grateful for. Minutes passed and smiles could be seen in abundance.

"Now, let's go back to evening meditation. After, we'll bake corn on a fire, and you are all welcome to join us."

It was the end of the day. Participants walked together, nattering, treading carefully, and feeling in a state of concord, drained and energised simultaneously.

DAY SIX: A SPRINKLING OF COMPLIMENTS. RAISE THE ENERGY AROUND YOU.

The more you recognise beauty within yourself the more readily you will see beauty in others. You can look at a rose and see her thorns or you can see her flower. Choose your focus wisely.

The teacher with long colourful dreadlocks that had helped Kara on her barefoot journey stood up after morning meditation. Her hands met at her heart in a prayer and then opened like a blossoming flower to welcome participants. She had bare feet that were dusty and well travelled.

"Good morning, beautiful souls." She said, laughing and jumping up and down like a rock star at a concert. She bounced from one side of the stage to the other in celebration of the day they were about to share.

"Good morning, dear participants." She repeated with building enthusiasm. "I like how your energy is rising every day. I feel it affecting me, so today, let's go wild. Today, let your energy spillover as you give compliments to every person you encounter."

To show that this was an actual task and that she was serious as well as excited, she repeated, "Compliment every single person you encounter! But you know what that means?" She said grinning. "You have to compliment yourself too. And try to give yourself a lot of beautiful compliments.

Whenever you find your reflection in a window, the water, or a mirror, greet yourself and say, 'Hello beautiful soul! You are good.'" She held her hand up like a mirror, then directed it to the floor to become a lake. "'You are really good! You are amazing. You, beauty, are the best body, mind, and soul.'" She lifted her hand to her cheek in a loving caress.

"Some poor souls find it very difficult to love themselves. If you have a hard time with this, when you catch your reflection, make a funny face, roll your eyes, make a funny noise, amuse yourself." She rolled her eyes, poked out her tongue, and morphed her face into a series of grimaces.

"If a compliment won't form, use this as an opportunity to stop taking yourself so seriously and to enjoy yourself. Ride with the day. It's an illusion, a game. Have fun.

As I said, some of you will find it difficult to praise yourself, but most of us have no problem complimenting others. Glorify yourselves and others today. Smile. Feel your energy rising higher.

For the morning, we will train here. What you do is up to you. Go with it and do what you feel: walk, paint, sit, write, sing. Then when you encounter another person, start a conversation and share something flattering and true. When you see your reflection, very important, compliment yourself. Give your soul some love." She jumped up and down again, her energy buzzing.

"Fun fact, we teachers woke up very early to put mirrors all around the estate. So you will find yourself more frequently than normal. Start loving yourself today! Let today be a day devoted entirely to you. And go on to be devoted to yourself until the day your soul leaves your body."

She swayed on her hips and lifted her hands to the air. "In the afternoon," she said, spinning,

"We have a bigger challenge for you. If you at least try to embrace this challenge, even if you don't succeed, you are a winner." She laughed like she'd told a great joke and appeared in a state of mania. This annoyed some and delighted others. "The challenge is that you walk to the village and start conversations and compliment the locals. Don't worry, they're used to it. So go for a coffee. Walk in the park. Go to the stores. And while you're there engage in a conversation and say something nice and true to the people you meet."

"Fun fact, previous participants found their happiness level rose with each compliment they gave, and their compliments became sincerer and more natural with each one said. And even more magical than that, the villagers felt happier and less heavy after being complimented. It's so wonderful that the local authority is trying to find a way to transfer this feeling to other villages." She joined her hands in prayer pose, raised them up to the air, spread her palms, and lowered her arms to her sides.

"This is our eighth camp of the year, and with every camp, the vibrations from compliments become stronger. The first time we asked participants to do this, it was challenging because people in the village were unwelcoming and unsure what to do. They didn't know how to react to unwarranted kindness. But, now, they help with conversations because they enjoy it. They offer direct, unapologetic responses, which are true. If they feel the compliment given isn't honest, they'll tell you." She grinned a mischievous grin.

"Every person you meet should get a little bit of your attention and a flattering remark. Compliment an old lady on her scarf. Maybe you think she knitted it herself, so you can compliment her skills. Tell the salesperson they're doing a good job and thank them for their exquisite service. It will become more comfortable with every compliment. Just make sure to comment on something you genuinely like, otherwise, you're not giving compliments but lies."

"And when you go back to regular life, after the 8-Day Experiment, you should continue this practice. Compliment the colleague you normally hate, the people in the shops at home, your family and friends. Let the words come from your heart, even the ones for your nemesis must be kind and praising. Thank them, and compliment them for their work proposal, their lovely coat, their coffee making skills. What can go wrong? I'll tell you: nothing!" She laughed whole-heartedly.

"It's impossible to like every person you come across. There are many soul families and we cannot all exist within one; energetically we can't all fit together. But try to learn acceptance in these differences and compliment despite them.

Now," she clapped her hands and jumped, her dreadlocks jumping behind her, "Go to breakfast and start your day. Remember, have fun and enjoy."

Participants slowly walked to the dining area, almost drained by the teacher's high energy. But as they started to compliment people they made eye contact with, the energy shifted. Initially, complimenting felt uncomfortable and forced, but the practice warmed quickly, as promised.

Lea almost crashed into a mirror that hung from the tree and was immediately faced with the one person she struggled to find nice things to say about. She looked at her reflection and made a silly grimace saying, "You are amazing. You are a fighter."
She felt immense sharing these words, smiled and went on to a promising breakfast.

Jan walked with Storm. Since Jan had been rude to Storm at the start, he felt his compliment should be especially meaningful. He searched for the words and eventually said a very vacuous, "This t-shirt looks good on you."

He knew it sounded stupid and should be added to with something more deep so dug for a pertinent remark. "Well, everything looks good on you, Storm. You're a handsome guy."

Storm smiled saying, "You've got a nice radio voice, Jan. You could calm anyone down if you wanted to."

Jan blushed. He'd always felt his voice was a bit funny, so Storm's words were a comfort as well as a compliment. They nodded to each other, recognising that they'd finally made peace.

Petra sat next to Kara at breakfast. "I love your hair, Kara. Is it like that naturally?"

Kara smiled. She also loved her hair. It was the one thing about her appearance that she felt proud of. "Yes, it's all-natural. I've never coloured it. And I love my hair too. Thank you so much for inspiring me. You are amazing."

Petra was content and grateful for this day. She was grateful for the fantastic nature surrounding them and the young people she could spend time with. *Everything's connected.* She thought. *When you enjoy yourself and appreciate yourself, you can see more beauty in others and are excited to compliment them. It's like surprising them with love.* She looked around at the faces from her group and acknowledged the changes they'd undergone. There was visibly less gloom, less heaviness.

Petra and Kara overheard a girl next to them tell a man across the table, "I adore your sense of humour." And they smiled together.

Nick stood with his hiking companion, fancying her even more today, and said with ease, "You are wonderful inside and out."

She giggled from under her eyelashes and said, "And you are very handsome."

They blushed and tingled with excitement. After breakfast, they took a long walk and used all of their energy and compliments on each other. Nick finally saw how easy it was to spend time with someone that shared his flow. There was no awkward silence, no stilted glancing, just an easy, steady, loving flow.

The teachers stayed seated on the stage until pre-lunch meditation. The bald, female teacher lit incense sticks with me, saying, "I think this group has been very successful. We can be proud of our role assisting them. The last ones are opening up and understanding the importance of acknowledging their feelings."

Gaya agreed, and they praised each other for their accomplishments. They discussed what to write in the email to participants once the week was done and how to help this group maintain their flow and practices.

The gong eventually sounded, guiding participants to meditation. The dreadlocked teacher led the session, her energy transforming into quiet consideration.

"This meditation is intended to open your heart and heal your hurt. Embrace the beauty of our planet and be grateful. Thank you, Earth, for plants, vegetables, for wind, for sea and forests. We must protect and love nature. We have to love the Earth for her abundance and generosity. We are but one part of nature. Relax. Focus on your heart, on it's natural rhythm. Sit or lie. Go into your heart. Place your hands on your chest and feel it's beating. Acknowledge the expansion of your feelings."

Jacopo lay down and followed the love swimming through his body. He felt abundance like never before. *I wish I could hold this feeling forever.* He understood the path that had led him here and felt solace knowing the path would now unfold with him as a conscious passenger. *It's time for a door to open, for a new beginning, to shake off old fears, and to carry on.*

I promise to try to maintain this warmth, to hold the bright light of my emotions up high.

Lunch was called and participants hummed with kind words. The second part of the day started when they walked to the village and became instantly aware of the bubble of the estate. It popped as they stepped over it's boundary. The estate was a separate universe absent of phones, TV, computers, and strangers. Shut away in this bubble, one can be happy. But it wasn't reality. Participants quickly saw that they had to relearn how to survive urban pressures, balance stress and external expectations, and to overcome their negative inner voices.

Tina was among the first to enter the village, on a mission to overcome her well trained cynicism. Over the week, she'd identified a bad habit of pointing out the shortcomings of others. In the past, her ego fed on criticising, and today, every time she complimented someone she was reminded of a sarcastic comment made outside of the camp. She took no pleasure in these memories, and they inhibited her complimenting with joy and a full heart.

When she'd come across herself in a mirror that morning, Tina toyed with admitting she is a judgmental person and that the person she loves to judge most is herself.
She tried to compliment herself but struggled, experiencing an internal duel between the lying, controlling woman she had been and the open one she wanted to become.

"You have a lovely face, but you have wrinkles. They're disgusting."

She tried many times, but each compliment ended in a criticism.

"You bake really well, but your frosting is far from perfect."

"You have a skinny figure, but your stomach's not on top form."

"You have a good job, but you could try harder to progress and achieve something with your life."

Today, Tina couldn't say an untainted kindness to herself, but that made her more determined to give beautiful compliments to others. She would find positivity in them rather than bringing herself down with devaluing, snotty remarks.

She walked into a shop and was greeted by a chubby saleswoman. *Oh, boy.* She thought, trying to silence her judgemental nature. She inhaled and stepped toward the smiling saleswoman. Tina, mute, looked at her with interest and focus.

"Good day. How can I help?"

"Can I get that juice, please?" Tina said, biding her time. "I just noticed the colour of your eyes. They're beautiful." She said genuinely, while paying for the juice. Tina was thanked and wished a good day, and with that, felt very proud of herself.

Next, she visited a local shop and continued the good work. The more she focused on the person in front of her the more her memories blurred.
She went to a coffee shop and ordered tea, although she wanted alcohol. She had a conversation with an old man who made her laugh, and she found herself saying, "You're so witty, mister," like she was a young girl again.

He smiled, bashful and pleased to entertain her. For once, she looked past the exterior of an old, dusty outfit and on to a kind gentleman who was a blast in conversation.

Lea sat on a bench under a large oak tree, closed her eyes, and prepared herself. She hated new social situations. She hated chatting with new people. She hated what she had to try and do now. When she opened her eyes again, she found a woman was sitting next to her.

"So, they made you come to the village and compliment people?" The woman asked, obviously no stranger to this task. "But it looks like you don't know how to start. Let me help. Give me a compliment and then it will be easier for the next person you talk to."

Lea gave a timid smile. "I like the way you think." She took the old lady's hand and shared the fear shaking her body. "And you are completely right."

"You know, most people in this village have lived here their whole lives. Their ancestors lived here for many generations before that. Our shop owner, however, moved here as an infant. He's an adult now and we still call him a newcomer." She laughed. "At first, when your teachers bought that land and created the camp, we were angry. The first time participants came up here, with the same task you have today, we were rude. We weren't used to outsiders. We even have problems with people from nearby villages in this municipality." She roared with laughter. "We're stubborn people.
But once we set our stubbornness aside, we realised we felt good on the day people from the camp came to give us compliments. Pretty much everyone comes to the centre for compliment day now.

It's not easy to change." She squeezed Lea's hand. "All we can do is try. Just compare yourself with yourself, and check you're taking steps in the right direction."

Lea hugged the lady and walked confidently to the village centre. She heard a young man laughing and stopped. Their eyes locked. His laughter carried on, and Lea noticed his eyes glisten.

"I love your laugh. It's vibrant, and your eyes sparkle." He bowed in thanks and went about his business. Lea took a moment to listen to compliments filling the air from all directions.

"Those earrings look good on you."

"Those glasses make your face glow."

"I love your knitted jacket. Did you make it yourself?"

"You are beautiful."

Compliments raised the vibrations of every person in the village forming a euphoric epicentre. Participants gradually began to walk back for evening meditation and dinner. They felt full of energy and ready for new challenges.

After dinner, most participants stayed by the bonfire, exchanging experiences and sharing with the teachers. For the first time, they weren't exhausted and so stayed long into the night.

When the sky was very dark and the fire burnt low, the dreadlocked teacher looked at the remaining participants and said, "The more you focus on one aspect of a good feeling the less you see other negative aspects. And the more you recognise beauty within yourself the more readily you see beauty in others. The cycle of feeling continues in this way, growing plentifully. Energy rises. You forgive yourself and others. Energy turns over and builds again. It's never-ending. It's all about focus. You can look at a rose and see her thorns or you can see her flower. Choose your focus wisely. Good night and sleep well."

DAY SEVEN: LET'S TRY THIS, EVEN IF IT'S OUT OF YOUR COMFORT ZONE.

We are used to delaying. We wait for things to happen and then we die.

A young, severe-looking male teacher stood in front of participants on the penultimate day and wasted no time. "Doubt and fear exist within us to remind us of previous experiences. They exist as markers of all that we have learnt, as warning signs against things that previously endangered our happiness and success.

Preventing doubts and fears from growing is a task that we must tackle. But in order to conquer these feelings, one must step out of their comfort zone. Today, it's time to grapple with your worries and doubts. It's time to walk all over them, to say thank you to them for protecting you up until this point, and to release them because you don't need them anymore." He spoke with precision and confidence, instilling willingness and resistance in equal measure.

"This morning is yours to think about fear. In the afternoon, we have prepared a few activities designed to shake you a little in order to overcome and conquer fear.
Common fears exist in things like heights, flying, snakes, spiders, and closed spaces. We will offer these to you today to get your heart pumping and your head thinking about how strong you really are."

Some participants felt uncomfortable hearing their identified fears. In general, the positive vibrations were raised amongst the group, but there was an undercurrent of nervousness mixing up the sediment.

"Some of your fears are not represented in that list, but don't let that stop you committing to the day. You can still embrace the challenge by choosing the least pleasing task available." He slowly paced up and down the stage. Participants' nervous eyes followed him.

"Today is an adventure, and there are a few options as to how your adventure will look. There is: paragliding, zip lining, handling snakes and spiders, or travelling through a claustrophobic tunnel.

Consider the things that stop you moving positively through your life. In tackling a fear, you can say to yourself, 'I can conquer anything along my path. Everything ends and this will pass.' In the end," He paused and held his hands out like tilting scales, "Everything passes, good or bad. And every situation you face is as you see it, bad or good. All you need to do is stay true to the path and follow your goals.

Trying new things is good because it confirms what we do and do not like. Deciding you do not like something and fearing it, only leads to missed opportunities. So try new things. Set a date or agree that once a month you'll try something new. That's not too scary. Right?" He gave the group their first smile of his session.

"I'm sure you all have a bucket list, with endless things to do, see, or places to visit. Embrace that list and push yourself to achieve some of it. If that means trying the Ethiopian cuisine your sister keeps willing you to and you keep avoiding, do it now. It's all about small, novel steps. Try the pottery class you never found time for. Sell your life's baggage. Buy a ticket.

278

Walk a trail in Australia or South America. Find the thing you've been postponing. Call your crush. Send flowers to the friend whose birthday you forgot and write a funny card: 'Thinking of you even when it's not your birthday,' or 'Happy b-day, Merry Christmas, and Happy New Year. Have fun on Independence Day.' Drive to visit the person you've been planning to see for a long time. Buy a bar of chocolate and call them to say you'll be there in an hour. Even if you only spend fifteen minutes together, go." The severe exterior was starting to melt away and show another warm-hearted teacher standing before them. His examples brought ease to listeners and allowed them to find new positive views for the day's challenge.

"We are used to delaying. We wait for things to happen and then we die. We leave this beautiful world without visiting the places we longed for. We get old. Our crushes get married. We watch the same TV shows year in and out. But it doesn't have to be like this.

Today, revisit your bucket list and tick something off. If you don't have a bucket list, write one. What do you want to do, see, experience, learn? Then pick something and join today's adventure. It's easy. It's perfect. It's good.

Don't let life pass you by." He paused so only the voice of the wind whistled by.

"Be honest with yourself. You have come here to grow. The best way to grow is to kick yourself out of your comfort zone. As a young boy, I worried about everything.
My parents never hurt me, but I was scared of them because they felt alien and cold to me. Whatever I did, I warned myself, 'You must not disappoint your parents.' And that warning stopped me from doing many things. I was scared of sports. I was afraid to break bones. My granny used to scream at me," he imitated the voice of an elderly woman.

"'You'll crack every bone in your body if you climb that tree!' And it terrified me. I never broke bones, but I did break my spirit.

The force that leads you to discover the world is within you. But I lived my life scared and full of doubt. I wouldn't do anything without consulting others. And, of course, the friends and family who advised me could only give me solutions that worked for them, based on their understanding of their own fears and doubts, not mine. So, ultimately, I couldn't discover anything about the world.

People told me, 'Don't change your job until you land another.' But my job was miserable. I earnt more then than I do now, but I felt stressed all the time, my health crumbled, and I became depressed to the point of medication. People told me, 'Don't leave your girlfriend. She is the best you can get.' But we'd grown apart, and I didn't love her. We'd been together since high school, and while she's caring and beautiful, we were heading in different directions. She wanted marriage and children, but I couldn't see myself with her in thirty years. So why stay? People told me, 'You don't have to exercise. You are alright the way you are.' But my back hurt. Back pain is fear, and I was afraid: afraid to step forward, afraid to break habits, afraid of finances, afraid to change.

These were their perspectives, values, cultures. These were their fears and doubts, and I tried to follow them for some time.

When the fear became too much, I just left. I left my phone at home, rented a cabin in the woods, and planned to kill myself. I rented the cabin for a week because it was cheaper than a day." A grateful grin spread over his face.

"Here, I made a decision for myself. I decided to use the time and write. Marking words made me see how silent I had been until that point.

280

As the words spilled out I became crazy with things to say. I took breaks and walked for hours. I climbed trees." He laughed. "I even swam in a lake in the middle of the forest, something I would have never done before. I became fearless. I still intended to commit suicide, but that made me unafraid of breaking myself falling from a tree or catching a disease from the lake. Nothing mattered anymore. Nothing does when you are dead."

"By the end of the week, I felt alive again. Actually, if I'm honest, I felt alive for the first time in my life. I questioned my plan and decided to try to change my life rather than end it. What could go wrong? I'd kill myself later if I reached the tipping point again. In that cabin, the only thing I was afraid of was what would happen if I didn't change my life." The teacher took a few deep breaths, his chest expanding and shrinking. His story was exposed, vulnerable and beautiful.

"Since then, I go to that cabin every three months. I leave my phone behind and write. I note what I do not like in my life and what I want to change. I always ask myself, 'Do you want to die?' And the answer has continued to be no. And so I promise myself again, 'You can kill yourself later if it gets too much.' And I take comfort in that."

From the young man's story, participants witnessed how a teacher develops. They saw he was not born Zen; he grew into it. All the teachers had. They each found themselves saying, *I have to change. I have to learn new ways of moving, eating, working. My journey is unique. Everyone has obstacles and our obstacles are often the same but how we tackle them is personal. It's time to change. No substance, gossip, party, organisation, activity should stop me thinking about my life. I have to focus on myself.*

"Many of you will not reach the same tipping point as me, but you all have a line that defines your happiness and safety.

There will be times where you reach the edge of that line and then return to your life and routines. If you don't change your routines, you will visit that place time and again. It is not possible to change a life without changing your routines.

Anyway, enough preaching. There are four tables that represent the four activities available to you. Go and apply for the activity that scares you. There's no point going for the thing you want to do. It must be the one that truly unsettles you. That is the one that will allow you to break patterns, that will begin to rewire your brain, to show your brain that you are able and that fear will not stop you. Look fear in the eye and say, 'Not this time sucker.'"

The four tables were labelled: animals, flying, heights, and narrow passage. Lines formed before each one.

Petra thought for a long while and then joined the queue for animals. She was not keen on heights either, but snakes, spiders, and rats were her biggest fears since childhood. Tina also hated spiders, checking for spiders was the one obligation Robert stuck to every week, and they found themselves waiting side by side.

Storm and Jacopo stepped to the line for the narrow passage. They both looked fearless and both hated being trapped in small spaces.

Jan and Kara stood in line for the heights table. They talked about fears and came to the conclusion they weren't afraid of heights but of looking down and seeing no floor below them.

Nick hated flying and was never able to take a plane without a sleeping pill or getting drunk. Lea developed her fear last year when she ended up on a flight with death defying turbulence. In theory, she knew the chances of being hit by a car crossing the street were higher than dying in a plane crash, but the substance of fear is rarely rational.

The group that signed up for 'animals' were led to the dining area where the animal owners waited. A young, long-haired man and his fiancée greeted them with smiles.

"Hello, ladies and gentlemen. Welcome to Face Your Fears, animal edition."

The group stood with disgust and panic dashed across their faces. Some meters away was a table hosting different size cages.

"Firstly, you have to know our friends over here are more afraid of you than you are of them. Animals don't attack unless provoked or hungry and see you as a potential meal. They don't have an agenda or wish to hurt anyone, not even the furry assassin cats." His attempt at a comedic intro was not working. On the contrary, some participants stepped further back and prepared to run.

"Do not be afraid. We will hold the animals and present them to you. Then you will slowly, one by one, approach the table and look at them up close. We will then start a second cycle where you'll try to pet them. You can also take one in your hand and hold it if you feel good. If you stay calm, they do too."

A cacophony of, "Blah, agrht, pfuj," escaped participants' mouths as the long-haired man let a giant spider crawl along his hand. Tina began to slowly back away, stomach flipping and readjusting itself. Without making a conscious decision, she screamed and ran away from her fear.

After a long motivational talk, she dragged herself back to the line. *You can do this. You must. It's time to conquer at least one fear. Like he told you, it can't hurt you.* She took a big breath. *You do not need to take it in hand. You can pet it with the tip of your finger. Yes, you can do it.* Her heart pounded. *Shit. Shit. Shit. Shit. Shit. It's hideous. Disgusting. Fuck. I don't want to.*

Her body shook. *I'm next. Fuck. What do I do? They all expect me to do it. Bleh. I don't want to.*

The young teacher guided her hand towards the spider, and they pet it together. After initially feeling horrified, Tina calmed down. It didn't feel as gross as it looked, and out of intrigue, Tina stroked it twice.

Walking away from the table, without screaming, she sat down and recorded the feelings that rushed through her. Every word was proud and triumphant.

Of the creatures on the table, Petra had the most immense repulsion towards the mice. "They're dirty and probably full of diseases. What if it bites me? Thank God, you don't have rats. I'd go crazy." She ranted.

"I have a rat. Should I bring it out?" The young man laughed.

Petra gave him an angry look and then focused on the task at hand. She tried to observe the caged mice with positive feelings and searched their eyes. She watched their little bodies move and heads tilt, and in watching, they became small animals rather than dirty rodents. After some time, she stretched out a tentative hand and quickly stroked one mouse. She refused to hold it. She'd survived and took comfort in that, then hurried to a nearby tap and thoroughly cleaned her hands.

The second group, who had committed themselves to flying, got into a bus and drove to a nearby hill where three paragliders were ready and waiting. Lea became hysterical with panic as soon as she saw them. Nick wanted to comfort her, but Gaya stepped in.

The teacher with a long beard led Nick away, explaining, "This is her process. She needs to conquer her fear, and you must focus on yours. You aren't here to be someone's hero.

Did you know, the majority of men who commit suicide are later described as strong, independent, and under control. Many of us press 'weak' feelings deep into our bodies." He placed a hand on Nick's chest and pressed like transmitting a feeling from his hand to Nick's heart. "But you don't need to do that. You don't need to cover your feelings with a mask; you do not need to be a hero. You need to face your fear and conquer it." He concluded with a warm smile and a nod to acknowledge Nick's bravery.

A few meters away, Gaya waited for Lea to calm down, while the rest of the group watched the paragliders in horror and anticipation.

When Lea appeared to have collected herself a bit, Gaya spoke. "I know facing your fear is hard. Would you prefer to wait here and see the others are alright or to drive to the landing spot and watch them land?"

Lea controlled her breaths, feeling her lungs fill and gasping for as much as oxygen as possible. After a few minutes, she looked for Gaya, who had not moved from her side. "I want to stay here and go last. And maybe I could talk to one participant after landing?"

Gaya agreed and praised Lea's plan and courage.
A participant was prepared for the first jump and lifted off. Then the second one flew. There was a brief pause as paragliders returned from the landing spot by car. A third and fourth member jumped, and so on, until it was Nick's time to fly.

As Nick prepared, Gaya brought one excited jumper to speak with Lea. She did not take the participant that had fainted after landing, knowing that could only cause chaos. The enthused participant wanted to jump again and told her, "I was flying. I was a bird.

Being up there was the most liberating thing I've ever experienced." Lea listened to his words and willed herself to be brave.

Strapped in, Nick focused on breathing. He felt the body of the professional behind him and tried to reassure himself. He moved his legs automatically when instructed, and in no time at all, the floor was lost under his feet and he was in the sky. Looking down, he panicked and then gathered his fear. *Not this time. I release myself from this fear. It's time to let go. I managed to let go of Linda; I can let go of this feeling too. Time for new beginnings.* He opened his eyes and saw the world below. Trees looked like blades of grass and the air cradled him.

Lea warned her professional paraglider that she'd probably scream the whole way.

"It wouldn't be the first time." He comforted her and laughed. He gave Lea instruction, and they started running. She clenched her eyes and ran as fast as she could. The instructor pressed her shoulders, notifying her they were up, and she felt suddenly feathery light. They were in the sky, gliding with birds, and she was no longer the screaming Lea who had gasped with fear on the ground.

The group facing heights walked to the other end of the estate where the forest became thick.
To their amazement, tucked away at the end of the estate was an adrenalin park. Kara, who had managed to uncover most hidden parts of the estate, couldn't believe she'd missed this. She felt dizzy looking up the tree trunks to platforms and ropes. She had been to a smaller version of this type of park and was devastated when her rope snapped. Her stomach squeezed and a headache snuck in like a drill behind the ear.

Jan instantly hated his decision to join this group. He should have gone paragliding or to pet some animals.

I have no bloody intention of killing myself in an adrenaline park. He cursed internally.

Instructors explained the procedure and how participants will be secured. They laboured on the point that their ropes were tested regularly and that each elevated challenge is protected with a net below in case they fall.

Kara had problems believing that this was safe and that the rope would support her. Even though she was much smaller, she still felt heavy. Jan remembered a time he'd almost fallen down a mountain side while hiking and didn't wish to repeat the sensation.

"Supporting each other is important." Added one of the teachers from the camp. "But every one of you is here to conquer a fear. We will make sure you are safe." He emphasised the word 'will' to show extra support. "You will get a helmet, and they will strap you on your safety ropes. These guys are professionals. They get at least two groups a week here, so they really know what they're doing. All the equipment is regularly tested and completely safe. So," He paused and smiled, "It's time to get in line. If you need to talk, we are here."

A line reluctantly formed. Participants nervously looked at each other and waited.

This is the hardest part. Thought Jan. *Waiting in line. Waiting for things to get better. Waiting for your heart to heal. Waiting...*

"I'm not sure these ropes can hold my weight," confessed Kara.

"You're not that heavy." Jan comforted. "If it didn't break under that tall, buff guy, it should hold you too. Don't worry. Let's breathe."

Kara had mixed feelings about this comment. *Should I be glad he thinks I'm not that heavy or angry for his lack of class? Best just start breathing.*

They became one shared breath, united bodies emptying their minds together, and it felt amazing. Kara even forgot where she was for a moment. Then, they were roped up in safety harnesses, and breathing ceased to help. They clung to each others' hands and simultaneously hyperventilated. They were directed to a ladder and automatically ascended. They didn't look down. Kara climbed cautiously with closed eyes: blind fear. She peeked them open from time to time to check how much further she had to go and then clamped them shut. Instructors guided them to a standing platform where Kara accidently looked down.

"Oh. Fuck. Fuck. Fuck. I am not doing this!"

The instructor, well trained, used a panic reaction and placed his hands on her shoulders. He applied pressure to the muscles in a few short squeezes, and she quickly felt energised and more relaxed.

"There are two ways to get down," he said, "Straight on this zip line to the bottom or by walking along that five-meter rope to the other side and taking a shorter zip line." Kara looked at the string he called a rope and imagined falling. She'd tried slacklining a few times but didn't feel confident enough to do that.
"I choose the zip line from the top. Let's get this over with."

He smiled and clicked her onto the line.

Kara used all of her strength to jump as soon as he declared it was safe to go and screamed, "Fuuuuuuuuuuuuuuuuuuuuck thiiiiiiiiiiiis," the whole way down. Every bird evacuated the forest and the group watched in amazement.

"I have never seen that before." The instructor laughed to Jan, who wasn't able to find any humour so high up.

When Kara was released from her safety ropes, she wanted to laugh and jump and shout, and so she did. She danced around singing, "The challenge is over. The challenge is over. The fear is dead." She laughed and sang and felt hopeful.

"Well, if I am challenging myself," said Jan, "I want to walk the rope."

He started slowly and inched one foot in front of the other until twenty minutes passed and he reached the podium on the other side. He felt on top of the world and, like Kara, screamed and jumped in his tree top platform.

The tree shook, making the instructor shout, "Stop! I heard a crack in the podium."

Jan laughed without fear and zip lined to the floor. When they set him free, Kara welcomed him with a hug. He squeezed her tight and they embraced and giggled for some minutes. They later admitted they wouldn't willingly repeat the challenge any time soon, but it was worth it for the powerful sensation rushing through their bodies. They felt even more powerful as the adrenaline wore off.

Finally, the group afraid of small spaces walked to the woods. They formed the second-largest group and were led by Gregor and the teacher with colourful dreadlocks. They paused in the woods and started to clear leaves. There was a narrow pathway, approximately ten meters long, that led to doors opening into the undergrowth.

Storm and Jacopo locked fearful eyes. The coffin-sized passage didn't offer any comfort.

The dreadlocked teacher laughed her recognisable laugh, which became a sinister, other-worldly cackle in the face of participants' fear.

Nick's new crush was in this group and her breath was out of control. She shook her head and chanted, "No. No. No. No. No!" A panic attack loomed. Gregor gently took her away from the group, reassuring and settling her.

The dreadlocked teacher guided the rest with a calm and solemn voice. "I promise you. This is a safe path. It was constructed safely. It's short. And its sole purpose is to show you you are strong, not to frustrate you.

Once, when I was skiing, I got buried in an avalanche. I managed to kick and push enough snow away from me that it created a space to wait for help. I managed to stay in my right mind despite being overcome with fear. I was already terrified of dark underground places and even driving through a tunnel felt like a horror movie for me. It was torture. It was a real phobia that affected me to the core. But I survived that avalanche. So now, when I drive into a tunnel and feel afraid, I tell myself, 'You can do this.' And I know it's true.

Underground darkness still scares me, but I will be the first to walk through this passage and conquer my fear again today.
You will see me when you come out the other side and conquer your own fear too. I will wait for you. Take your time, and when you go, think about how amazing it will feel to overcome this fear."

She turned and walked inside, shaky but strong. The group watched her emerge on the other side and wave, beaming with accomplishment.

"Hey, ho! Let's go!" She sang and laughed.

Storm went first, knowing that getting it over with was the best way for him. *Just rip off the bandage and go.* The path was so small he had to lean forward as he went and at one point his head was almost between his legs. He breathed fast, almost out of control, and remembered waves pulling him deep into the sea, trapped inside an airless world.

"I survived that." He told himself. "I can do this; this is a short path."

He walked faster and kept focused on the end. A few minutes passed in slow motion, and then, he was out. Storm hugged the teacher and enjoyed knowing it was over. He wouldn't repeat it if someone paid him and, for once, seemed unsure what he'd gained from the journey. He was relieved. *But what else?*

Jacopo was eighth in line. He'd been shut in a closet as punishment in childhood, and since then, he resented small spaces. As the people before him disappeared one by one, he gave himself a pep talk to prepare for what lay ahead. "Jacopo, just a few steps." He promised. "You are not a coward."

And with that, he stepped forward. At first, he walked slowly, allowing his eyes to adapt to the darkness. But as soon as he witnessed a flicker of light at the end of the tunnel, his pace quickened, striding into an almost run. Jacopo jumped into Storm's arms and hugged him so tight, he felt a pang of excitement. Jacopo kissed Storm on the cheeks and continued to hug everyone else that had won over their fear. He did the same for new participants that appeared after him.

The final person to go through, overwhelmed by the fear built from waiting, had a panic attack inside and had to be talked out of the ground. He shivered as he emerged from the tunnel and was welcomed by much applause and love.

At the end of the day, when groups of eight reflected on their expeditions, Gregor felt proud. Some shared stories of powerful, transformative moments. Others were quick to say they wouldn't repeat the day but they did feel something, showing Gregor they had learnt more than they perhaps realised.

After lunch, the young, severe teacher led a much-needed mediation. "Some of you had bad reactions to the tasks today and did not finish. Fear is strong." He said. "If you feel fear is still with you, we will have an additional workshop for you now, so please stay here. The rest of you have the afternoon free. We will run an orgonite workshop this afternoon. If you are interested, come and create, but if you need time to analyse your fears, there will be another workshop tomorrow. Take the afternoon at a pace that feels good for you."

Personal, one-to-one reflections were held to support those that suffered through the day. Others enjoyed their free afternoon, satisfied and tired. By evening, the energy was low and the process of working on deep-rooted fears was taking its toll. Most retired to their rooms and went to bed.

After a stressful day, the best thing to do is sleep and release the dampened energy, thought Storm as he lay his head down.

DAY EIGHT: NEW SETTINGS

There is no end and no beginning. Every end is a beginning and every beginning an end.

Petra sat on her terrace, smitten before the impending natural beauty of sunrise. She delighted in the dance of colours morphing from dark to light red and then a passionate orange. Peacefully sitting through the early hours of the day filled her heart with joy. The air felt extra special as it entered her blood stream and filled her body like a free flowing river.

Did I read it or did someone tell me? She questioned. *I can't remember. You can stop eating if you watch the sunrise and sunset. Was it both or were you supposed to pick one? Hmm, I can't imagine not eating anything. How was it? Ten minutes every morning to guarantee you are rising with its energy? Who has time to watch the sun so much twice a day? Maybe, if you don't eat, you have a lot of extra time. I don't know. I don't know. Why do I think that's so silly?*

There was no resolution to her thoughts but it was no bother. The sun found its place in the sky and the gong invited her to morning meditation. Afterwards, the only teacher that had not yet shared stood up. He was an older man, tall and skinny.
At first glimpse, he seemed almost intimidating in his size, but there were sparks in his eyes that greeted all that looked up to them.

"Good day, dear participants. You have survived every challenge placed before you and worked hard. Congratulations. It is difficult to address your feelings, fears, and patterns. When you leave our estate, incorporate all the practices that you've found helpful and commit to them. Set goals. Make them realistic. Exiling your negative practices will bring you ultimate pride.

"This morning, we gave you new notebooks to take with you when you leave the 8-Day Experiment. Use this notebook to record goals after leaving this place. First, establish a broad picture of what your goal is. Then, break it down into small steps or tasks. If your goal is to be happy, write down what could make you happy and work from there. If you want to achieve something, like starting your own business, put the business as the top goal and the things you need to do to get there as goals underneath. You can also write personal goals like, 'Improve my relationship.' Set goals that are measurable and have a timeline in which they should be achieved. Make sure they are relevant and specific. Create a to-do list, and ensure the most relevant goals are at the top.

Then, when you have your goals arranged, prepare a plan for how to execute them and write down your steps. What do you need? What skills do you need to learn? What books should you read? And so on.

You have to stick to your plan and follow the steps. If you don't achieve the goal, it doesn't matter, but you must commit to the path. Every person has a different path. Find yours. If you're a night owl, don't wake up at 5am to fit all your goals in.
If you are a morning person, we encourage you to go with your early hours and work out or catch up on reading. Listen to your body and desires. Create your own flow, your own agenda.

There are eight of us here, and each one of us has a unique system of working. Promise yourself that you will create and follow your own plan.

294

Dedicate time every day to reaching your goals. If that is losing weight, dedicate time to exercise or prepare healthy meals. Be kind to yourself, even when you slack off and lose a day or two. Don't let the day turn into a month of ignoring your goals. Forgive yourself. Pick up where you stopped, and carry on. In the long term, you will see the positive results you wish for."

Some participants were taking notes, so the old man stopped, offering time to catch up.

"For your career, ask yourself: Where do I see myself in a couple of years? Is it still in this job or do I want a change? What work do I see myself enjoying?

For fitness and weight loss: How can I increase my stamina? What do I want to be different about my appearance? What diet will satisfy my needs and improve how I feel inside and out?

If you're focusing on a relationship: How can I change my behaviour and reconnect with my people? Has my relationship come to its end? How will I sever the tie respectfully? What steps can I take to protect my partner from pain?

For mind-set, ask: Am I being pessimistic? How can I change my negativity? Is there a new hobby or affirmation, if you believe in them, that could help? How do I want my actions to change? Can I respond differently? Does mediation, listening to music, or walking in nature help me?

When considering your finances, ask: How can I improve my current situation with my existing income? Where can I make cuts? Can I create a passive income or take on part-time jobs to develop other skills I want or need?

Do you feel this world is fucked up?" Participants were taken aback by the swear word but enjoyed his rebellious tone.

"Do you feel you have no influence to change things? Start in your community and that feeling may change. Be honest about what you consider crucial. Is it helping people or animals, the environment, or even protecting cultural heritage? There is not one worthy cause. Many areas need help, and you could be part of that. When you start, you'll find other avenues to pursue and may then view 'change' differently.

Do you have artistic skills you want to improve? Sign up for a dance class or painting workshop. Start writing poems. Find out what makes you happy and full. You never know, you could find new levels of satisfaction. Maybe, you're the next big thing. It doesn't matter; what matters is to have fun exploring.

If something makes you nervous, if thinking about extra work puts you off, if you don't want it, if you have unresolved fears, remember that the first step is hard and the next is too, but with every step it gets easier. Enjoy life. Enjoy nature. Enjoy your body. Stop hating yourself for the past. The beauty of life is that every day is a new start. Pick up where you left off and go on with the next step. Be kind to yourself.

Harder is pressure. Challenge is enjoyment. Things that are meant to be, come easily. You want every task you tackle to be exciting. Be excited about the pit stops, the small steps, the conclusions. Remember, you are doing more than all the years before now when you merely thought and did not act.
You are the master of your life and your responses to it." He said humbly and waited a breath.

"You have until lunch to write your goals into your new notebook. Lay a new path for your life. After, we will get arty and build orgonite mementoes of the week. In the evening, there will be a burning ritual where we'll gather and burn your first notebook from the week. This releases the feelings and struggles of the week and allows you to move forward lighter.

You can also burn baggage you no longer need to carry with you: pictures of an ex from your wallet, gifts that hold negative connotations, items you don't want to see anymore. And you can do this when you get home if you feel like it. Burn old letters, clothes, anything that pulls you down and isn't needed anymore. It's time to reset." Participants couldn't help smiling at these words. It was time. They were ready.

"The energy from the 8-Day Experiment will stay with you for some time, but eventually, it will become smaller. That's when the real work starts, when you discover where your focus lies and you set your goals alone. For now, go. Have fun."

Excitement rose in the group, as they set out to plan new, better, focused lives, full of positive habits. Our group spread across the estate, most returning to their usual spots.

Kara ate breakfast quickly and skipped off to her positive practice of walking in the woods before starting to write. She felt good in the forest, happy to enjoy its glorious nature. After reaching her step count, she took refuge on a rock and opened her notebook.

Goals, 8-day retreat

Health goals:
- Eat more vegetables and fewer carbs. Steps: sign up to a cooking workshop (vegan or gluten free).
- Improve fitness and run. Steps: I will try to add five-hundred meters to my running distance each month. Goal: 7k.
Relationships:
- Be clear about what I want and need.
- Plan more time to spend with my granny.
- Talk to friends and explain how I feel.
- Write affirmations for a future partner.

Job
- Expand business. Steps: call old business partners and network more.

Jan sat on a bench by the lake and started writing. Initially, he noted his goals without hesitation. The harder part was adding steps to achieve them, and it took some time to fill those spaces.

Goals
Family: find a solution to our current negative relationship. Steps: write some proposals for improving things, talk about them with Ema, start moving in a direction that rebuilds the family as a unit.
Job: Get a raise. Steps: note and present the projects I've been successful in over the years. Highlight my value. If the boss doesn't agree, start looking for another job.
Health: start drinking vegetable smoothies to increase vitamin intake. Steps: research how to make a smoothie and buy a mixer. Start climbing again. Efforts: find a sports hall with a climbing wall.

Less is sometimes more. He told himself. *And these few are important.* He looked at his goals and his fingers wrapped around the page in a gesture of love.

Nick sat under his tree, thinking hard about what his plans should be. *What's my priority?*

LOVE: to be open to new possibilities. Steps: go on dating websites, call girls you like.
HEALTH: go to fitness sessions and develop some muscle tone.
JOB: ask the boss for new cases and to be the lead lawyer on them.

Nick's goals were short and sweet, as was his way.

Lea, for the first time, went back to her room in need of complete solitude.

Goals for next year:
SAFETY: Sign up to a self defence class.
JOB: Look for jobs in new cities or even countries. Maybe I'd feel better somewhere new.
MENTAL HEALTH: Meditate every day and look for good psychological help.

Close to Lea, Petra sat on her porch and sipped tea. She watched the forest for a long time. She'd decided the only important thing was to feel content, so she was in no rush.

Day 8 – New goals, new settings
One and only goal for now until the end of my life: be happy every day, in every situation, with all the people I love.
Steps:
-        Travel more: sign up to a travel club for seniors and go away (at least) twice a year.
-        Health: try to be vegan. Efforts: learn exactly what that means and what I need to eat.
-        Health: join a yoga class.
-        Chess: learn to play. Steps: join a chess group at the local senior club.
-        Family: spend more time with grandchildren.

Storm stayed at the stage, returning to his practice from the start of the experiment.

GOAL: HONOR RIDER'S LIFE
OPEN A BUSINESS CONNECTED WITH SURFING AND BOARDING IN RIDER'S MEMORY AND NAME IT AFTER HIM.

STEPS:
1. FIND OUT WHAT NICHES THERE ARE IN BOTH SPORTS
2. MAKE BUSINESS PLAN
3. FIND FINANCIAL PARTNERS
4. CREATE SOCIAL MEDIA ACCOUNTS @StormforRider on Instagram

He lay back to embrace the sky above. *No more running away from Rider's memory.*

Tina sat on a bench on the opposite side of the lake from Jan. She had a long way to go before fixing the mess of her family and her affair, but she knew herself better on this final day of the retreat. *At least that will help guide me.*

Try to be happy.
Find something just for me. Steps: first, figure out what will make me happy. Then, see what comes.
Try to reconnect with Robert. Steps: talk more and organise a getaway together.

Jacopo was sad, excited, and paranoid all at once. The feelings bubbled inside him and made it difficult to sit and concentrate.

My goals for the next period of life:
Fitness: get bigger. Steps: change food and find a new fitness instructor.
Love: go out to clubs, to events, on dating apps. Explore.
Family: send a letter to family and one message every week until they reply.
Rocco: invite him for coffee to resolve the past and finally be honest.

* * *

In the afternoon, they took part in orgonite craft workshops. Cupola shapes and pyramids formed. Some created necklaces and bracelets. Creativity and friendliness filled conversations as participants focused, complemented, shared, and constructed side by side. The afternoon passed in a flash, and it was already time for some to pack their bags. For those members that were leaving early, their focus for life after the retreat was already apparent.

Following the evening ritual, it was time for fire and burning. Participants gathered, notebooks in hand, by bonfires surrounding the meditation area. Gaya stood in the middle of the stage and waited patiently for the crowd to become quiet.

"Dear participants, today you set out new plans for your life. These goals are written in the notebooks we gave you in the morning, and they will go forward with you on your journey.

Now is the time to burn your notebook from the week. You might be attached to these items, but it's very important that you release your past. Fire is a cleansing energy and burns everything away. If you want to burn other items that hold old energy now, you can. And continue this practice when you get home. Write and burn. It is freeing.

As you know, the first time doing something is hard. The first time letting go of feelings is especially so. Take your time.

We ask you to create eight lines around the fires. When it's your turn, say goodbye to the old you and embrace the new.
Say thank you for everything you have experienced up to today and release that history."

All sixty-four participants lined up to form eight lines around the fires and one by one burnt their notebooks.

Nick took a leather bracelet from his wrist. It was his first gift from Linda, and it stayed with him every day apart from when he took a shower. "Linda," he said, holding her memory over the flames, "Thanks for the illusion. It's time to meet new people. You are not a bad person. We both lived the lie." He dropped the bracelet into the flames and watched it shrivel and disappear. He then ripped page after page from his notebook and threw them in. Relief washed over him with every page and every memory joining the air.

Petra was silent as she took pages from her book. She watched the carefully scribed words fly from her to the fire, hypnotised by the power of the flames.

Next to her, Kara deposited her notebook whole into the flames and it erupted in a flailing bundle of pages. "Goodbye old patterns and negativity."

Storm threw his notebook in from a distance, sending embers into the air. He made a hang loose sign with both hands, saying a casual, "Later," before walking away.

Lea had discovered her engagement ring while packing and now held it in her hand. *It's a sign. Be brave.* She threw the notebook, whole, into the fire. She stared at the ring and contemplated what to say. Many words ran through her mind. She looked up, away from the ring, to see her favourite teacher across the fire, and her mind was silenced. *I don't need to waste any more words on him.* She dropped the ring into the fire and turned away before it could land. "Goodbye Patrik."
Jan stood close to the fire, slowly pulling page after page and placing it in. He was at peace, without thoughts, and happy.

Tina watched the others, before asking for support from the dreadlocked teacher. "I want to burn them right." She said and received an unwelcome laugh in response.

"You just throw it in and say, 'Bye, bye!' That's it." Another manic laugh.

Tina was not entirely pleased with the answer but carried on, following Jan's example. She carefully pulled pages out and sacrificed them to the flames. She said thank you and goodbye to every single one.

Jacopo cried as he plucked pages from his notebook and reluctantly released them. He had become aware of so much on the 8-Day Experiment, and it was hard to let his understanding and discoveries go. *This is just the tip of the iceberg. I will keep searching and know myself better. It could be never-ending.* He smiled, releasing the last pages of this chapter of self-discovery.

Once every page was cinders, the teachers took each others' hands and said in a unified voice, "Thank you for your energy, your work, your story. Thank you for your tears and laughter, for your fear and power, your depression and happiness. Thank you for everything you have taught us. You are amazing teachers. Nothing lasts forever. Remember that in the bad and good times so you always appreciate the moment. It's all a part of the game.

We appreciate you. Goodbye from all eight of us." They lit candles for the last night of this 8-Day Experiment and celebrated their dear participants.

Gregor, overjoyed, sent me crashing to the floor in a fatal blow. As drops of lighter fluid leaked from my plastic case, I was spent. The next day, I was gathered up by the cleaning crew and buried in a rubbish bag.

A new lighter will illuminate the path for the next story, and so the process renews.

There is no end and no beginning. Every end is a beginning and every beginning an end.

You will love others more easily once you appreciate yourself.
Fall in love with yourself.
Never lose your light-er.
Live your vibe.

AUTHOR'S NOTE:
For the purpose of conclusion

The presented work is a work of fiction and should be read as such. With the exception of Urša, no character is based on a living or dead person. If you find events similar to your own or characters similar to yourself, that is just a reflection of life. The intent is to heal your wounds.

There were two reasons to start writing this book.

Firstly, to put out the noise from my head and record my thoughts in a suitable, focused, beneficial way. Now I see, it was also a kind of natural therapy. This book came from a hard period of my life and that is reflected in the range of emotions of different characters. In them I detached myself from my pity and sorrow. If I'm honest, the book wrote itself. I just landed at my computer and let my fingers do the rest.

Secondly, I always liked writing. When I started reading, a dream formed and grew with age: I wanted to publish stories. More specifically, I wanted to publish short stories and scripts in a joint publication - I was ambitious. I tried to publish a novel when I was fifteen, but when I didn't succeed, I stopped writing altogether. So this was a challenge to prove I can write and publish a book, even if it's self-published.

I hope you found this work helpful, had a good laugh reading, and picked up some useful tips. For me, it was one of the most exciting paths to travel and a big success to have finished. It was essential to reach this goal, and the knowledge I gave it my best in the time and space of 2019 and 2020 is humbling.

Hopefully, I will publish another book and that will signify that I am successfully walking down a positive path of learning.

I wish you all the best, and remember to love yourself.

Maja MOLAN

ABOUT THE AUTHOR

Dear Reader,

My name is Maja. I am an infinite searcher for solutions and answers to my insecurities and 'flaws'. I search in books, workshops, meditation, astrology, religion, and ether. Yet, I never fully grasp answers.

I travelled to Fuerteventura in 2019 after having a hard year, both personally and professionally. The urge to write overtook me there and since then it has swallowed me whole. Only two months have passed from the moment I woke up with the idea for my first book, Infinite Search - Life of a Lighter, until the last word was written. I came to that island broken, and with this book, I started to heal.

My message to you, dear reader, is grow as a person, human being, and conscious inhabitant of the earth.

I am on the path of infinite searching. Join me.

With love,

Maja Molan

Printed in Great Britain
by Amazon